OTHER STORIES BY TR DILLON

MR. KUNZ

MR. BALEY

THE HALL OF BRAINS SERIES

> THE HALL OF BRAINS
> THE BOY WHO WENT TO EARTH
> THE BOY WHO UNLOCKED THE UNIVERSE

PURE ATTENTIONS: A NOVELETTE

WHENCE: A HORROR STORY

BURN BOY AND OTHER STORIES

> "BURN BOY"
> "THE YAHWEH PROJECT"
> "FRIEND, OUT"

FIVE STORIES

> "PROX"
> "NOT BENTON"
> "THE LAST COMPETENT MAN"
> "MERRY GO ROUND"
> "LONGWORTH"

"THE MARKIE MARK" IN THE ANTHOLOGY WHISPERS OF THE APOC

"LAND OF THE BLIND" IN THE FORTHCOMING ANTHOLOGY THE CURATOR

The Memory Witch

Book One:
The Chronicles of
Cloth and Crystal

TR Dillon

ISBN 10: 0-578-40450-8
ISBN 13: 978-0-578-40450-9
RJA Enterprises, Oakton, VA

Prologue

Elan was there, of course. Six years old. That morning the men in black hoods and blood red coats murdered her father and brother and burned down their villa.

It was luck, it seemed, Elan was spared. She and Gregor, her elegantly gaunt gray-haired tutor, were studying edible plant roots in the cellar. Dressed in the trim black suit of his profession, Gregor had laid out eight kinds he'd collected earlier that morning and three mushroom species as well. Elan loved the cellar. Cool and dark and damp, it was the only room they allowed dirt on the floor. When no one was looking, Elan would sneak down, take off her shoes and socks, and scamper around making tracks with her tiny feet on the ancient red bricks.

That day, Gregor heard it first and frowned. He rose abruptly and cocked his head. Then he put his face into Elan's and whispered hoarsely, "Radorelan of House Montescue, you are to stay right here until I get back. Do not leave. Do not make a sound. Are we clear?"

Elan nodded, her eyes wide. Gregor had never before addressed her by her formal name, *Rador,* meaning beloved daughter in a family where Fluence runs in the blood. Elan knew little of Fluence, except that the common people – the dearths – called it magic. The dearths in the village whispered that Alaric, her father, was the last of the era's great sorcerers.

As soon as Gregor was gone, Elan, wearing a plain smock underneath a silver-trimmed sweater with pearl buttons, removed her shoes and socks. She spelled her name in the moist grime, remembering this time to capitalize the E. Then she found a black beetle and dropped it near Gregor's hand-picked roots to see which it preferred to eat. Finally, she fished out a comb and, humming softly, began untangling her long straight cherry-red hair.

Elan coughed and then coughed again, harder. The air was now hazy, especially near the ceiling. Then she noticed garish sounds, and they became louder. She heard voices from outside, shouting and moving, followed by stomping and running and horses' hooves. And then noises directly above. Furniture being moved. Glass breaking. Thuds and bangs. An enormous *boom.* Exclamations and curses and cries.

Now scared, Elan eyed the rickety wood-slat stairs that led out of the cellar. She wanted to go find Gregor or her father. Or even Willem, her nine-year-old brother. But Gregor had tasked her as Rador-elan to stay put, and girls named Rador-elan kept their word. So, nervously, Elan sat cross-legged on the cellar floor, careful not to dirty her sweater, and waited for Gregor's return. She no longer cared about the beetle or spelling words with her feet. Something momentous was happening. Something terrifying.

The door flew inward, pungent black smoke pouring in like angry ravens, and Gregor rattled down the stairs. His ashen hair askew, Gregor breathed hard through his mouth as sweat rolled down his temples. He snatched Elan's arm and pulled her into a corner where rough hand-hewn wooden corncribs leaned against the wall.

"Help me pull them down!" Gregor ordered.

Working alongside Gregor, Elan grabbed and yanked, and cobwebs swept across her face as the corncrib crashed.

"Now the next one!" Gregor barked. "Hurry."

The second corncrib teetered and dropped, Elan barely ducking out of the way. Behind it was a pitch-black hole in the wall. Frigid dank air blew into Elan's face. It smelled like cold soup that had gone bad.

"What's in there?" Elan asked, shivering.

"It's a tunnel," Gregor gasped, his hands on his knees while he caught his breath.

"Where does it go?" Elan said, frowning.

"To safety," Gregor said. "Now give me your sweater, Elan. There's no time to waste."

"But it's my favorite," she complained.

"That's why I need it," Gregor said, checking his exasperation as he roughly pulled it off her arms from behind.

"And your butterfly barrette," Gregor said. The acrid smoke was so heavy and thick Elan could barely see the stairs.

"I'm scared, Gregor," Elan said.

"I know, my little caterpillar," Gregor said. "But right now I need your barrette."

Elan pulled it from her pocket, and Gregor grabbed it. "Now wait for me in this spot," he said, pointing to her feet. "This very specific precise spot. I'll be two minutes, no more, no less."

Covering his face with one arm, Gregor staggered off into the smoke, kneeling to pick up Elan's shoes and socks on his way out. Barefooted, Elan sat miserably against the wall, arms around her knees, and angled her head toward the tunnel. She gulped the icy air as smoke erased the cellar from her sight.

Elan closed her eyes and thought of her mother, Catherine. Elan wondered where she was. And why she had left and never returned. Catherine had been gone less than a year, but already Elan had trouble remembering what she looked like. Or the sound of her voice. When Elan asked, people smiled sadly and said her mother was beautiful.

Then Gregor, clutching a valise to his chest, burst through the smoke.

"We must leave now," he wheezed, grabbing Elan's shoulder, pushing the red-haired girl towards the gaping black hole.

"What about Father?" Elan asked.

"He's who ordered us to go," Gregor said, fumbling to extract a torch from its casement against the tunnel wall. He stared hard at the straw wrapped in old cloth, his lips barely moving, and the torch ignited into a bright yellow flame. The tunnel was supported by oaken beams as thick as a full-grown man. Tree roots dangled from the ceiling, and the bare dirt underfoot was a viscous mud from the prior week's rains.

"Where is he?" Elan said, trembling.

"Let's traverse this tunnel first, then we can see to Alaric," Gregor said, his eyes searching the tunnel as he pushed her harder. Once inside, Gregor handed her the torch while he wrestled a fallen corncrib back upright against the opening.

"No one can know we've used the tunnel," Gregor said, "or even that it's here."

"All right," Elan replied shakily, handing back the torch and grabbing Gregor's other hand. She was cold but too frightened to feel it.

The pair squished down the tunnel, one plodding step after another. Elan gripped Gregor's hand so tightly it turned chalk white. Then Elan's right leg disappeared halfway into the mud, and she screamed. Gregor lifted her up with a one-armed heave.

"Upsy-daisy," he said, as casually as he could muster. "We must keep going, Elan."

"I can't feel my toes," she said.

"Nor I," he responded.

"I think there are snakes in here," Elan said, whimpering.

"Rest assured, dear child, that they are more scared of us than we are of them."

"Are you sure?"

Gregor didn't answer, instead thrusting the torch forward in search of the tunnel's exit. A faint light glimmered in the distance. Their breaths were visible in the torch's flickering light. Batting away a low-hanging tree root, Gregor dropped Elan's hand and put his arm around her shoulder. They would march in lockstep toward the light. And whatever was waiting for them beyond it.

The tunnel's end was a tight jumble of boulders. Gregor pressed against the topmost rocks. Nothing moved.

"The people who built this tunnel," he announced, his voice breaking, "took such pains to make sure no one could see it from the outside that they may have made it impossible for us to exit."

Then, as he pushed with his shoulder, a small rock in the top right-hand corner gave way and fell back. Light poured in, and Gregor shoved harder. Another rock fell away, and then a third. Gregor pounded with his fists, but nothing else moved. He placed his head into the opening, then turned back.

"I think we'll both fit," he said. "Barely."

The two wriggled through, first Elan, then Gregor, still clutching his valise. Once outside, they clambered and crawled over the rocks until they fell into the tall grass bending sedately against a pleasant breeze under a warm late-autumn sun.

The tunnel had emptied them beneath a grassy hillock on the far side of the villa's east pasture. It was late morning. Flat on their backs, Gregor and Elan basked in the sunlight.

Then Gregor sniffed the drifting smoke. He rolled over and clawed his way upwards to a vantage point, Elan following. Across the field, leaping flames and pungent smoke engulfed the villa's five structures, one of them the old farmhouse, the other four still unfinished. Everything was built of wood – stone was simply too expensive in the flatlands. Alaric had spent hundreds of hours poring over blueprints and drawings, making one set of changes after another. He had personally supervised the hiring of local laborers and the purchase of materials. Now everything burned with fetid alacrity while nineteen hooded men in red uniforms clustered around two stooped, exhausted figures in the cobblestone courtyard.

"Father!" Elan murmured.

"And Willem," Gregor finished, his breathing terse and rapid.

A tall thin man with talon-like fingers and a hood shielding his face grabbed Alaric by his right shoulder and spoke to him harshly. Like a judge proclaiming a sentence. Gregor and Elan craned their necks to listen, but they could not hear the words. Then the thin man casually pulled a rapier from his waist, looked briefly to the sky as if seeking an indulgence, and pierced Alaric through the heart. The rapier emerged briefly from Alaric's back before the thin man retracted it coolly. Another red-uniformed attacker did the same to Willem. Both figures stiffened and dropped, dead before they hit the ground.

Elan howled, while Gregor, recoiling as if he'd been struck, clapped his hand over her mouth. At that moment, the remaining ceiling of the farmhouse collapsed in a heap, the crash drowning out all other noises, including Elan's cries.

Gregor quickly slid them back down the hillock, Elan clutched in his arms. When they reached the bottom, he pleaded with her, tears in his eyes. "You can't make a sound, Elan, or they will find us, too."

Elan flailed wildly with her legs and arms, but Gregor did not loosen his grip. "If you need to do something," he said, "bite my arm. Here, bite it. As hard as you want. Just don't cry out."

Gregor removed his hand, and Elan lunged at his arm. Wincing, he stroked Elan's bright-red hair as, bawling and shaking, she bit down hard. "There, there," was all Gregor could think to say, so he said it over and over.

After Elan's agonized grief subsided, she buried her head in Gregor's shoulder. He hugged her fiercely, then wiped her cheeks before pulling her abruptly to her feet. "I am so very sorry, my little caterpillar, but we must be away. We need to be far from here before they come looking for us."

Gregor fished shoes and a jacket from his satchel for Elan. Avoiding the rutted cartpaths and open fields, Gregor steered them toward the creekbed, which led for miles along gently rising ground to the forest's edge. The locals, the dearths, never ventured beyond the treeline. It was the westernmost edge of the vast Northern Reaches leading into the Dirovian mountains. The dearths believed the Reaches were a place of ancient magic inhabited by strange folk. A place where dearths entered and never came out or came out changed. It was, they said, a place where trees had eyes and animals talked. It was all nonsense of course, but on this day it meant the forest was a place of safety for Gregor and his pupil.

Gregor tried engaging Elan in conversation, but the girl said nothing. He tried holding her hand, but she pulled it away. Gregor finally gave up, and the two trudged side by side through the afternoon in grief-stricken silence.

They reached the treeline by early evening. They had seen no soldiers searching for them. As dusk rendered the dense forest impenetrable, Gregor found a secluded spot near fallen trees for a campsite. There he studiously set wards to ensure that no creature, living or dead, would see or hear or smell them that night.

"I don't imagine any soldiers will dare come this far into the woods," Gregor said with nervous levity, "but in light of today's events, I'm not taking chances. These wards will make us invisible. As my grandfather used to say, exhaustion is no excuse for negligence."

Gregor glanced repeatedly at Elan as he spoke. Perched grimly on a log, staring straight ahead into nothingness, the girl did not respond.

Gregor triggered a small fire the same way he had lit the torch in the tunnel. Within moments, light and heat spread in all directions.

"As a matter of principle," Gregor said, "I do not favor using my fluential abilities to trap and kill animals, or any living thing, for that matter, but tonight, I believe, qualifies as an emergency. We need to eat. I shall be back shortly with dinner."

Elan said nothing, her eyes now focused on the flames. She locked her knees together and pursed her lips.

Minutes later, Gregor returned carrying two rabbits, which soon found their way onto a makeshift spit over the fire.

"You may be wondering," Gregor said at last to the mute girl, "where we are going. Unfortunately, there is only one feasible option. For planning purposes, we must assume the soldiers are hunting us. We can't flee to the village since that's the first place they'll look, and we frankly don't know if the dearths would protect us. I suspect they would not, and they may even be in on the plot. Any other route over open ground is highly dangerous, especially since we are on foot and the soldiers have horses.

"So our destination is the Montescue family Keep above the snowline in the Northern Reaches. The structure is a thousand years old at least, but it's built from stone and brick, so it should serve our purposes well. It will take us days of uphill climbing through the forest, but I remember the way, and I know sufficient spells to ensure we'll stay warm and dry. Unfortunately, I don't know any trick to get us there faster. We are going to have to walk, and it's not a short distance."

Gregor paused to see if Elan would respond. She did not. Nothing moved except the firelight reflecting in her eyes. Her face was dry. She had not cried since those first moments after the soldiers killed Alaric and Willem.

Gregor set a juicy piece of rabbit by Elan's side, then noisily opened his valise. He extracted a bulging paisley handkerchief, its four corners bound together by string. Gregor opened the bundle to reveal a large handful of glittering white crystals. Elan glanced once at the crystals, then resumed staring fiercely into the firelight.

"Your father and I planned to wait at least a year, perhaps longer, to broach this with you," Gregor said hesitantly, jiggling the crystals in his open hand. "But waiting, I think, no longer makes sense. It's about who you are. Something important. You need to know, and in light of today's events, the sooner the better, I think."

Gregor paused again to see if Elan would show interest. She did not. He sucked in his breath and pressed forward.

"As you know, Alaric and I closely examined your brother, Willem, and determined that he lacked fluential capabilities. He was, bluntly put, not a sorcerer. Initially, we reached the same conclusion as to you, Elan. That is, until that day shortly after your mother left. The day we realized whenever you were underfoot, people were struck by memories of events long forgotten. Some pleasant, some not. But vivid memories, as if the person had been transported to the past. And then it hit us. You have the ability to summon episodic recollections."

Elan stared impassively at Gregor.

"You are," he continued, "what the dearths call a memory witch."

Elan turned back to the fire.

"The books suggest that your talent will require considerable training, and your abilities cannot function in a controlled manner without cloth and crystal. The cloth, we have. The crystal, well, Alaric started gathering it. This is what we have to work with, and it will certainly do for a start."

The crystals tinkled merrily in Gregor's hands, and they reflected the firelight in fantastic color combinations. Elan appeared not to notice. If anything, she bent herself more intently toward the campfire. The forest was remarkably quiet and still. As if a long forgotten relative had returned without warning.

Gregor sighed, bundled the crystals back into the handkerchief, fixed the string in place, and deposited the bundle in the valise. Then he sliced the roasted game and slid a piece into his mouth.

Elan's voice was small, but she spoke clearly. They were her first words since seeing her father and brother murdered. "So, you will teach me to be a memory witch?"

"I will train you to be a *sorceress*," Gregor said

between bites. "We are not a *witch*. The term is coarse."

"How long will it take?"

"Years, my little caterpillar."

"I'm going to learn to use my powers," Elan said after a lengthy pause. "I'm going to find the men who killed Father and Willem."

"Excellent!" Gregor said. "We can bring them to justice."

"No," Elan said.

"No? What else is there to do once you've found them?"

Elan shifted on the log. Her face was dirty, her smock torn, and her bright-red hair gnarled and stringy. She wore blood on her arms, and her legs were stained with mud from the tunnel and green grass from the hillock.

"I'm going to kill them," Elan said.

Gregor's jaw dropped.

"One at a time," the small girl said. "Until they are all dead."

Then she reached for the rabbit and tore off a piece with her teeth.

TEN YEARS LATER

1

Elan

Like always, I come wide awake at dawn and listen for that telltale hum. The sound of Gregor's wards protecting the Keep. Making it invisible. Gregor is an artist, and wards are his canvas. No one does it better. When the thick forests of the Northern Reaches quiet at night, I can hear the sizzle if I hold my breath and listen carefully. Like a swarm of insects approaching from a distance.

I fear the day I will wake up to silence. It will mean Gregor is dead. Wards are personal extensions of sorcerers, and they expire with them. And these last years have been hard on Gregor. He lies about his age, but he has to be nearing eighty. Still, on this day, the day I leave the Keep to avenge my father and brother, I hear the familiar sound, and I sigh in relief. The wards are in place, which means Gregor is alive and likely downstairs making tea.

My eyes brim, and I feel my face growing wet.

No tears! I think. *I must be strong and resolute. Gregor must believe I am up to the challenge.*

I use a towel to wipe my face, then my eyes, then my face again.

I haven't told Gregor I'm leaving, but he's guessed. I can tell. The way he raises his eyebrows and looks sideways at me. How he cocks his head and purses his lips. As if he knows there's something I want to tell him. *Need* to tell him. And of course, I've chopped enough wood for two winters, and the food stores are overflowing. So it's no secret what's about to happen.

Ten years is enough time to prepare for a mission of vengeance, and my anger is no less fierce than the day those hooded men murdered Father and Willem. I haven't forgotten my vow. I will hunt those men and kill them. One by one.

Gregor's view has always been the same: Not now. *Next year*, he'd say. But then next year would arrive, and it would be the same. *You're not yet ready*, he'd say. *There's still more for you to learn.* I would have left last year except for Gregor's accident. His broken leg. I waited another year, like Gregor asked, and yesterday I turned sixteen. Father and Willem have waited long enough. I leave today.

I dress in men's clothes, the plainer the better. Dark trousers, a simple white woolen pullover, and walking shoes. I haven't worn a smock since the day we arrived at the Keep. Gregor and I have kept to ourselves. There's been no one to dress for. No boys to look pretty for. And even if there were, I have no intention of marrying or having children. Thousands of years of Montescue sorcerers, born and bred to the Fluence, will end with a single red-haired memory witch hunting the men who murdered her family. I don't think much about death, but neither do I fear it. My only regret is leaving Gregor. I am all he has.

I push open the windows from my second-floor bedroom, lean my elbows against the icy stones, and peer into the distance. The blademetal sky looks like snow, and it's cold enough. I thrust out my head and see deep frostlines on the Keep's western face. Gregor says the Montescues built the Keep a thousand years ago. The mountainfolk say god built it. The curved lintel over the entryway says in archaic letters, THE SACREDE HOUSSE MOUNTESSCUE. All I know is the Keep feels like the lone survivor of some long-forgotten time. A thick-walled castle, built to withstand a lengthy siege, waiting for its lords and ladies to return.

The forest is dense around the Keep. I have always regarded the army of thin angry trees as my personal bodyguards. The branches, leaves, and pine needles protect me. There are people who want me dead, but I'm safe so long as I stay here at the Keep. Protected by the trees in the bosom of the Dirovian mountains. But when I leave on my mission of vengeance, I will be out in the open. Vulnerable to whatever the world has in store for me.

I wipe my face again. *I said, no tears!*

I pluck off my sleepcap, and my long red tresses plunge to the small of my back. My hair is my only indulgence, and over ten years, it has grown a deeper auburn and now is the color of rich maple leaves in autumn. I finish packing my travelbag, take a deep breath to steel myself, and head down to the kitchen.

On the outside of my right wrist is a ragged red burn in the shape of the letter D. The mark of my patron saint. I close my eyes and kiss it lightly.

I enter soundlessly as Gregor sips his cup and stares out the window into the dormant garden. His cane leans against the wall. Gregor wears his svelte black tutor's attire, now homemade. His face is thin and sallow, and his scalp, littered with dark red spots, sports scattered gossamer tufts of white hair.

The kitchen is larger than we need, but then the Keep is designed for more than two people. The massive coal-black wood stove crackles, and the kitchen is toasty and honey-scented. Another of Gregor's spells. When I was ten, I implored Gregor to make all the rooms warm all the time. He clucked and raised his chin. "I wouldn't think of it, dear child. Keeps are *supposed* to be cold."

Gregor's eyes remain glued to the window. "So you've decided to leave," he says.

"Yes," I say nervously. I set my bag on the wide varnished oaken planks of the kitchen table.

"You're not ready, dear child," he says, then takes another sip.

"I'm as ready as I'll ever be," I say.

4

"Perhaps," Gregor concedes.

"You're a wonderful instructor, Gregor, but there's nothing more you can teach me."

"Experience is the best teacher, Elan, and you've had precious little of that."

"I've seen a lot," I say.

"Through other people's memories," Gregor says. "Which is not the same thing as experiencing the world yourself. Living is something you do, not something you see."

"Not all of those memories were easy," I say quietly.

Gregor's head swivels. "Oh, dear child, I still worry you blame me for making you see them. I debated for weeks, months, but in the end . . ."

"I needed to see them, Gregor."

"Yes," he says, setting down his cup. "You did."

When I first learned my powers, Gregor offered himself as a practice subject. I would select a fabric and lay it against his arm, then use a crystal to enter his mind through the fabric's color. Different colors accessed different sets of memories. Back then, I liked white and yellow the best. They were usually associated with pleasant memories. I met Gregor's long-dead parents and his sister and older brother. I would laugh at their jokes, but I squirmed when his brother taunted and hit him. Gregor never visibly reacted to the punishment his brother inflicted. For some reason, those memories disturbed me more than him.

I especially enjoyed seeing Gregor tutor my father, Alaric, as a boy. One day, young Alaric tried to climb the Keep like a cliff by using makeshift grappling hooks. He nearly killed himself, and the scars from his attempt are still visible on the Keep's south face. Bolstered by my father's example, I learned to climb the old stone walls. Over time, I became so adept I could do it without any assistance. I would flatten myself against the wall, and my feet and fingertips would find the crevices I needed to crawl upwards. Gregor would avert his eyes, but I never fell.

"If you weren't a memory witch," Gregor said more than once, "you would be an acrobat."

Later, Gregor arranged excursions to villages in the flatlands, often more than a week's distance away, but never the same one twice. We would lease a horse and carriage, Gregor posing as an itinerant apothecary, me as his granddaughter. We would stay at the local inn, and while Gregor sought to acquire more crystals for my training, I would mingle with the dearths in the tavern, a piece of cloth in my left hand, a crystal fisted tightly in my right. I would brush against the locals, always quick to vanish so no one could connect the little mischievous red-haired girl with the long-forgotten memory that leapt unbidden into their heads. I used white and yellow cloth, then green and light blue, to witness the happier times in people lives.

When I was thirteen, Gregor, his face unreadable, produced new colors for me to practice with. Not on him, but on the unsuspecting locals. The dearths. It was rude, I know, a violation of their privacy, but there was no other way for me to learn. Gregor's new-chosen colors were midnight blue, deep pulsing crimsons, and ten shades of black. And for the first time, I began seeing the memories that people suppressed. The episodes they buried as deep as their souls permitted. The cruelty staggered me. The angry violence. Parents beating children. Children beating children. A savage variety of atrocities.

And no one buried memories deeper than the women. Sometimes I'd have to tug and pull for the episodes to appear. Like bodies surfacing from inky depths. And the perpetrators were nearly always men, sometimes strangers, but often men the women knew and even loved. Fathers and brothers and husbands and sons. Inflicting raw unquenchable pain, intimate and penetrating.

That first night, I cried myself to sleep. Our room, typical for a flatlands inn, held a single bed with a wafer-thin straw mattress and threadbare pillows. Mouse droppings littered the corner, and a lewd body odor hung in the air. The episodic memories were bad enough, but the women I touched had reacted so viscerally to those hated and haunting memories. They groaned and gasped and sucked in their breath. They shivered and shook. Some fell to their knees, and one vomited. Another cried out like she had been stabbed. Through it all, Gregor had sat alone in a dark corner with his cup of tea, taking it all in, his keen aristocratic eyes focused on me.

Instinctively, I understood why Gregor had

tasked me with the new colors. A memory witch needs to see the full spectrum of human life. Particularly one who is intent on setting off alone to hunt a band of murderers. I needed, as Gregor knew full well, to understand what people are capable of doing to each other. Especially to women. The good, yes, but the depravity as well. And how people somehow find the courage to push down the pain and move forward with the hard work of surviving.

That first night, I was distraught. "Do all men treat women that way?" I asked Gregor.

He started to answer, then bit his tongue. "Enough," he said at last. "Not all, not even most, but enough."

Standing in the kitchen at the Keep on the morning I departed, I stare at the beloved frail old man sipping his tea, and I smile.

Remember, no tears!

"If it weren't for you, Gregor, I wouldn't be in a position to undertake my quest."

"So you're saying," he says, smiling back, "that if I'd done a worse job, you'd be staying?"

"No."

Gregor laughs. "I knew that, of course," he says. "You were going to leave, one way or the other. So better to prepare you as best I could. But you need to understand, Elan, the Riege is no place for a young woman traveling alone. It's not just that men will harm you if given the opportunity. It's that they will *seek out* the opportunity. You must understand that. You must protect yourself at all times."

The Riege is the enormous landmass extending from the Northern Reaches all the way to the Paemok Desert in the southeast corner and the Impassable River on the western border. Its southernmost point is the capital city of Kimbar, where King Marcellus and his red-coated retinue rule from the purple palace. This far north in the vast flatlands nestling the Northern Reaches, the king's grasp is light and feathery. He can send an army this far north if he wants to foot the cost, but he doesn't want to. He has enough other claims on his treasury. So the flatlands are a place for travelers to be cautious.

"I understand," I say. "My plan is to travel to Montauk, then catch a king's carriage, one after another, all the way down to Kimbar. I have the money to pay for it. I'll sleep at local inns, stay inside as much as possible, and keep to myself."

"And in Kimbar?" Gregor asks.

"I'll use my powers until I find a memory of that day. Or someone's memory of talking to a person who was there that day. Or someone who made the uniforms or supplied the horses or . . ."

"Yes, yes, dear child, I understand," Gregor says, waving his teacup. "You will shake the royal tree as hard as you can until something falls to the ground. He won't like it. Not one bit."

"Who?"

"King Marcellus," Gregor says.

"You've taught me to use my powers without being detected," I say. "No one will know I'm there."

"I've taught you," Gregor says, setting his tea-cup down harder than he intends, "how to mini-mize the likelihood of detection. But if you ply your trade day in and day out at every inn and pub and greasy spoon in Kimbar, sooner or later some-body is going to figure it out. And then, well, you know . . ."

"Torches and pitchforks," I say with raised eye-brows.

"Yes, torches and pitchforks," Gregor says. "If the dearths think you're a witch, they will form a mob and come for you. They will burn you or hang you. Perhaps both."

"Let them try," I say fiercely. "I'll use my pow-ers."

"It's your powers that make you vulnerable!" Gregor says with exasperation.

We exchange glares in a strangely comfortable silence. We've had this discussion before.

"And how will you travel to Montauk?" Gregor says, leaning back as he closes his eyes and rubs his temples.

"I will hitch a ride with mountainfolk headed to the flatlands for winter provisions."

A smile sneaks onto Gregor's face. "You refer, of course, to the Vorstadts."

"Yes."

"Your make-believe family!"

"They're nice people," I say.

"You don't know that," Gregor says.

"I've watched them for years," I say.

"You don't know anything about them," Gregor says, "except that they travel to Montauk every year at this time."

"I'm not here to argue with you," I say.

"I never argue," Gregor says. "I instruct."

We laugh at our private joke. "So you're leaving, and I can't stop you," Gregor says. "Is that the size of it?"

"I'm sorry," I say.

"Well, I have something for you then," Gregor says, fishing two handkerchiefs from his rightside pocket. He hands me the paisley handkerchief. The one he brought with us from the villa. I gently pry it apart and smile at the shining crystals.

"It's all I have left, my little caterpillar," Gregor says. "I have no need for them if you're not here."

"Thank you, Gregor."

"And one more trinket," Gregor says. "Let's call it a keepsake." He places the second handkerchief on the table, then opens it to reveal a glorious rubystone. It sparkles in myriad crimson shades, and audibly I catch my breath.

"This is for you," Gregor says. "From Catherine."

"My mother?"

"Do you know any other Catherines?"

As I reach for the gem, Gregor quickly covers it with the handkerchief, then ties it with string.

"What, I can't have it?" I ask.

"Rubystones are risky!" Gregor says. "They can be enchanted. A sorceress is well advised to steer clear of them. I'm only giving this to you now because it's yours, and you are leaving, and I may never see you again. And if you are ever desperate for cash, you can sell it for a pretty penny. To reduce temptation, I've tied it up in this handkerchief."

He dabs at his face.

"You're not crying, are you?" I ask. I am about to break down myself. I bite my lower lip as hard as I bit Gregor's arm on that awful day.

"Of course not. Tutors never cry."

"They instruct," we both say at once, laughing.

Gregor stands and hugs me before I can react. "My dear child," he whispers into my ear. "Please promise me you won't use the rubystone. You must promise. I won't sleep at night unless you do."

"You realize, Gregor," I whisper in return, "that I know almost nothing about my mother."

Gregor stands back. "Neither did your father, truth be told. Catherine bewitched him, and I mean that in the basest sense. Nobody knew her or her family, or even where she came from. Then, after bearing two children, she disappeared with nary a goodbye, except for this gem she earmarked for you. It's a crystal, but please promise me you will never use it as a sorceress."

"I promise," I say. Then I kiss Gregor on both cheeks, hoist my travelbag, and exit the kitchen quickly, wiping away my own tears so I can taste his lingering on my lips.

2

Gregor's Journal

The day I've dreaded for ten years has arrived. Elan is gone, and I am alone. At least she stayed at the Keep until she turned sixteen! Alaric would be proud of her, but as for Catherine, I cannot say. Training that lovely girl has been both the joy and bane of my existence. A joy to see the sorceress she has become. And could become with yet more time. A bane to think that her powers may be the death of her, and soon.

I should begin, as they say, at the beginning. I was certain Alaric would be the last pupil I trained to be a sorcerer, especially after Willem arrived without any fluential talent. I was, of course, mistaken about that.

Elan was born at the tail-end of the tenth Ebb. The Fluence washes over the Riege in waves. During the Flow, which lasts up to a century, the magi multiply and gain strength. Then the Ebb takes hold, and the Fluence recedes fast and hard like a wicked undertow. The Ebb lasts fifty years at most, and then the magi are gone. The families born and bred to the Fluence continue on, of course, their primary objective to survive the seemingly interminable Dry until the next Flow begins. Until they can start begetting sorcerers anew. The dearths, most of whom can neither read nor write, quickly relegate the feats of the magi to stories told by toothless old men to disbelieving youths over campfires or one too many ales. The dearths are always caught by surprise when the next Flow starts and the magi reappear.

It is said that each Ebb, as its dying gasp, spits out one last great sorcerer. The history books, many written in languages no one speaks anymore and which only the trained few can navigate, recount the amazing achievements of these magi. The most famous, Tay-marcus of House d'Uberville, created the Impassable River during the third Ebb to protect the Riege from invasion by the vicious sun-stained Karator nation to the west. The Karators had battered the Riege with one invasion after another, and the next one likely would have done the trick. The miraculous emergence of Marcus d'Uberville saved the Riege from annihilation.

Sorcerers were already few and far between when Alaric was born. He was precocious as a youth, and so the born-and-bred quickly anointed him as the last great mage, an accolade which

Alaric, never bashful, accepted at once. His objective was to alter weather patterns to eliminate droughts in the flatlands. A worthy goal, but one that proved elusive for a wizard even of Alaric's talent. And then came the day the hooded soldiers arrived on horseback. Alaric died, and I escaped with Elan to the Montescue family stronghold in the Northern Reaches.

Alaric and I were slow to see Elan's talent because the tenth Ebb was nearly finished. No infants from any born-and-bred family, Willem included, had fluential powers, and many adult sorcerers struggled with diminished or lost competence. So we assumed the Dry was upon us and threw barely a second glance at Elan. All that changed when she was five. It was literally a few weeks, perhaps mere days, after her mother, Catherine, had fled the villa. Elan discovered a chest full of old clothes, including some of Alaric's, then tried, laughing and squealing, to pull a boy-sized tunic over Alaric's head.

A memory seized Alaric. He was immediately transported to the day he tried to climb the family's Keep with pigsty hooks and twine. It was as if he'd gone back in time. Other household members had similar experiences with Elan's horseplay. Alaric and I put our heads together, consulted a few crumbling ancient texts, and came away with a unified reaction.

We were terrified.

A memory witch, to use the dearths' crude vernacular, was the most hated and feared of all magi.

Always a woman, she was the only mage capable of entering minds and picking through their contents. Many became unbalanced, some became vigilantes, and the rest went stark-raving mad. None of them lived long. They never married or bore children. No matter how hard they tried to be stealthy, inevitably their training failed, and they slipped up. And then the mob arrived with torches and pitchforks. Burnings. Hangings. Disembowelments. In some cases, the dearths simply tore them apart, limb from limb, with their bare hands.

The most powerful of the memory witches was Rador-amelia of House Martòn during the fifth Ebb. The stories of the carnage she inflicted on the Riege were too incredible for Alaric and me to fully credit. Amelia escaped Kimbar to the flatlands just short of the Northern Reaches, where a massive manhunt finally pinned her down in the now-forgotten hamlet of Manuel. They used a herd of rampaging horses to take her down – apparently entering the minds of animals was beyond even her powers! – before cutting her body into a hundred pieces and, according to legend, burying them throughout the Riege. Then the dearths burned Manuel to the ground, and House Martòn disbanded, its members fleeing for their lives. The dearths' ensuing inquisition against the born-and-bred during the fifth Dry was vicious. Only a handful of families survived to the sixth Flow. That was a thousand years ago. Amelia was the last memory witch on record, and she perished one month shy of her fourteenth birthday.

The born-and-bred have always viewed memory witches as a horrid anomaly. A fluential imperfection. An unfortunate mistake, if you will. Memory witches' lives always ended badly and frequently poisoned relations with the dearths for years if not decades afterward. In Amelia's case, the born-and-bred were nearly exterminated. Were a memory witch to reappear, the dearths would have no need to track her down and kill her. The born-and-bred likely would do it for them.

Among dearths, the exploits of Amelia and other memory witches persist primarily in the form of old wives' tales. Along with goblins and dragons and, of course, stone-faced red-tinted Karator warriors, memory witches are among the monsters parents summon when they seek to scare their children into obedience.

For scholars, modern references are mostly found in appendices to historical tracts and sometimes not even then. It's the ancient texts, some copies of copies of now-lost handwritten parchments, that discuss memory witches in vivid detail.

I was particularly struck by an oversized tome, its front and back covers, upon closer examination, made of pigskin pulled tight over thick cherrywood slats, which was entitled Unfortunate Lives of Fluence (Illustrated). Its author is identified only as A Sorrowful Survivor of The House Marton. The book documents the lives of famous sorcerers who bent towards evil, and Amelia's is the last life documented. Her short reign of terror is narrated in page after page of bloody detail. The author claimed personal knowledge of certain events, which effectively dates the book to the onset of the fifth Dry.

One passage, repeated several times throughout, puzzled me. It said that Amelia ultimately dispensed with the "Ceremonie of Clothe and Cristals." But according to every other history, cloth and crystals are the necessary instruments of a memory witch's powers. She needs both to enter the mind of another person and summon memories. So how could Amelia dismiss such a "Ceremonie?" The Sorrowful Survivor offered no explanation.

I told Elan none of the history of memory witches, of course. I feared it would become a self-fulfilling prophecy. She would expect to cause damage and end badly, and so she would. Thus are teenagers. And it wouldn't have stopped her from leaving to avenge Alaric and Willem. If anything, it would have prompted her to leave soonest, and my goal was to keep her in training as long as possible. There at the Keep, far from prying eyes. Whoever wanted Alaric and Willem dead probably wanted Elan dead as well. And I thought if my training was unflinching, perhaps, just perhaps, she might survive traversing the Riege in search of the hooded horsemen. It offended my sense of professional acumen to think there was any fluential power that could not be harnessed by a tutor working at the top of his game to instill discipline in a pupil over a sufficient period of time.

Now that Elan has departed, I've developed the

habit of pausing whatever I might be doing to monitor my wards protecting the Keep. Elan told me she could hear them as a kind of distant hum. For me, they're a ringing in my ears. Faint, but high-pitched and always there. I fear that moment I will listen and detect only silence. It will mean Elan is dead. A tutor has fluential abilities, but they are tailored to his pupil. Once he lacks a pupil, he becomes no better than a dearth, powerless and feeble. My life-long powers, including the ability to set and maintain wards, will continue only so long as Elan, my final pupil, survives.

Although the fire that destroyed the villa also claimed Alaric's library, the Keep has its own rather substantial collection. The volumes are much older, many written in long-neglected dialects. I did manage to salvage one item from the villa's library before I fled with Elan through that horrid cellar tunnel. A single page from a single book. In the Sorrowful Survivor's tome, there is an illustration of Amelia. It is, I assume, highly idealized. It shows Amelia in flowing robes and sandals, her face hard and masculine, devoid of female emotion. She stands on a pedestal with chaos strewn around her. Toppled buildings, raging fires, screaming children, and more than a few headless bodies. But Amelia is not looking at the carnage. She stares in rage and fascination at a gem – surrounded with jagged lines to show how it radiates power – which she holds high in her right hand. The reader can easily identify the gem. It's the only aspect of the print depicted in color.

In her right hand, Amelia holds a rubystone.

At night, when my fears for Elan rage nearly out of control, I wrap myself in blankets, sip centuries-old brandy, and stare at the illustration by firelight. Amelia died a thousand years ago, so I tell myself the rubystone Catherine gifted to Elan can't possibly be the same one.

Can it?

3

Elan

The mountainfolk call it a longjacket because it drops below my knees. Gregor says it is my coat of many colors. I've always called it my leathers. Gregor stitched it together from burnished black leather, fabulously glossy and smooth, that he discovered in long-unused closets at the Keep. Then I sewed pockets on the inside lining to house my fabrics. Every color god created, plus a few he didn't! Gregor started me with four bits of cloth: snow white, sun yellow, grass green, and eggshell blue. Now my collection runs in the hundreds, no two the same. A memory witch needs cloth, and the coat carries my supply.

I shrug the coat over my shoulders as I head from the Keep. I don't want to advertise my gender, so I'm careful to sneak my hair down the inside. I tell myself I won't look back. I am leaving to fulfill my purpose in life, and I doubt I shall return. So I must rid myself of emotion and doubt. The past is behind me and needs to stay there.

The pine trees, tall and elegant, escort me down the hillside. But when I reach the jagged rocky outcrop with veins of ragged red ore, I know I have reached the point of no return. Those rocks mark the outer rim of Gregor's wards. One step in front, I can turn around and see the Keep in all its ancient magnificence. One step past, and all I see when I turn around is a thick forbidding please-leave-and-don't-come-back forest. The Keep has disappeared.

I sigh and crane my head, thinking perhaps Gregor is watching from a window. He'll wave, and I'll wave back. But I don't see him. The Keep is silent and still. Only the barest puff of smoke above the kitchen indicates it is occupied. So I step past the rocks and, just like that, the Keep is gone. Like it never existed at all. So much, I think, like Catherine. I no longer have any vivid personal memories of her. Her looks, her voice, her movements, her clothes. I caught stray glimpses of Catherine in Gregor's memories, but he was reluctant to show me more. So I pushed mother out of my mind as best I could, only to have Gregor surprise me with the rubystone. Mother's untouched and apparently untouchable gift.

When I was twelve, I interrupted my lessons to ask Gregor if I looked like my mother. It was a question out of the blue. "That's neither here nor there," he grumbled.

"Gregor, I just want to know," I said.

He stared at me for what seemed like the longest time. "You have her face," he said at last, then quickly resumed the lesson.

All that is behind me now. My immediate destination in the Reaches has no name. Some call it the crossroads. It's what mountainfolk mean when they say they'll meet you "there." It's a wide spot on a decent lay of flat land near a stream where two cartpaths intersect. Well back in the trees are a lice-infested ramshackle inn and a general store. It's below the snowline, barely, and two days' walk from the Keep. Montauk is a day's ride by horse and wagon if you start at dawn.

Each fall equinox, Gregor and I traveled "there" for supplies. Avoiding the inn, we camped on the steep tree-stuffed hillside and slept soundly on thick layers of pine needles. Gregor's wards and spells kept us invisible and warm.

And each year I saw a family – the Vorstadts, I finally learned – arrive by wagon. They would eat and sleep around a campfire. I'd sneak down, hide in the dense prickly shrubs, and watch and listen. A family! Something I once enjoyed but would never have again. I yearned to read their memories, but Gregor warned me against it. *Using your powers is always risky, so don't unless you have a good reason for doing so.* Sheer curiosity, Gregor made clear, was not a sufficient reason. In Gregor's mind, torches and pitchforks were never more than a few moments away.

Still, over the years, I've learned a lot about the

Vorstadts. Adam, the garrulous father, proud of his mustache, a little rounder and balder each passing year. Molley, the mother, always bundled in a thick shawl, saying little beyond pithy instructions and reminders to the boys. And Jasper and Frederick, about my age, now strapping restless young men with big ideas and no fear. They farm a snug valley just above the snowline, and every year at the same time they travel to Montauk for supplies.

For years I've fantasized about being a Vorstadt. I fit perfectly. The daughter Adam and Molley always wanted. A sister for the boys. Under his jovial exterior, Adam would watch over me, and I imagined he had a lovely singing voice and played a string instrument. At night, I would lay my head in Molley's lap, and she would comb my hair tirelessly. The boys would tease and jostle me but would rise protectively in my defense should a stranger get too close. And the hideous men I saw in all those women's fearful memories, the ones capable of inflicting such searing brutal pain, would be kept at a great distance. I would have a family to protect me.

The last several months I developed a plan to hitch a ride with the Vorstadts. I rehearsed and refined my story endlessly. *I am traveling to Montauk*, I would tell them, *to catch a king's carriage to live with relatives in Kimbar. My grandfather dropped me off yesterday, but my ride never showed, and the people at the inn mentioned your lovely family. I have a few coins to pay with, and I travel with my own food and water pouch, so I won't be any trouble. All I need is a small space in the back of someone's wagon.* Of course, I know their wagon is always empty on the ride down to Montauk to make room for the supplies they plan to buy and haul back.

My hike to the crossroads takes two days. I camp overnight on the hillside above the inn, careful to set wards, as Gregor trained me, to avoid being seen. I can hear his voice in my head. *Exhaustion is no excuse for negligence.* I smile at the familiar wagon, darkened with age and repairs, anchored in the same spot as previous years. It creaks in the wind like it could fall apart any moment, but somehow it returns year after year. The horses are old and tired and as dark as the wagon. The Vorstadts look and act the same, Adam joking with the boys, Molley silently wrapped in a brown shawl with tassels. If only they had a daughter, I think, they would be a perfect family. If only they had me.

The next morning I say my well-rehearsed lines to Adam, dressed in his usual worn coveralls, as the Vorstadts load the wagon. Stunned, he peers at me for a moment, tweaking his mustache, then he laughs and accepts my proposal on the spot. I smile because it's what I knew he would do. Then he catches himself and glances at Molley like he's tossing her an egg. Their eyes meet, and it is a look I have never seen before. It must, I think, be some kind of private language a husband and wife develop after years of growing closer together.

"Whatever you think best, Adam," Molley says quietly, lowering her eyes.

"Then it's settled," he says with high spirits. "I'll gladly take your money, and you can ride in the back to Montauk. There we'll part ways as friends."

The boys guffaw and punch each other, then fall down wrestling and rolling in the fragrant pine needles. I laugh like I imagine a sister would laugh. Then I bite my tongue, not wanting to become too familiar too quickly. The Vorstadts must never guess I know who they are. That I've watched them closely for years. That I know all their stories. They must believe, I tell myself, we are strangers meeting by chance for the first and last time.

The ride to Montauk with the Vorstadsts is far less comfortable than I'd imagined. When Gregor and I visited flatlands villages as part of my training, we rode in a fine tall carriage. There were cushions on the seatbox up front and a downy mattress out of the sun under the stiff canvas hood in the back. On each side was painted a tall man in a black hat and mustache, holding a light blue bottle that said _ELIXIR_. The words "Gregor Rensmann & Sons" were written in a wild cursive hand, and underneath, in smaller square letters, the phrase "Licensed Apothecaries." I rode up front as my eyes adjusted happily to the wonders of a world without trees and mountains and snow and wild animals.

But there are no cushions in the hard wooden well of the Vorstadts' wagon. Nor a hood overhead to block the sun. The Vorstadts wear wide-brimmed hats and do not offer one to me. *If there is ever a next time*, I think, *I will remember to bring a hat*. I perch myself in the back corner, absorbing every bump and rattle in the rutted cart-path. I loosen the buttons but dare not take off my leather coat lest they see the cloth and crystals I carry, so I become overheated, sweat streaming down my face and trickling down my back. Family conversation ends quickly. After staring at me open-mouthed for a few minutes, the boys doze off. Molley rides like a statue next to Adam, never once turning around.

For an hour or so, Adam peppers me with questions over his shoulder. Where do I live? Who am I seeing in Kimbar? Where am I staying in Montauk? And many more. I offer him as little information as I can. Gregor told me the best lies are unembellished. Adam accepts all my answers with his twinkling eyes and infectious bushy smile.

We arrive in Montauk at dusk. I have consumed several gallons of water from our river stops. My clothes are drenched in sweat under my leathers. My temples throb, and I ache all over. Every muscle, every joint. My bottom has no feeling. I can trek through the bristling forests of the Reaches for days without tiring, but a one-day trip under a blazing sun in the back of a wagon to Montauk has finished me. Tracing a finger on my coat, I realize I'm slathered with grime from head to toe. My red hair is stringy, and my face wears mud like makeup.

There are no big cities in the flatlands. Nothing like Kimbar or Elden or the other trade centers in the south. Montauk, with a few thousand residents and a compact business district, is the largest for some miles in any direction. And it has grown since Gregor and I visited three years earlier. I remember the chall – the Order's place of worship – from that visit. The chall was a modest one-story wooden building where the Order's brothers and sisters lived and worshiped. It offered no luxuries and few comforts, but everyone was welcome. With its emphasis on piety and poverty, the Order has governed religious life in the Riege for a century or more.

But now there is a hunger for new construction in the air. The chall has expanded to include nearly an entire city block, and upper stories are being added. In the center is a towering spire that, replete with a sonorous black bell, dominates Montauk. The front door is a work of fine craftsmanship, and hand-wrought iron sconces cast an eerie light. Black-clad brothers and sisters are everywhere on the streets, and the bell tolls as we approach Montauk's main inn. It is the first time I have ever heard a challbell.

It is noisy, and there are people and wagons and horses everywhere. Passersby look at our lumbering wagon for a few moments, as if sizing up the newcomers, before something else diverts their attention. Everyone seems to have some other place they need to be at once. In the street a drunken man with a torn tunic and long greasy hair slurps ale from a cracked wooden cup. He pulls his sword and, its blade glinting, duels with a phantom opponent until he loses his balance and topples over.

Suddenly I am terrified. I am in a strange wagon surrounded by strange people in a strange town. If they knew who I was, or what I was, they would kill me. I have never been so scared and alone in my life. Maybe Gregor was right. Maybe I'm not ready for my mission. Maybe I need more training. Maybe the Riege is more than a young inexperienced memory witch can hope to navigate alone.

And then the stables by the inn come into view, and I breathe more easily. Soon I'll be inside the inn and safe from the dangers of Montauk.

It is only one day, Father, I think, *but so far, everything is going according to plan.*

4

Elan

A dour dirty stableboy slides open the doors to the stables as Adam deftly maneuvers the horses and wagon inside. Smelling of manure, the structure is large and dark and damp. Adam guides the wagon to a back corner, where the stableboy takes the horses. The Vorstadt boys and I tumble wearily out the back. The last few beams of a setting sun sneak through cracks in the roof. As Adam motions me over, I realize my time with the Vorstadts is over.

"Where will you stay the night?" Adam asks.

"I planned to stay at the inn," I say.

"The stableboy says the inn is full. Montauk is always jammed at equinox. The Order also has a celebration planned for the new chall. We have a standing reservation at the inn since we come every year, but it's only one room, and there's four of us. I wish we had space for another."

"I'll find something," I say. I try to remember Adam's route into Montauk and the layout of the business district. I've slept beneath the stars before. All I need is a park or a garden or an empty building. Somewhere out of sight so I can set wards and remove my leathers without being seen. If I have to wear my coat one minute more, I'll scream.

Adam slaps the wagon hard with his left hand. "You can sleep in our wagon if you want. I doubt anyone will care. The stableboy won't come back here. It won't be comfortable, but it will see you through the night until your king's carriage tomorrow."

I look around. There is ample straw, and burlap bags hang limply over empty horse stalls. I could easily make a mattress.

"Thank you," I say with relief. "That would be lovely."

"The boys and I will push the wagon nearer the far corner," Adam says, winking. "That way you'll have some privacy. We'll see you in the morning."

After Adam leaves, I climb into the wagon. I am dead on my feet, but first things first. I am a trained memory witch, after all. I need to set wards. Exhaustion is never an excuse.

Gregor drilled into my head that wards are about mathematics and geography. *Only a fool believes wards emerge ready-made from spells.* Incantations seal the package, but first you calibrate power, directions, and angles over a unique geography. Gregor prepared diagrams and flow charts to determine the proper number and location of wards. It was six months before he felt he was properly warding the Keep. For wards to work, the entire area must be sealed. One tiny opening can ruin everything. What works in a house will not work in a field. A flat pasture requires a different configuration than a forested hillside. I laugh, as I can almost hear Gregor talking.

For ten minutes I attempt to ward the wagon's well. My first try leaves it open underneath, my second try, an opening above. I seal those two, but then the wheels leak. By the fifth try, nothing is sealed, and the entire configuration collapses around my ears like a tent with bent poles. I am so tired, and the sunlight through the roof is nearly gone. All I want to do is cry.

Then I peer into the stable's darkest corner. Two sturdy walls, a dirt floor, and a low wood-planked ceiling. Perfect. Even I can ward that space. So I clamber down from the wagon, throw my travelbag against the wall, and push armfuls of straw into a pile. I'm so exhausted, I don't bother with the burlap bags. I've slept on plain straw before. One more time won't kill me. Setting these wards is so easy I laugh. When I repeat the sealing spell in my head, it all comes together in perfect unison. The sound it makes is like slurping warm soup straight from the bowl.

I throw off my leathers and fall in a heap on my bed of straw. In the nearly pitch black stable, I am invisible and protected from whatever the world can throw at me. I don't care about the odor. I sniff my armpits and realize I smell just as bad. Another minute and I will be sound asleep.

Except I hear heavy footsteps. I become instantly alert. In the damp gloom, I see a large man approach the Vorstadts' wagon. He swings a creaking lantern in his left hand, and with his right he unbuckles his belt and begins removing it from his trousers. He climbs onto the rear left wheel, bracing one boot on a spoke, and steps into the well. The lantern weaves crazily. Like a drunken firefly.

"There's no one here, Adam," the man calls out roughly.

I can see him more clearly now. He's half a head taller than Adam, with a full beard and a sweaty jowly face. His hair lies in greasy strings down nearly to his collar. His unbuckled work-pants sag around his hips.

"She should be there sleeping." It's Adam's voice from the gloom.

Instinctively, I crawl tightly into the stable's corner. I try to calm my breathing. I don't make a sound, even though my wards, if I've done them properly, should keep anyone from hearing me.

"I said, there's no one here."

Adam's head pops into the lantern light. His eyes, like beads, survey the wagon's empty well.

"I paid good money for thirty minutes," the man says sharply.

"Jasper, give me your lantern!" Adam barks. Jasper appears from out of nowhere and hands him a second lantern.

Adam aggressively searches the surrounding area, his lips pursed tightly in anger. He walks to the corner where I'm huddled and jabs the lantern toward me. His eyes stare at me, and I think I've been discovered. He's so close I can smell his foul breath. See the beads of sweat on his forehead. But then Adam turns away and retreats to the wagon.

"That little hussy," Adam snarls. "That dirty red-headed two-bit grifter. She's not here. She gave us the slip."

"I want my money back," the man in the wagon says as he rebuckles his belt. "And I mean, now."

Adam grumbles, retrieves some coins, and hands them to the man.

"It's not my fault, Anse," Adam says. "She rode with us from the crossroads. I arranged for her to sleep in the wagon. Jasper stood guard outside. I paid the stableboy to vanish. She should be here."

"Except she's not," Anse says, pocketing the coins. He climbs down from the wagon, then suddenly punches the left rear wheel, shattering a spoke. "That's for my trouble," he says.

"Does this mean I'm not going to get a turn?" Jasper asks plaintively.

"Shut up, Jasper," Adam barks, still holding the lantern as he backs away from Anse.

"I should rearrange that fat face of yours," Anse says, leaning menacingly toward Adam. "You promised thirty minutes."

"I'll make it up to you," Adam says nervously. "I promise."

"You better," Anse says, then stalks off.

After Anse is gone, Adam wheels and slaps Jasper hard in the face. The boy falls to one knee.

"You were to stand guard!" Adam yells.

"But I did," Jasper protests.

"Not well enough," Adam says. "The girl's gone, and now Anse is mad at us. Look what he did to the wagon."

"Where do you think the girl went?" Jasper asks.

"Well, she's not on her way to visit relatives in Kimbar," Adam spits out.

"She's not?"

"Of course not, you fool. Her cockamamie story made no sense. Granddad dropped her off and just left her at the crossroads? Not likely. And she shows up wearing a fancy leather coat that's probably worth as much as our farm and pays for the trip in three hundred-year-old coins? No, she's a runaway or a thief, probably both. We could have done what we wanted with her. There's no one would miss that girl."

Adam stomps off. Jasper, head down and sulking, follows seconds later. In the corner, I hold myself tightly, elbows to my ribs, knees glued, shaking all over. I don't want to cry, but I'm not strong enough to fight the tears. The memories of all those women wash over me. The memories that emerged only from the blackest cloth. Gregor warned me. Seeing evil through other people's eyes is one thing. Seeing it through your own is another. Having it *happen* to you is the worst. I realize how close I just came to being one more victim on an infinite list.

Gregor was right about the Vorstadts. I knew nothing about them. I think back to that morning – the look Adam and Molley shared before we started – and now it's clear to me. Molley knew! She knew what Adam was going to do. Her eyes told Adam she wouldn't interfere. It's why Molley turned her back on me all day. Why she never said a word. She needed me to be a stranger. I guess that's how she sleeps at night.

Suddenly I know what I have to do. I am on a mission, and there is no room in my life for indulgences. Not even one. I search my travelbag for shears, then, with one last fierce sigh, I close my eyes, lean back my head, and begin cutting. My hair barely makes a sound as it wafts through the air onto the straw. I don't need to see my reflection because I don't care how I look. It no longer matters. Nothing is going to stop me. Nothing is going to hold me back. I will find the men who murdered Father and Willem, and I will kill them, and I'm prepared for it to be the last thing I ever do.

And so long as I live, I vow never again to trust a man.

Anse's lantern still glows next to the wagon, and I spy a mallet leaning against a horse stall. It has a long weathered wooden handle with a sheared-stone head. It is almost too heavy, but I manage. I drag it over to the Vorstadts' wagon. One by one, I destroy the spokes on each of the four wheels. For a moment, I think the wagon will collapse of its own weight, but it doesn't. It stands there, trembling unsteadily like a newborn colt.

Then I drop the mallet, pick up my travelbag, and head off into the unwelcome night.

5

Gregor's Journal

There is no training manual for memory witches. Alaric's library offered little assistance, and why should it? Memory witches were to be stamped out, not encouraged. Certainly not taught. But the Montescue family hired me to tutor Alaric because I was the best. So I improvised and adapted. In front of Elan, I acted like I knew precisely what I was doing. Like I had been training memory witches all my life. To teach well, you must be confident above all else. But in fact, I was making it up as I went along.

The key was understanding how the Fluence works for a memory witch. The Keep's library contained older books, some predating Amelia's reign of terror by centuries. No instruction manuals, but useful information nonetheless. For example, a memory witch should never use cloth and crystal to access her own memories. The books were unequivocal about that. She could get lost in her own mind and never emerge. Which left me as the only possible subject for experimentation.

Cloth offers a channel into the subject's mind. The color is important, yes, but also the texture, the weave, the density. It gives the sorceress access to specific memory sectors. It's the crystal that enables her, once inside, to sort and select a particular memory. When Elan first practiced on me, I could sense her entering and scrolling through my recollections. It felt like another being was inside me, and I nearly vomited. After a while, it was more like a prolonged tickle. With my instruction, Elan perfected her technique. By the time she turned sixteen, I could still feel her enter my mind, but only because I knew her touch. To an unsuspecting dearth, it would be the barest caress, a mere flicker of feeling. Like the softest moment of breeze on a napping tulip blossom.

I wasn't worried about ordinary dearths. Most of them couldn't read or write. They wouldn't feel a thing if Elan accessed their memories. It was the trained minds that worried me. The born-and-bred, and of course the elite dearths, however few there were. Unless they were asleep, they would know instantly a thief was inside their skull. Pitchforks and torches would not be far behind. No amount of training and practice could fully insulate Elan from discovery by a self-aware mind.

It took me years to figure out how the crystals worked. How could a sorceress scroll through a person's memories in a moment? And then one day, I knew. It was staring me in the face all along. Some discoveries require merely unpacking the obvious. The crystal enables a memory witch to stop time! Or at least slow it to a nearly imperceptible crawl. This allows her to peruse a subject's mind for that certain specific memory in what seems to be the merest instant.

And her skills work by kinetic repetition, not spells or potions or incantations. The more Elan practiced with crystals, the more power and control she wielded. It was like a muscle. The more you exercised, the stronger it became. After ten years, her powers are now so strong she can read a person's entire lifetime of significant memories in the blink of an eye.

Still, during those early years I felt something was missing. Elan's powers were growing, but she was nowhere near as capable as Amelia was purported to be. And then I found it. I want to call it a book, as it was bound, but it was a mere ten pages. Hardly enough to merit inclusion in a library filled with ancient texts of great length and learning. The title was unprepossessing: Sortes Of Cristals. It had no author or date, but the parchment was old, and it was handwritten in thick homemade black ink. It appeared to be a reference volume. Something you'd write to keep track of everyday information. A kind of reminder.

It was the last page that made all the difference. The first nine pages listed various types of crystals in the Riege, including a few found only in the Dirovian mountains. On page ten was the picture of a boy, a drawing, really. I don't think it was meant to be anyone in particular. Just an average everyday run-of-the-mill boy. And beneath the picture was the following:

> "It is by now well knowne that a memorie wiche may use, combined with Clothe, the Cristals listed in these pages. Further, folk legend says that for each memorie wiche the Fluence provides one person, in the form of a Boye of equal years, who by purpose and desyne functions as the one Cristal to focus, magnifye, and perfect her powers. This Boye will be her *Anaiah*. The memorie wiche must remane ever Alert because the Fluence will offer to her the *Anaiah* but once."

So that was it – a human crystal! Which makes sense, of course. The bond between a sorceress and the hard granular crystal she holds in her hand is inanimate and unforgiving. Incapable of growth. But the bond between two people! If the legend is true, if the Fluence designs and births a boy to be the perfect match for a memory witch's powers, there's no telling how strong she could become. Especially a sorceress, such as Elan, who's been trained to exercise rigorous self-discipline.

The word *Anaiah* comes from an ancient Riegian dialect that no one speaks anymore. Some call it the language of the first words. It dates back to the time of the original settlers, preserved today only in oral fables and myths. People laugh to hear them told. Those were times of powerful men and women clothed in radiance and possessing enormous powers, or so the stories go. If memory serves, the *Anaiah* was their word for answering a prayer.

On that blessed day of discovery, I read page ten over and over again. Well past midnight and into the darkest hours dredging the morn. While the volumes on memory witches were loath to address what obviously was considered to be an old wives' tale, maybe there would be other references. I piled high the books from the Keep's library, then studied every passage by the light of twenty candles as if I were reading it anew. None of the books mentioned the *Anaiah*. The link, it turns out, came down to a different word. Always capitalized. A memory witch must remain always and forever "Alert." That was the word used in <u>Sortes of Cristals</u>, and the same word appeared in other tracts from the Montescue library. It was like a secret code.

Passages I previously dismissed as obscure now shone with meaning. They contained subtle instructions to help a memory witch identify her *Anaiah*. A sorceress should be Alert to sudden but temporary changes in the weather, especially involving lightning or wind. Or unusual animal activity, birds and domestic pets in particular. Or anything involving sparks, lightning, fire, or flares. Or unusual splashes of colors or color combinations. Or, and this was stressed repeatedly, any unusual physical sensations, such as chills or palpitations, that startle or yield a flash of insight. I think Master Eusebius of the Second Ebb put it best. A memory witch must be "perpetually Alert to any Connection that opens the possibility of her ultimate Perfection."

At that point, the pieces fell together like a Tormentian puzzle. Somewhere in the Riege was a boy the same age as Elan – the only boy, if the books were correct – who could serve as her human crystal, her *Anaiah*. We lived in isolation at the Keep, and the Reaches provided no opportunity for Elan to meet boys. Which meant the Fluence was waiting for Elan to undertake her mission of vengeance. And then it would throw this boy directly into her path. Like a lamb in front of a galloping carriage. And I imagined the longer Elan's training took, the faster the Fluence would work once she ventured out. It would be a matter not of days but of hours. Elan would have to be Alert indeed.

During her years of training, Elan exhausted all the crystals I brought with us from Alaric's villa that awful day. And a few she cracked; one even splintered into pieces. A memory witch is hard on her crystals. She uses them until they are empty vessels, then discards them casually. A fractious thought formed slowly, and I brushed it away, but it kept sneaking back. What toll would Elan inflict upon her human crystal? Would she exhaust the boy? Squeeze him dry? Break him?

Would Elan kill her *Anaiah*?

One night I woke up in a heavy sweat. My dreams pointed it out to me. Tapped me on the shoulder and whispered into my ear and told me to go find it at once. So, by the light of my silver-plated chamberstick, I fished out the Sorrowful Survivor's illustration of Amelia and examined it with a magnifying glass. There by her left foot was a boy's body, arms crossed, lying on a rocky slab. Coins covered his eyes. Of all the many bodies strewn about, only this one was identified. I squinted to read the letters – P. GUISCARD. Was P. Guiscard her *Anaiah*? Did the mob kill him with pitchforks and torches? Or did Amelia use him too hard once too often? Was that what drove her mad? And what role did the rubystone play? All questions to which I had no way of finding reliable answers.

I waited until Elan was fourteen to tell her of my discovery. I thought she would be excited. She wasn't. In fact, she dismissed it out of hand. She would initiate a mission of vengeance. It was hers to undertake alone. Without anyone's help. Especially some boy's. She nearly spat out the word. Elan did not expect to survive, so she didn't care about perfecting her powers. And she didn't believe in folk tales anyway. Legend said her father would be the last great sorcerer of his era. And we all know how that turned out.

"Nevertheless, you must be on the lookout," I admonished her.

"I will be," she replied. "For the men who murdered my father and brother."

"No," I said. "For your human crystal. Your *Anaiah*."

"Boys are a myth," she said.

"I'm talking about one boy," I replied. "One special boy."

"Yes, yes," she said absentmindedly. "Weather, and animals, and colors, and sparks, and chills, and other ridiculous things."

"Just promise me you'll stay alert," I said, smiling. "Otherwise, Stanislaus will pass by, and you'll miss your opportunity."

"Stanislaus?" she said, rolling her eyes.

"That's the boy's name!" I said merrily.

"You made that up!" she shrieked, laughing.

"It came to me while I slept," I intoned, closing my eyes, fingers to my temples. "Even now, I see it so clearly. Stanislaus! I'm certain that's his name."

Elan laughed so hard she fell off her chair. It was midsummer's eve, and she lay on her back there on the fertile soil of our garden, chortling as she stared up into the sky through the tenacious gnarled treelimbs of the Reaches. "If I ever meet a boy named Stanislaus, I shall heed your warning," she said at last. "Otherwise, I think the legend is stupid, and I shall ignore it. My fate is to be alone forever."

"As you wish," I said.

"And Stanislaus is a stupid name," she said, chopping with her hand for emphasis.

"I heard you the first time," I said.

"And anyway, a boy would just slow me down,"

she said.

"If you say so," I replied.

Periodically I would review with Elan the tell-tale signs that her *Anaiah* was nearby. I'd show her the pages in the books to prove I wasn't making it up. She would sigh and groan and hold her head and pretend to cry.

"Why are you crying?" I asked.

"For Stanislaus, of course," she said. "He's going to spend his life looking for something he never finds."

"Poor boy," I said.

"Poor Stan," she agreed.

6

Elan

First I think it, then I speak it.
"I am stupid."

I close my eyes and hold my head. "I am *so* stupid."

I didn't know anything about the Vorstadts. Not really. I saw only what I wanted to see. I projected onto them my fervent wish to be part of a loving family. They were missing a daughter — missing a sister! — and I thought I would slot right in. Only Gregor's training saved me. I had no natural aptitude for setting wards, but Gregor insisted I learn. *Safety first, Elan.*

"I am an idiot."

And then I destroyed their wagon wheels with the mallet. All four of them. It gave me grim satisfaction, but now the Vorstadts will be stuck in Montauk for another day. Adam will be furious, and he'll hunt me. How will I get out of town? The king's carriage is no longer safe. Adam will be there lurking. Waiting for me to make a run for it. If only I'd let their wagon alone, they would have bought their supplies and left by midmorning. And I could have caught a late-afternoon king's carriage ride out of town. But now I'm stuck in Montauk.

"I am *such* an idiot," I mutter.

It is evening in Montauk, and I hide deep in the shadows far away from the inn. I am desperately tired. There are still so many people on the street. I can see them by the light of the high torchlights every few meters. Walking and chatting. Yelling and slapping backs and occasionally pumping fists. One or two singing, probably drunk. Then I look closer. It's not people I see. There are *men* on the street. Their breaths explode into the dense chilly air. No women chance the hospitality of Montauk on this night.

I think of Molley. By now she knows I escaped her husband's trap. Is she happy for me? Relieved? Or does she fear Adam's rage will now be directed at her? Either way, I don't care. She passed on the opportunity to play my surrogate mother. Molley is dead to me. She deserves what she gets.

I know where I can stay the night without being disturbed. I overheard workmen talking loudly as they left the chall. The top floor beneath the bell tower is still under construction. There's a back stairway, and work has stopped until after the consecration. I don't know what a consecration is, and

I don't care. All I know is that if I find those stairs, I can sleep in the steeple tonight. I'll sneak across in a few minutes when the street quiets. I'll deal with tomorrow when it arrives.

"Excuse me, miss," a man's quavering voice says. Somehow he snuck up without a sound.

I startle, then inhale quickly. My left hand reaches for black cloth, and my right clasps a crystal in my pocket. I will not go without a fight. Whoever he is, he should be prepared to face his worst memories.

"Good evening," I manage.

"Best be inside, miss," the man says, leaning towards me. He smells of tobacco and dust. "It's not safe on the streets at night for a young woman by herself."

Torchlight reflects off his weathered face and scalp, and I see he's as old as Gregor. He wears coveralls and holds a broom. I breathe easier. He's a streetsweeper.

"Thank you, sir."

"Lots of strangers in town for the equinox," he says. "Even more for the consecration. Itching for something to do. You don't want to be anywhere near at hand when they start drinking."

"I understand," I say. "Thank you for your concern. I only wanted some air."

He nods, his thick fingers trembling with palsy.

"I had a daughter once," he says quietly.

The wistful crack in his voice tells me his daughter is dead. I have an urge to wield cloth and crystal to read his memories. To find out what happened. I can do it in an instant. But I don't. Gregor's voice rings in my head. *Never enter a person's head out of curiosity. Have a good reason, and get out as fast as you can.*

"I'm sorry for your loss," I say.

"It's been years," he says. "Feels like yesterday."

"What happened?" I ask.

"She joined the Order, then disappeared. The missus and I, may she rest, never heard from her again."

"Did you contact the Order?"

"Sure."

"And what did they say?"

"To stop asking."

"The Order says it stands for piety and poverty."

"Yes," he says, then turns his head and spits. "That's what they say."

"What's this consecration about?" I ask.

"You really don't know?"

"No."

"You must not be from around here."

"I traveled to Montauk three years ago with my grandfather, but the chall was smaller then. The steeple wasn't here either."

The man looks both ways, and his voice softens like the shoulder plume of a Béson bird. "No, but then the Order arrived. In force and with money. Plenty of money. They've taken over Montauk. Taken over the flatlands. Every village. Every hamlet. They've built these monstrosities everywhere. Montauk's one of the biggest. The royal presence is nearly gone. People say King Marcellus is sick. Weak. His agents are like ghosts. A few are still here, but they don't show their faces much."

My nose wrinkles at the mention of the king. The royal colors are red, and it was men in red uniforms who murdered Father and Willem. But I have another more pressing reason for concern.

"There's still a king's carriage, isn't there?" I ask nervously. Even if I have to wait a few days for Adam Vorstadt to leave town, my plan for traveling to Kimbar still depends on that carriage.

"Yes, but not much else. Consecration is the day after tomorrow. They're christening the new chall during the Festival of the First Brother. Hard to believe Mordecai is still alive, but he is. And more powerful than ever. Mordecai runs the Order with an iron fist. The consecration is a big deal. Everybody's who's somebody in Montauk will attend. Praelat Ortun arrived from Elden today, and Bishop Fiske will conduct the service. Fiske has been in Montauk on and off for forty years at least."

Elden is where the Order was founded a century ago. A sea-faring city due west of Kimbar. There on the Tablas river, a few miles south of where the Egwa river splits off and heads northeast. A handful of penitents, known as brothers, made their long and dusty way to the flatlands in bare feet and rags. The Order has always had a hard time putting down roots in the flatlands. Cities are where it flourishes, but there are few of those out here. Still, the brothers recruit with energetic humility, and their successes are dispatched to Elden for training. Some return, but many do not.

"Thank you for the information," I say. "May I ask your name?"

"Samuel, miss."

"Thank you, Samuel. What was your daughter called?"

"Clara. Some days it's all I can do just to recollect her face."

I say nothing, and we stand there in amenable silence. Then he tips his nonexistent hat, mumbles good night, and shambles off down the street. I stare at the chall's massive steeple, quietly ominous beneath a starless night sky.

People lose each other all the time in the Riege. It is our way of life. Samuel lost his daughter. I lost a father and brother, and before that, a mother. Most people accept their losses. How else can you keep living? But I am not most people. Father and Willem are dead, and I can't change that, but I can track down the murderers. And kill them. And I don't care if that means some child or wife or parent loses a loved one. Sometimes you have to fight back. Sometimes you have to make people pay for what they've done.

I watch Samuel trudge slowly down the street. He stops and leans heavily against a thick hand-hewn railing where the men picket their horses. Gregor would disapprove, but I know what I have to do. I walk soundlessly toward the railing, throwing my travelbag over my shoulder and staying as much in shadow as I can. I reach into my leathers and select eggshell blue with a fine weave while twirling a crystal in my right hand. I've done this so many times I could shut my eyes. I circle behind Samuel. Then, at the perfect moment, I glide behind and past him, brushing his wrist lightly with the fabric, and I'm there. Inside his head. The world freezes as the crystal directs my search for his last memory of Clara.

It is the day she joined the Order. In Montauk, or what once was Montauk. Late morning on a sweltering midsummer's day. Years and years ago. The sky is azure. I see a breeze tickling the hems of dresses. There is no steeple or challbell. The street is lined with ramshackle buildings. Samuel's wife, plain as a pancake, sniffles. Clara is not a pretty girl, red-faced with pimples and stringy hair. She wears the Order's sack-like dress and black bonnet. She tries not to cry but fails. Her teeth are crooked. She throws her arms around Samuel and hugs him tightly. Two brothers watch patiently, hands behind their backs, their feet as dirty as the hard-packed clay street.

And I'm out. *In and out*, Gregor says. *In and out, then get the hell away.*

By the time Samuel reacts, I've already darted into the nearest alleyway and its long lean shadows. Samuel whirls, nearly falling, and looks around. Like he fell asleep and awoke from a dream. Then he puts his hands to his face and pinches himself. His breathing is fast and shallow and hard. Staring up into the night, he mutters exclamations. He even hops a bit, then clasps his hands. I sense tears. Joyful tears, not the other kind. I think I hear him say the girl's name, but maybe I didn't. Maybe that is just my wish fulfillment.

Have I done Samuel a favor? I think so, but I can't be sure. Memories cut both ways. I've seen almost everything. Gregor made sure of that. What I know is this: Samuel was losing his daughter's face, and I've given it back to him. Whether it causes joy or sorrow is his business.

A fight breaks out in front of the tavern, men brawling into the street, throwing wild punches but doing little damage. This is my chance. As everyone scurries to get a closer look, I glide head down across the street to the chall and then behind. A stray dog scampers away, annoyed at my intrusion. What the workmen called a stairway is a thin rickety ladder nailed against the outer wall. I climb it easily and without a second thought. In moments I'm at the upper floor's threshold. The room is dark, but I toss my travelbag inside and step through the opening.

I could conjure a light – Gregor taught me that spell when I was ten – but I don't want to risk the attention. I carefully step across the lumber and bricks and tools and buckets until I am at the window sill, minus the glass, overlooking the street. I glance down. The brawl has ended, and passersby help the loser into a sitting position. He dabs at his nose, but there is no blood.

A brilliant lightning strike illumines the street,

and a strong gust blows the torchlights sideways. Then the rain descends like a swarm of insects. Within seconds, the street is empty of people. Empty of *men*. The gurgling gutters on the roof beat rhythmically against the wall.

Gregor warned me to be alert for sudden weather changes. *Alert with a capital A.* So for five skeptical minutes, I watch for a boy. Sixteen years old, if the ancient myths are true. I don't believe in myths, only what I can hold in my hand or see with my own eyes. It comforts me that no boy appears. He probably doesn't exist, and even if he did he'd have to be stupid to venture out in this deluge. And the last thing I need slowing me down is a stupid boy.

Or any boy, for that matter.

Several lightning bolts in a row brighten the skies, and thunder crashes over the flatlands. I look down one more time. For Gregor's sake. Just to say I heeded his admonition. On this night there is no boy. So much for folk tales. So much for my *Anaiah*.

And as much as I like Samuel, his kindness doesn't change how I feel about men. I will never trust another one.

I crawl into the brick-framed fireplace, the mortar still fresh and fragrant. The wards take only a moment to set. I close my eyes, but I cannot fall off. I think back to Samuel's final memory of Clara. And those two brothers – the Order – watching behind her like buzzards. I can't get them out of my head. Their impassive faces glisten with dirt, but their eyes are molten beads. I've seen those eyes on other men in other memories – *women's* memories – and I know Samuel is right.

Clara is long dead.

7

Elan

A gaggle of girls wakes me. Thirty or forty have gathered in front of the chall. The storm has passed, and sunlight drowns my makeshift fireplace bedroom beneath the bell tower. The air is fresh. Out the window I see wagons traveling with agonizing care over the rain-rutted street. Directly beneath my window, a brother sourly dispenses sack dresses and black bonnets to the girls. There is a practice this morning for the consecration, and Bishop Fiske himself will preside.

I grab a crystal and red fabric, then hide my leathers in the fireplace and skitter across the floor. After clambering down the ladder two rungs at a time, I run into the alley and around the corner. The girls have nearly finished donning their somber garb. I push through the crowd and see a bonnet on the ground. I snatch it and pull it quickly over my head. Then I approach the brother, who hands me a dress, and in seconds I wriggle into it.

There, I think. Let's see Adam Vorstadt find me now! I'm invisible so long as I stay with this group. And I recall what Samuel said about the bishop. He's been in Montauk forty years. If Fiske has memories of that awful day ten years ago, I need to know. I'll have no better opportunity than this practice for the consecration. I'll be one of dozens in identical shapeless dresses and black bonnets. I have the cloth and crystal I need. Even if Fiske senses an intrusion, he'll never know which girl did it, and I'm well-versed in vanishing.

Gregor would not approve. *Never use your powers on the Order. Many are trained minds, and they're mean. It's too risky.* But I rarely learn anything from reading dearths. They weren't there that awful day, and they don't know anyone who was. Bishop Fiske is someone who might know something. If I'm to be stuck in Montauk, I might as well find out.

I have trouble tying my bonnet, and another girl, tall and skinny with a long nose, walks up to me. She is red-cheeked like Clara, but without the pimples.

"Here, you have it inside out," she says, pulling it off my head. My sheared red curls glisten in the sun.

"What happened to your hair?" she asks.

"Bad haircut," I say, then mimic a laugh.

"Well, don't let the brothers see it," she says.

"They don't like bad haircuts?"

"No, they like red-haired girls," she says, wide-eyed. "If you know what I mean."

"Ah, thanks for the tip."

The girl tucks my hair under the bonnet, then ties the straps so tight they cut into my skin.

"Ouch!" I say.

"You'll thank me later," she whispers. "So how long have you been singing?"

"Singing?"

"You know, in a choir like this."

I glance across the street, and there is Adam Vorstadt. His lips are a tight angry sullen line, and his nostrils flare like a bull's. My guess is he's just been to the stable and discovered the damage to his wagon. He accosts people walking past. He holds his hand as high as his chest, and then he thrusts a shock of my red hair clippings at them. He's describing me. People shake their heads and scurry away.

"All my life," I answer sweetly.

"What choir do you sing with?" she asks.

"Umm, just with my family," I say. "My brothers and sisters."

"You're so lucky," she says, rubbing shoulders. "I'm an only child. I'd give anything to have brothers and sisters."

I think about the Vorstadts, and Jasper and Frederick in particular. "Well, be careful what you wish for," I say gaily.

The brother herds us with impatient hand motions into the sanctuary. The windows are high, and it is dark and cool. No one speaks. The only sound is the rustle of our dresses as we make our way past rows of pews to the south transept. Canvases hang on the stone walls showing black-garbed men and women in various poses of devotion. Silver candlesticks line the walls.

The tall skinny girl leans over. "We're going to sing 'Holier Unto Thou,'" she whispers. "That's my favorite."

"Mine, too," I say uneasily. I cannot recall ever singing. Even one note. Gregor considered it frivolous. At the Keep, I'd hum my own melodies while doing chores or bathing, or just walking in the forest, but I'd never put words to the tunes.

Suddenly Bishop Fiske appears. He's a tall emaciated man in black satin robes with red-and-gold velvet stripes. He wears a trim gray-flecked black beard and close-cropped bristly white hair. He holds his chin up, so he surveys the group through the bottoms of his eyes. He does not smile. He starts speaking, but I don't hear a word. I focus on his wrists. His sleeves are too short, which exposes his skin. His arm is covered with dense hair, so I'll have to catch the tender underside.

Fiske begins handing out the music, and I seize my opportunity. I clutch tightly to a coarse-textured red cloth. Gregor and I found it in a tiny flatlands village years ago. It is a unique shade of red. It's the only fabric I've run across that lets me search for memories of my father. For memories of that awful day. I've seen a hundred episodes of people hearing about the death of the famous sorcerer who lived in the fancy villa, but none from an eyewitness. Nothing from someone who knew something. Maybe today will be my lucky day.

It's no more than a feather's flick. My slipping between two taller girls and reaching out to brush Fiske's underskin with the fabric. But that's all it takes, and suddenly time stops, and I'm inside his head. Massaging the crystal between my right thumb and forefinger, I shudder in disappointment. I know instantly he was not at the villa that day. But there is one memory lurking down deep. There at the very bottom of his soul. I pull, but it resists. I pull again. Then I suck in my breath and tug with all my might. The memory explodes to the surface, like it had sunk into the sludge at the bottom of a deep fast-moving river.

It is the first moment after dawn. Young boys, maybe fifty in all, stand in a row on a green grassy hill in their heavy white nightshirts. A layer of dew glistens. The boys are in bare feet with their hair askew, like they were rudely awakened and rushed from warm beds. Their breaths are visible as they blow into their hands. Fiske stands behind them, and he surveys the line-up from left to right, then right to left, then left to right again. I sense fear and unease and onerous regret. A river, or is it the ocean, gleams with whitecaps in the distance. At the edge of the clearing is an enormous bronze statue of a person with open arms. Then a younger man steps beside Fiske. Portly, and with prominent jowls. He glances at Fiske, then smirks and raises his hand.

And the memory ends. I realize it was a mere shard. Some memories are like that. They come in broken pieces. Getting the entire memory might be possible, but I do not want to stay longer inside Fiske's head.

As I disappear silently into the mix of choir-girls, Fiske groans horribly. Like someone reached into his chest and wrenched out his pulsing heart. He collapses to one knee, wailing in a language I do not understand. As the music sheets drop to the floor, Fiske staggers to his feet and runs unsteadily to the back of the chall.

Fiske's memory puzzles me. Who were the boys, and why were they standing there at dawn? And what does this have to do with my father? I glance at the coarse red fabric in my hand to make certain it is the correct one. In the past it has searched unerringly for memories related to that awful day. Why did it fail this time? Or maybe it didn't fail. Maybe the problem is me, and I simply do not understand what I saw. But what possible connection could there be between fifty boys in nightshirts by a river and the murder of my father and brother ten years ago in the flatlands?

"Oh my word," a choirgirl says hoarsely. "Here comes Praelat Ortun himself!"

The magnificent robes cannot hide the fact that Praelat Ortun is a fat man with short legs. His robes are pitch black speckled with what looks like authentic gold leaf. A clutch of silver chains rings his neck. Ortun wears a delicate white cap and holds a golden rod, which he uses as a walking stick. The Order's mantra is piety and poverty, but his robe alone must be worth a fortune.

I take one look at Praelat Ortun's face, and I recognize him as the other man in Fiske's memory. His jowls are larger and hang lower, so he's older now, but it's unmistakably him. I need to see the rest of Fiske's memory. To try to make sense of it. To figure out how it relates to Father's and Willem's murders. Fiske has disappeared, but Ortun should have the same memories. I know it's risky, but I may never have this opportunity again.

Ortun wants to know what happened to Bishop Fiske. Of course, no one knows but me, and I slide as far back into the group as I can. Several choirgirls say Fiske had some kind of seizure and then stumbled off. Ortun starts questioning choirgirls one by one. Sooner or later, he's going to get to me. I can feign ignorance, but will the praelat see through me? Will he see the truth in my eyes? I could make a run for it, but I'm not ready to do that. Not yet. I tell myself I must stay calm. I must control my breathing. My heartbeat. My emotions. If I am to succeed on my mission, I must have nerves of steel.

Suddenly Ortun is interrogating the tall girl with the long nose. She stands right next to me. Out of fear, she reaches for my hand as Ortun peppers her with questions. I take it and squeeze. I'm next in line.

There is a commotion behind the chall, and a brother, the same one who organized the choirgirls out front, rushes into the transept. His face is contorted, and he yells. Something about Bishop Fiske. Something awful. Something terrible. Ortun waddles quickly toward the back, and the choirgirls follow like a flock of birds.

I am in the rear and can barely see through the open door. I catch a glimpse of Fiske's feet swaying. The choirgirls gasp and cry out. I drop to my hands and feet so I can crawl to the front of the assemblage.

Bishop Fiske has hanged himself in his office. I see instantly how he did it. There is a beam across the ceiling. He dragged over a chair, stood on it, tied rope around his neck and the beam, tightened it, and then kicked away the chair. He lost one shoe in the process. Oddly, the look on his face is one of expectant peace. As if he'd finally conquered the devil after a long intense struggle. I think of the boys in nightshirts, and I know that memory is what caused his suicide. What I don't know is why.

At the sight of Fiske, Ortun drops to his knees and bows his head. His cap, made of delicate knitted white feathers, nearly topples off his head. I see it at once. I'm *trained* to see it. That patch of white skin on the back of his neck. I still have the cloth and crystal in my hands. Ortun is right in front of me. All I have to do is reach out. He may have a trained mind, but I'm good at what I do. And I've never been caught red-handed before. So I swipe the cloth against the back of his neck, and I'm inside his head.

But on this occasion, time doesn't stop. Ortun

wheels and grabs my wrist. I try to slide away, but his grip is tight. Ortun's mouth twists, and his eyes are full like moons. "So, we have a *witch* among us. I should have known."

My brain freezes in fear. I need to get away as fast as I can, but my body won't move. My legs, my arms. Even my breathing stops. Ortun puts his sneering face into mine, and all I can do is react. I strike hard with my head, and Ortun's nose bursts like an overripe tomato. Blood spatters his garments. Roaring in anger and pain, he drops my wrist as his head rocks back. I turn and launch myself through the gibbering choirgirls.

"Get her!" Ortun shouts. "Get the witch! Bring her to me!"

I run like the wind into the nave, then weave my way through pews, overturning tall black candlesticks to hinder pursuit. I glance back once and see two black-robed brothers close behind me. I am fast but not faster than they are. I do not know where I am going. I throw myself down steps, and I hear them do the same. I can almost smell their breath. They are one lunge away from tackling me. Zigzagging through a hallway and around a corner, I shoulder through a massive wooden door, black with age and varnish. I slam it shut and swing down a sturdy oaken plank. The brothers pound on the door from the other side, but the plank holds. I have locked them out.

Then I turn around and discover I've locked myself in. It's a sizable windowless courtyard with no other doors. There is a garden, an ornately carved ivory bench, and a pond with orange fish. And armaments of all kinds arrayed under improvised wooden storage sheds. Broadswords, short swords, knives, axes, machetes, dirks, blades of all lengths, shapes and kinds. And various helmets and rows of full body armor. And, yes, a rapier. Like the one used to murder Father and Willem.

The pounding on the door tells me I have little time. The stone walls rise three stories on all sides. It takes me a moment, but I realize I've seen walls like this before. The Keep! The one I've climbed a million times back in the Northern Reaches. I smile grimly and toss aside my dress and bonnet to begin climbing. The stones protrude just far enough for a narrow foothold. But then I have narrow feet. After that, a fingerhold. Then one more foothold, and another fingerhold. In no time I'm at the top, and I pull myself onto the roof. My legs and wrists burn with exertion, and I feel the heat from the shingles absorbing the late morning sun through my trousers and white pullover. I traipse across to the bell tower like an acrobat, then lower myself down and through the window into the unfinished room where I spent last night.

My leathers are in the brick-framed fireplace where I left them. Quickly, I set wards like Gregor taught me. The fireplace is easy, and right now I need easy. If anyone comes looking for me, they won't see anything amiss. Once the wards are in place, I curl into a ball on top of my coat. I hold myself and cry because I'm scared. And because I've made a mess of things. And because I don't know what to do. Maybe I should find my way back to the Keep. Gregor would take me in. Maybe I need more training. Then I cry some more because I vowed not to feel sorry for myself. But I do.

And I weep because I killed a man. Big round raindrop tears.

I didn't tie a rope around Fiske's neck and kick away the chair, but I might just as well have. I'm the one who made him see something he couldn't live with. Memories have immense power. You can't always control them or predict how people will react. I am so exhausted I fall asleep before I'm done crying.

It is dark when I wake up. The night air is heavy and wet. My plans are in pieces and so is my life. I have no idea, absent a miracle, how to avenge Father and Willem. In addition to running from Adam Vorstadt, I am now a fugitive from the Order. Every black-clad brother and sister in Montauk is looking for me. Which means taking the king's carriage out of town is no longer possible. I can't stay in Montauk, yet I can't leave either.

And the image of Fiske's swaying feet is seared onto my brain.

If I can't deal with Bishop Fiske killing himself due to a memory, I think, *how will I be able to kill the men who murdered Father and Willem?*

I have no more plans and nowhere to turn. If the Fluence has something more to offer me, now would be a good time. I lean over and lightly kiss the burned D on my right wrist. The mark of my patron saint. I fall down to my knees and press my forehead against the window sill. I've never prayed in my life, but this night I pray.

Father, Willem, wherever you are, I thought I could avenge your deaths on my own, but I can't. I need your help. I need a miracle.

I venture to the window and peer out at the empty street. The torchlights are snuffed, so it must be after midnight. The moonlight reflects off a large puddle from yesterday's storm. Tiny sky blue birds gather and peck. I smile as their numbers grow. In seconds there are a hundred or more. They are beautiful. And the world is perfectly still. No wind. No movement. No sound. Utterly peaceful.

Suddenly, the birds alight from the pond as a single body. They circle three times in the air, and then they are gone. I have no idea what could have startled them. I don't see or hear or smell a thing.

Then a boy about my age walks, head down, around the corner. I feel lightheaded. Both my arms tingle brightly, and I take a deep breath.

"Hello, Stan," I murmur.

8

Gregor's Journal

Elan always assumed King Marcellus was behind the murders of Alaric and Willem. Her logic was simple. Kingsguards wear red uniforms, and so did the murderers.

"But they wore hoods," I said. "Which means they didn't want to be identified. So if they are kingsguards who don't wish to be identified as such, why wear red uniforms?"

"Maybe that's exactly what they wanted us to think," Elan said. "They disguised themselves by appearing to be exactly who they were!"

And round and round we went.

The truth is, we had little to go on. As far as I knew, Alaric had no enemies. He was no threat to the king's reign. He lived in the most distant and obscure part of the Riege, and his aim was to improve weather conditions to aid struggling farmers. He had no desire to wield power, and the Montescue family's history was business, not politics. He did not support the Order, but neither did he interfere with its dogged proselytization of the flatlands. His infrequent trips to Kimbar and Elden gained Alaric nothing but a wife, Catherine, an acquisition, in my view, of dubious value.

Alaric was, of course, widely regarded as the last great sorcerer of his era. But the Ebb was nearly finished, and the Fluence was no longer of concern to the dearths. In time, even Alaric's powers would have dissipated. What would anyone gain by killing Alaric and his children, both of whom were believed to lack any significant fluential inheritance?

Elan and I spent hours poring over my memories of that awful day. Her own were no more than vague images tinged with strong emotion, and in any event she was forbidden from entering her own mind to quarry details. As for my recollections, I did not show her everything. There were things she didn't need to see. Things I didn't want her to know. And that, I must confess, was a mistake. I excelled as a tutor. But as a guardian, I was, it turns out, quite fallible.

Oddly, when selecting fabrics for Elan to use in practicing her craft, at first we could not match the red in the murderers' uniforms. There was something different about it. We tried a thousand shades of dyed fabrics, but none worked. Until one small village – its name eludes me now – we visited when Elan was thirteen. At last we found a garment that gave her access to memories related to Alaric's death. But her elation turned to despair over time, as none of the dearths she read knew anything about what happened. There was, of course, that moment when people heard the news, or the idle chatter that passes for gossip in flatlands taverns, but nothing concrete. Nothing firsthand or remotely useful. And all the servants from the villa had long since died or vanished to parts unknown.

Elan examined and reexamined every detail of my memories. There were nineteen mounted attackers. She identified the types and colors of the horses, the comparative heights of the riders, and various sundry characteristics of the hooded villains. But we never saw a face. We only assumed they were men. Elan studied the attacker who killed Alaric with special intensity. But he hid himself well in his uniform and under his hood. We could meet him at midday on the streets of a flatlands village and never know it was him.

Throughout these sessions, I held back certain memories. It was, I told Elan, for her own good. But then I became too clever. It was the week of Elan's fifteenth birthday. She wanted to see one particular memory over and over. The one in which I gathered items for the valise. Shoes and socks and a jacket for Elan to wear. Alaric's collection of crystals. The rubystone. A tunic Alaric gave to me as a keepsake for Elan. Other sundry items.

I tried limiting the memory as best I could manage, but there, off in one corner for the barest of instants, was the toe of a girl's shoe. Elan's shoe. One of two I had picked up in the cellar, along with her socks and sweater and barrette. I didn't notice it in the memory, and at first neither did Elan. But once she saw it, the questions came fast and furious. She recognized the shoe. It was hers! What was it doing there? And the angle of the toe was strange. It was as if someone was wearing it. Who would be wearing her shoe, and why were they lying on the floor at such a terrible time? And what had I done with her sweater and barrette?

I refused to tell her. I was her tutor, she was my pupil, and that was that. It was my decision, not hers. But of course we were beyond that. She was far more than a pupil to me, and I more than a tutor to her. Elan refused to let the matter drop. It was her shoe, she said. Her clothes. She was entitled to know. In the end, I had no choice. I had to tell Elan what I'd done with her things that day at her father's urging. And explain how it may have saved her life.

Alaric retained a number of servants at the villa, mostly at Catherine's insistence. He kept them on after she left, perhaps hoping for her return. Not wanting to admit she was never coming back. Two days earlier the cook had been visited by her daughter and granddaughter, a four-year-old named Dezzie. I had told Elan the servants escaped unharmed, but that was a lie. They all escaped but one. During the initial attack, as the farmhouse was being set afire, Dezzie fell and struck her head on the shaved-rock corner of the fireplace hearth. She died instantly. Once the hopelessness of our situation became clear, Alaric devised a plan. He would leave to find Willem, and I was to escape with Elan through the tunnel.

It was Alaric who suggested dressing Dezzie in Elan's clothing. The farmhouse would burn to the ground, and the attackers – Alaric, it must be said, having no more clue who they were than I did -- would find the charred remains of a young girl wearing Elan's shoes, sweater and barrette. They would conclude Elan died in the fire and, Alaric hoped, see no reason to hunt for her. Dezzie, Alaric assured me, would forgive us this desperate use of her corpse.

Well, Elan went into hysterics. "That girl gave her life for me, Gregor! How could you not have told me?"

"She most certainly did *not* give her life for you," I said. "She didn't *give* her life at all. It was taken from her forcibly by murderers."

"She died for me!"

"She didn't even know you, Elan. The two of you never met."

"She died so that I could live."

The argument escalated into shouting, and then Elan announced she was leaving. It was, she declared, time. Nine years of lessons from a deceiving tutor such as myself were enough. Her mission would start that night. The next thing I knew, she was in her leather coat with some travelbag thrown over her shoulder. She was really going to do it! Right then and there! Caused by a toxic mixture of anger, guilt, impatience and re-gret. And maybe a touch of self-pity thrown in for good measure.

I met her at the top of the main stairway in the Keep. She was not leaving, I informed her, until we had discussed the matter thoroughly and she could see precisely how unwise her plan was. I even showed her the small teeth marks on my arm. A reminder that I'd let her bite me to quiet her cries after seeing Alaric and Willem murdered. I'd sac-rificed, too. Our lives were bound together in the same plan.

I restrained her, and she pushed me away. I grabbed her, and she pushed harder. Then I lost my balance and tumbled down the stairs. I heard and felt that awful snap and knew instantly I'd broken my right leg.

Well, if I'd wanted to stop Elan from leaving, I'd discovered the trick. She reached the bottom of the stairway almost before I did. She lifted me like I weighed nothing at all, then carried me to my bed. I'm not a healer, but I knew some spells. We found other spells in books. Throughout the night, we worked by candlelight trying to repair the dam-age. In the end, I think we can be proud of our handiwork. The break never fully healed, but in a few weeks I was able to walk, after a fashion any-way, with the help of a cane.

And Elan didn't leave. Not that night. Not that week or month. She stayed another year, and as I look back on it, that last year was when she blos-somed. When she truly became a sorceress. She was no longer my little caterpillar. Her powers became instinctive and mature, even if her judgment was sometimes that of a still maturing sixteen-year-old girl.

That night, as I lay in bed with my leg raised on pillows, Elan stole away. She dug out a small piece of iron from the kitchen in the rough shape of a D and tossed it into the fire. Then she pulled it out with tongs and applied it, red hot, to the back of her right wrist. Elan did not cry out or make a sound. Or at least none that I heard. I only discovered the mark a day or two later, that ugly red burn on her arm. I wide-eyed her. She wide-eyed me.

"I do believe Dezzie would be pleased," I said at last.

"Saint Dezzie," Elan corrected.

I nodded. "Saint Dezzie it is."

Neither of us spoke of the matter again.

9

Elan

I follow the boy, my *Anaiah*, to the stables by the inn. Not my favorite place. I deal in memories, and those few from the stable are not my favorites. The smell of manure and animal urine is overpowering, and I bat away the black flies. As it is well after midnight, the stableboy keeping watch by the entrance is asleep on the straw. And fortunately, I don't see Frederick or Jasper standing guard. Nor any other people up and about at such a late hour.

The stables are dark except for dim lights in the distance. That must be the boy. He's in the private quarters where the rich people park their properties. The area is cordoned off with thick rope, and I duck under it. I don't have a lantern, and in the gloom I bang into a table, which causes horseshoes to clatter to the ground. I stop and wait for footsteps, or shouts, or a swinging lantern headed my way. But there is nothing. Slices of moonlight streak through the stable roof. I continue to the stall with light under the door. I barely make out the sign above: THE PROPERTIE OF MASTER TONSIL DEPSIK.

I pause at the threshold. I don't know what to say to this boy. Should I tell him I distrust all men, but I need his help desperately so I can avenge my father and brother? That I'm a memory witch, and I believe he was born to be my human crystal? My *Anaiah*? Should I offer to pay, or would he be insulted? At a minimum, I will need his assistance to travel to Kimbar. I realize everything – my entire life – depends upon what happens in the next few moments. There is nothing to do but go forward.

I open the door and walk into a bright opening. As my eyes adjust, I see the room is lit by a series of lanterns placed at intervals along the walls. In the middle is a gorgeous-to-touch black suede carriage and two horses. Suddenly, out of nowhere, I'm confronted by a boy, holding a thin pole upright with two hands. Like he means to swat away my head. He wears a white shirt tied at the neck with pleated cuffs, and a black leather vest several sizes too large.

"So you've come to kill me," he says grimly.

"What?" I say.

"Just like the rest of my family."

He holds the pole even higher, but then its top detaches and falls onto his head. He doesn't move. He just stands there, gripping a pole that's flopped onto his head.

I stifle a laugh, putting a hand to my mouth.

"Don't laugh at me," he says.

"I'm not laughing," I say, laughing.

"Yes, you are."

"No, I'm not."

We stare at each other for long seconds. I want desperately to giggle, but somehow, I stifle it.

"That pole has fallen over onto, well, it's on your head," I say, my hand still on my mouth, my eyes on the pole.

"I know that," he says.

"You can put it down," I say. "I won't mind."

"You won't kill me?" he says.

"No," I say.

"Promise?"

"Yes."

He lowers the rod. He's a slender boy, about my age but slightly taller, with floppy brown hair and an intelligent oval face. And one very black eye.

"Why do you think I'd want to kill you?" I ask.

"You're that memory witch they're all looking for," he says.

"And you know this how?" I ask. I'm cross to think people can identify me as a memory witch merely by looking at me.

He points to his head. "Your hair. That's like the worst haircut in history."

Now I'm flustered. "Well, I did it myself, and I didn't have a mirror, and I was really tired, and I was in a bad place at the time, so this is how it turned out."

"You did that to yourself?" he asks doubtfully.

"I did," I say defensively. "And you still haven't said why you think I want to kill you."

"Because you killed my family," he says.

"I most certainly did not," I say.

"Yes, you did."

"No, I didn't."

"They were killed by witches," he says.

"Then those witches should be punished," I say. "But I am not them."

"But you *are* a witch," he accuses. "A memory witch."

"Yes," I say, after a pause. "Well, I'm a sorceress anyway."

"What's the difference?" he asks.

"One's tone of voice," I respond pointedly.

Try not to argue with him, I think. *After all, I desperately need his help.*

We stare at each other again.

"I'm sorry about your family," I say somberly.

"Thank you," he says.

"Did they catch the witches who killed them?"

"No, but I think they died. They were very old."

"Well, I'm so sorry," I say.

"Thank you," he says again.

"Let me introduce myself," I say, walking slowly towards him, holding out my hand. "I'm Elan Montescue."

He reaches to take my hand. "And I'm . . ."

We touch hands, and lightning erupts. The next thing I know, I'm flat on my back. I think I'm seeing stars. A million tiny bright multicolored stars.

Every color in the rainbow, and perhaps a few more besides. But then I realize it's not stars. It's my fabrics. The explosion tore off my leathers and tossed all my bits and pieces of cloth into the air like confetti.

On my hands and knees, I scramble to gather the fabrics. They're all over me, the stall, the carriage, the horses, everywhere. And that special red fabric. The one that lets me access memories related to Father's and Willem's deaths. I need that one most of all. I don't see it anywhere. I can't lose that one.

"Please help me, boy!" I yell frantically. "I need to collect all these cloths and then organize them by color and weave."

He rises groggily to his knees. "Stille," he says.

"What?"

"I said, Stille."

"I'm sorry, I don't understand."

"My name is Stille. Stille Vespers. Please don't call me 'boy.'"

"Oh, sorry."

"That's what Master Depsik calls me."

"I promise I won't call you 'boy,'" I say, my right hand over my heart. "But right now I need you to help me gather my fabrics. I can't fulfill my mission without them."

"All right," he says, rubbing the back of his head.

We gather the fabrics in silence. I work furiously. It took Gregor and me years to build this collection. I'm not going to lose it now. Not one piece of it. Without cloth, I'm not a memory witch. I'm not anything at all. I peek up, and Stille, on his knees, is staring at me.

"Yes?" I say.

"I've never seen anyone work that intensely before," he says, then resumes gathering.

My piles grow. Color, texture, weave, size. Stille has his own pile, but I'll deal with that later. I need to find that one special red fabric. I see something glitter from under the carriage. There it is! I rush over on my hands and knees, then fall to my belly as I slide underneath. I reach out to grab it.

Stille's hand appears from nowhere. He must have seen the fabric at the same time and had the same idea. Our hands touch briefly, and sparks fly. Not an explosion like before, but a loud crack.

"Ouch!" Stille says, pulling back. His head smacks the underside of the carriage. "Augh!" he says, rolling backwards.

I grab the fabric, crawl out from under the carriage, then rush to Stille's side. "I got it!" I say with a big smile. I show it to him. "I couldn't afford to lose this one."

"That hurt," he said, rubbing his hair.

"The spark, or banging your head?" I ask.

"Both," he says, grimacing.

"Sorry about that," I say, then I hold the fabric to my cheek.

"Every time you touch me, it hurts," he says accusingly.

"That means we're supposed to be together," I say as cheerfully as I can muster.

"What?" he asks. "How do you figure?"

This is not the time, I think, *to inform him of his destiny from birth as my human crystal.*

"Well, it just does," I say.

Until this night, I never believed in human crystals. The idea seemed preposterous. And stupid. But the birds, the tingling, the explosion, the sparks. There's only one explanation. Gregor was right. The Fluence has flung this boy into my path, and I need him if I'm to get out of Montauk and find the men who killed Father and Willem. It's only been a few days since I left the Keep, but already I'm out of options. I need Stille Vespers' help, and I need it now.

"Here, let's try it again," I say offering my hand.

"No way," he says, skittering backwards.

"Oh, come on," I plead. "Just one more time."

I offer Stille what I hope is a winsome smile. Not that I've had much practice flirting with boys.

"No!"

"Oh, all right," I say. "Maybe later."

"I don't think there's going to be a later," he says.

"Why not?"

"Trust me, you don't want anything to do with me. When I leave this stable, I'll be a wanted man."

"How so?"

"The carriage and horses belong to Master Depsik. And I'm taking them without his permission so I can go home. Back to Kimbar."

When the Fluence decides to intervene, it really knows what it's doing. I find my *Anaiah*, and it just so happens he's going my way. Fate has taken a hand. All I have to do is persuade Stille to let it guide us.

"You don't say!"

"So you should steer clear," Stille says. "A few minutes from now, I'm going to be a criminal."

"Correction," I say. "In a few minutes, we are both going to be criminals."

"I'm sorry?"

"Because I'm going to be riding with you in that carriage," I say, pointing. "Which means we'll both be thieves running from the law."

"You want to come with?"

"I'm going to Kimbar, too."

We size each other up. His hair flops over his eyes, and I resist the urge to smooth it back in place. My hand reaches, and I consciously pull it back. It's as if something is pulling me towards him. I vowed never to trust a man again, but Stille is different. Somehow I know he will never hurt me. In his mind, the question is whether I'll hurt him.

"Are you going to keep touching me?" he asks.

"No," I say, holding my hands up.

"Promise?"

"Promise!"

"I'll let you ride along on one condition," Stille says.

"And that would be . . ."

"We have to fix your hair. We won't get out of Montauk with you looking like that."

"Well, there's not much I can do about my

hair," I protest. "I was born with it."

"I can take care of that," he says. "As long as you don't mind, well . . ."

"As long as I don't mind what?"

"Me touching you," he finishes.

I take a deep breath. The last time a man wanted to touch me was here in these stables, in far different circumstances. But I need to get to Kimbar, and my own plans have fallen to pieces, and the Fluence placed this boy here to help me.

And besides, I kind of like Stille.

"I don't mind at all," I say sweetly.

10

Elan

I think I'm in heaven. I ignore the dank foul smells in Master Depsik's private stall, the heavy claustrophobic air, and the bits of floating straw that make me want to sneeze. In sixteen years, I have never been touched. Not really. Not like this. It may be the middle of the night in Montauk, but I lean back, close my eyes, and let Stille wash my hair with warm water while massaging my scalp with his long fingers.

"I'm not hurting you, am I?" he asks.

"Um, no," I say, keeping my eyes tightly shut.

Then he pushes my head upright, dries it with a thick clean towel, and begins snipping.

"What are you doing?" I ask.

"Evening you out," he says.

"My haircut was even," I say defensively.

"It looked like you stuck your head in a

thresher," he says flatly.

I feel his fingers in my hair and on my scalp, and I decide to let him continue doing what he wants.

"Now for the dye," he says.

"Wait!" I say. "Are you sure you know what you're doing?"

"I lived with my uncle in Kimbar before coming here," he says. "He hated gray, so I dyed his hair every two weeks."

"Do I get to choose the color?"

"Sure. There's dark brown, and dark brown, and dark brown."

I laugh. He does have a sense of humor. "I'd like dark brown, please."

"Coming right up," he says, and his fingers return to my scalp. I focus on breathing. In and out. I am relaxed. My body tingles, and it's not because Stille's my human crystal. I don't want this hair-and-scalp experience to end one moment sooner than it has to.

"There!" he says, pulling his hands away. "Finished. We need to give this time to dry, but we can't wait too long. Morning has arrived. We should be off within the hour."

The stables awakened an hour earlier. Horses and wagons and people coming and going. The harsh noises of wheels being repaired, carriages refurbished, and horses hooved. But we are safe in Master Depsik's private stall. No one bothers us.

"Stille, can I ask you a question?"

"Sure," he says, washing the dye from his

hands.

"How did you get the black eye?"

"Master Depsik hit me."

"You should have hit him back," I say.

"I can't," he says. "Assaulting the Chief Scribe is a crime."

"You should explain your situation to the magistrate," I say.

"The magistrate is Master Depsik's cousin," he says.

"I see. How often does he hit you?"

"Most every day. More when he drinks."

"And how often does he drink?"

"Most every day. Master Depsik likes his whiskey."

"I'm so sorry, Stille," I say. "That sounds horrible."

He shrugs. "Lots of people have it worse."

"How long have you been in Montauk?"

"Eighteen months, give or take."

"So why leave now?"

Stille points to his eye. "My uncle contracted for me to work here for two years. Said it would be good work experience, and then I could return to Kimbar. Yesterday Master Depsik left his account books out on his desk. I peeked and discovered that my uncle died six months ago, and his estate paid up my contract. I confronted Master Depsik and got this for my boldness."

"So you're leaving."

"Yes. I should inherit my uncle's house in Kimbar. It's small, but big enough for one person. And

I can do piecework to earn money. People like me are more common in Kimbar, but I should be able to make a living."

"What do you mean, 'people like me?'"

"I'm a scribe. I can read and write. The guild rates my penmanship and calligraphy as exceptional. Master Depsik will be angry when he discovers I've gone. He won't be able to function. And of course, I'm stealing his carriage and horses."

"For once, he'll have to do his own work," I say.

"That won't happen," Stille says. "Master Depsik is illiterate."

"So how did he become chief scribe?"

"The usual way. Influence. Money. Schmoozing. He pays people like me a pittance to do the work. My official title is candleboy. That carries the lowest salary. He pockets the rest."

Stille approaches me, then, peering intently at my hair, fluffs it twice. Once on each side, and twice in back. I've never had a boy this close to me before. Certainly not one fondling my hair. I have to remind myself to breathe normally. The Fluence, I think, must be laughing. It creates Stille as my crystal, but I'm the one who has to explain everything to him. Persuade him to accept the task of helping me become the best memory witch I can be. And fulfilling my mission to avenge Father and Willem.

I've never paid any attention to boys. Not that I've encountered many. It never made any difference to me whether they liked me or not. I didn't dress for them or flirt with them or try to catch their eye, especially given Gregor's warnings. But now, suddenly, it matters enormously whether this boy likes me. This one special boy. If he doesn't, my life is lost.

Stille continues to examine my hair, and I clear my throat. "So how is it?"

"It'll do," he says. "A little more time wouldn't hurt, but that's one thing we don't have. We need to be as far away as possible when Master Depsik wakes up."

"He's still sleeping?"

"Based on how much he drank yesterday, he'll be asleep until late afternoon. If we're lucky, he'll wait overnight to visit his chambers. Which is when he'll discover I've left. We should be to Heedle by then."

"What's Heedle?"

Our eyes lock and dance merrily for a moment. "Our immediate destination," he says, then smiles. "You'll see."

Stille may be skinny as a rake, but he has an interesting face, and he's so easy to talk with. And, I think, he has a nice smile. I have to admit there are worse things for a boy than having a nice smile.

He strides to the other side of the carriage and pushes out an antique blue-and-white trunk with his foot. Knee high, it's the kind used for dowries. The interlocking vines and flowers on the trunk's lid are exquisite.

"Take what you need from in there," he says.

"What I need?"

"Clothes."

"In case you haven't noticed, I'm wearing clothes," I say, jutting out my chin.

"Young women in Montauk," he says, "do not wear men's clothes. If we want to get past the Order, you'll need to dress like a girl."

"I see," I say.

"You know, frilly and empty-headed."

He ducks as, grinning, I fling a rusty horseshoe at his head. "Watch yourself, Stille Vespers," I say. "If you're not careful, I may just come over there and *touch you*."

The clothes in Master Depsik's trunk are gorgeous. Expensive antiques. I select a simple unblemished white dress I can slip into easily, formal black slip-on shoes with heels, and a saucy blue hat with red ribbons.

"How did Master Depsik acquire these?" I ask.

"From his mother," he says. "He's looking for a wife, but so far, despite his money and position, he's had no luck. So here they remain."

Stille packs his travelbag, so I walk to the other side of the carriage. "I'm changing now, so you can't look."

"Okay," he says.

I peek around the corner. He has his back to the carriage. "I mean really," I say.

"Fine," he calls out, not turning around.

I remove my pullover and pants. Both are grimy and smell bad.

"You aren't looking, are you?" I call out.

"Nope," he says.

I finish with the dress, then tilt the hat at a

saucy angle. The shoes are a problem. I've never worn anything with heels. I walk unsteadily around the carriage, and Stille stands and turns.

"Well, ta-da," I say with a frown. I'm not sure how I look. I've never worn anything like this before, and it feels strange. And balancing in these shoes is hard on my ankles.

Stille's eyes widen and his jaw drops. "Wow," he says. "You look gorgeous."

I blush, which always ruins my complexion. But I suddenly feel better about myself. Stille has a way about him.

Stille strides to the carriage, throwing both our travelbags into the back. I grab the black-suede fittings on the carriage for balance. The horses are motionless except for the side-to-side tails. They don't even look back. There are three steps up to the seatbox. I have no idea how to manage them in heels.

"Here, let me help you," Stille says, holding out his hand like a gentleman.

"Thanks," I say, and our eyes meet again. And then our hands touch, and sparks erupt like a dry torch by a firepit. I fall hard onto my bottom, and my hat flies off. Stille lands flat on his back. Stunned, we sit there for a few seconds. Then I start laughing. I can't help it.

"This is not funny," he says, still on his back.

"Yes, it is," I say.

"It isn't, and it's your fault," he says. "You promised you wouldn't touch me."

"You offered your hand!" I exclaim. "I thought

you were being gallant!"

"It's all because you wore that dress," he accuses.

"Which was your idea," I respond.

"Well, no more touching," he says. "And this time I mean it."

"Fine," I say, pulling myself up. I take off my shoes and climb onto the seatbox in my bare feet. I slip the shoes back on once I've settled. Stille comes around the other side and takes the reins. He stares at me as I keep my distance.

"Don't worry," I say primly. "I'm not going to touch you."

~~~

Stille maneuvers the carriage through the stables and out into the street. Montauk is a beehive of activity due to the consecration. I've never seen this many people in one place at the same time. And the Order is everywhere. Previously I've encountered brothers only in ones and twos. Today they travel in packs. And the women, dressed in shapeless ugly black dresses and bonnets, are out in force as well. It feels like the entire city is there watching us ride past.

"Shouldn't we use a back road?" I ask.

"No," he says. "That's what the Order would expect. When you're running away, you need to do it in front of everybody. In broad daylight."

"So what's our story," I ask, "if the Order blocks the carriage?"

"We are brother and sister," Stille says, nearly dropping the reins as his hands gesticulate expansively, "on our way to attend a nearby wedding. It is a happy day, and we are buoyed by the beautiful couple's hopes and dreams. We'll be back for the final ceremonies at the chall this evening."

"All right," I say dubiously. From what I've seen of the Order, they aren't much into hopes and dreams. They're certainly not into beauty. But then it's not my carriage, and the reins aren't in my hands.

As we pass the inn, I see three men imprisoned in a pillory. Bent over and stripped naked, their genitalia dangle as their heads and hands protrude through heavy wooden stocks. Beads of sweat drip from their noses. Their long greasy hair hangs low, and their mouths writhe in open agony. Sitting nearby in front of a hand-made placard, a brother from the Order holds a thin leather switch and urges passersby to inflict punishment on the men.

"Don't look at them," Stille says, his eyes fixed on the rutted dirt road.

I don't look – well, not exactly – but I glance sideways, and my heart catches in my throat. It is Adam Vorstadt and his sons, Jasper and Frederick.

A mother and daughter pass by on the promenade. The brother speaks briefly to them. The girl looks quizzically at her mother, who nods aggressively. The girl takes the proffered switch, then strikes the men several times. Her eyes light as the men wince under each stroke, and Frederick even cries out.

"Why are they being punished?" I ask, my throat tight.

"The sign says they gave shelter and transport to a witch," Stille says. "Do you know those people?"

"Yes," I breathe softly. "They brought me here. I paid them."

"Well, they're now the ones paying," he says. "Paying for their sins."

"What sins?"

"Helping a witch."

In the flatlands, the Fluence dates back for several thousand years. The born-and-bred used to be everywhere. I have vague memories of the grand parties Father used to throw at the villa. They made me wear a little dress, and Willem a proper gentleman's suit. I was too young to know it, but I met some of the most powerful sorcerers in the Riege. It occurs to me I haven't seen a single sorcerer since I arrived in Montauk. The born-and-bred are gone.

"The law doesn't prohibit sorcery, does it?"

Stille sighs. "The king's law? No. But the Order? Different story. They hate the Fluence, and they've outlawed sorcery. They're brazen about inflicting punishment on the streets. Out in the open. They pretty much control the flatlands."

"And the king approves?"

"The king isn't here, Elan," Stille says. "The Order is."

We ride in silence to the clop-clop-clopping of Master Depsik's horses.

"And the born-and-bred families are long gone," Stille continues softly, not turning to me. "Retreated to the big cities down south. The Order chased them out some years ago. There are no witches in Montauk. Or in the flatlands."

"Except me," I say.

"Yes," Stille says. "Except you."

I should feel vindicated about the Vorstadts, but I don't. What they did to me in the stables – what they tried to do, anyway – was a crime. But that's not why they're being punished. It's for hauling me to Montauk. There was nothing wrong with that. I paid them cash, and they gave me a ride. They didn't even know I was a sorceress!

"Did they treat you well?" Stille asks.

"No," I say.

"Well, then."

"But that's not what they're being punished for," I say.

"Justice works in circuitous ways," he says sadly.

Minutes later, we approach a blockade as we try to exit Montauk's central business district. To think how many nights I plotted ways to access this city on my quest to avenge Father and Willem! And now all I want is to leave this evil godforsaken place with my head still firmly on my shoulders.

In front of us is a simple wagon. A husband and a wife up front, and two daughters and a small boy in the back. A family, just like the Vorstadts. Three black-clad brothers from the Order interrogate them. Their hand motions are sharp and authoritative. The brothers do the talking. The husband and wife protest briefly, exchanging quick worried glances. They avert their eyes as they turn their wagon around. They head back to the consecration. Attendance is not voluntary.

I know our story won't work. The one Stille invented. If that family didn't make it, the two of us – a mere "brother and sister" – certainly won't. The Order will never let us leave. They'll send us back. And then someone will recognize the carriage and horses. Or someone will recognize me. Or Master Depsik will make a drunken appearance. The brothers will take me away, and they'll stash me somewhere dark and cold and unprotected. And then do god knows what to me. And Father and Willem will never be avenged. And Gregor will die alone in the Reaches.

And, I can't help thinking, *I'll never see Stille again, ever.*

A brother approaches our carriage, but I do not let him speak first. I know how to intimidate a brother – invoke a superior authority! "God be with you," I say heartily. "We've just come from Praelat Ortun. He asked us to speak with the brother in charge. Would that be you?"

Stille's tongue seems to catch in his throat. The brother nods.

"It was such an honor to see the praelat," I say, "despite his horrible injury! May god smite his attackers! The praelat has such courage to continue with the consecration. This young man" – and here I grab Stille's right arm and clutch it to my bosom

– "is my intended. We are to be married today at our local chall just outside Montauk. Praelat Ortun gave us his personal blessing, and we are to return tonight for the final ceremony. But first we have to get married, and everyone has already gathered."

The brother's jaw is on his chest. He looks at the other brothers who have gathered. They stare at each other. One scratches his head.

"If you'd like," I say, "we can go back to Praelat Ortun to get something in writing, but he said that wouldn't be necessary."

"You say, um, you say this man here, um, this man is your intended?" one brother blurts out.

"Yes," I say, clutching his arm more tightly. His arm is inside his shirt, so there are no sparks. "He's my sweetheart."

"Is that true?" the brother asks.

"Um, yes, Brother, it is true," Stille says, smiling wanly. "This young lady, my intended, I mean, my fiancé, we are headed out, you know, to be married, and, I think . . ."

"Fine," another brother says, waving his hand. "Go on, and god be with you."

"We'll see you in a few hours!" I yell, leaning out over Stille, calling to the brothers. For some reason, I want Stille to know what it feels like to have me near to him. Is that me or the Fluence? Stille snaps the reins, and the horses move forward. We are instantly forgotten as the brothers attend to the next vehicle.

The horses pull Master Depsik's elegant carriage smartly through the outskirts of Montauk.

Stille says nothing for a half hour until we reach the open road.

"So, getting married at our local chall?" he says at last.

"The brother-and-sister story wasn't going to work," I say decisively. "I had to think of something."

"I see," he says, his eyes fixed on the road.

"And it worked," I say.

"It sure did," he agrees.

We ride longer in silence. Surrounded by vast lush open fields to the south and dense forests to the north. Now I fret that I've ruined things. That Stille thinks I see him as a potential boyfriend or, worse yet, a husband. And I haven't yet told him about my mission and what it means for him to be my *Anaiah*.

"I invented the getting-married story on the spur of the moment," I say.

"I believe you," Stille says.

"I mean, I'm wearing a white dress. You know, like a bride."

"If you say so."

"I was improvising, that's all."

"Sure."

I grind my teeth. Stille is being deliberately infuriating. "Well, don't get any ideas," I say archly.

Stille snaps the reins playfully, and the carriage accelerates.

"I was going to say," he says, "the same thing to you."

11

Gregor's Journal

The key to Elan's survival, I determined, was to maximize her speed in entering and exiting the subject's mind. The quality of the crystal played a role, of course, but in the end it was a matter of repetition. The more she practiced, the more skilled she became at locating and retrieving memories. And the faster she worked, the less likely the subject would feel her intrusion. Even trained minds, if asleep or distracted, won't notice a memory witch working at the height of her powers.

Unfortunately, being Elan's only practice subject took an enormous physical toll on me. I didn't fully realize the cost until one overcast day when she was ten. We'd had a particularly intense set of lessons, and it was time to see to dinner. We'd been practicing, as often was the case, in the

Keep's garden. I recall the lavender of the jimberry trees in full blossom. Elan traipsed into the kitchen, and I intended to follow. Except that I could not rise from my chair. My legs no longer worked. Elan fetched blankets, and we both slept in the garden that night. My mobility returned by morning, but our regimen would never again be the same.

A tutor's magic is largely unexplored territory among the born-and-bred. Without a sorcerer as a pupil, I have no fluential abilities. I'm little better than a dearth. Probably worse, truth be told, since I lack many basic manual skills that dearths develop as children. I can light a fire with a spell. Deprive me of that ability, and I can fumble all day long striking flint against sharp stones while eliciting nary a spark. But what I can accomplish in the service of my professional obligations knows nearly no limit. And so it was with Elan.

After consulting a few texts, I created a sizable floating translucent sphere. It hovered above Elan in the garden. The "ball," Elan called it. It wasn't always that shape, of course. Sometimes I preferred cubes or cylinders. The ball had a specified number of interlocking chambers. Initially, we began with twenty. I placed a light in one chamber, and Elan's task was to wield the crystal and her powers to move the light through all the chambers in proper sequence. That first week, she failed to move the light even one chamber. By the end of the month, she was at ten chambers. The day she pushed the light through all twenty was a red-letter day. We celebrated with hot cider laced with cinnamon and a touch of brandy.

Elan assumed we were done with the ball, but of course, we were just beginning. The purpose of the exercise was not merely to guide the light through all twenty chambers. It was to do so as swiftly as possible. Frequently, her concentration gave out before she completed her task. As her stamina increased, so did her speed. I believe it took more than a year, but ultimately she moved the light through all twenty chambers in roughly one second.

Elan again assumed we were done with the ball, and again she was wrong. The next day, I used the same incantation to fabricate a new orb. Just as sparkling and translucent as the first, but larger. Fifty chambers, this time. And so we began again. It was during her last year with me that we reached ten thousand. The sphere was massive, and it hovered above her like a small moon. The light moved so swiftly all I saw was a single spark. The hint of a spark, really. It lit up the entire sphere for a hairblink. Far less than one second.

One day early on when Elan experienced difficulty moving the light, she found a stick and pointed it at the ball. "Move," she commanded. The light ignored her. "Move," she said more loudly, wiggling the stick.

"What, pray tell, do you think you are doing?" I asked.

"I'm using a wand," she said.

"That," I said, pointing, "is a stick. It used to be

part of a tree until it died and fell off. What it has to do with our exercise today is beyond me."

"Some book stories talk about wands," she said.

"Yes, and they talk about fairies and goblins, too," I said. "But they aren't real."

"I want it to be real," she said.

"Wands are toys for babies," I said heartlessly. "Go around waving a stick in the air if you like, Rador-elan of House Montescue, but you won't accomplish a thing. The Fluence will ignore you, as it should. Use your mind and the instruments the Fluence has selected. In your case, cloth and crystals."

Elan tried again with the stick, and again it failed. She flung it into the trees.

"Now to task, my little caterpillar," I said. "Use your mind to move the light. As the Fluence intends. The crystal is your tool. Bend it to your will." Elan never tried using a stick again.

I had no way to know for sure, but I fully believed then, as I do now, that Elan is the fastest memory witch in history. If other tutors devised novel instructional methods such as mine, the books are silent about them. And I shudder to think of young women venturing out into the Riege lacking sufficient speed to exercise their powers without detection. No wonder they all ended badly. I even pondered what improvements could be expected if Elan found her "Boye" – her human crystal. Surely she couldn't get any faster than I had helped make her! Ultimately, I banished my thinking about such possibilities. What I knew about the powers and limitations of a memory witch would barely fill a thimble. Who was I to speculate what improvements – or perfections, if you will – could be implemented with the aid of an organic crystal such as her own personal Stanislaus?

But even my fluential abilities as a tutor had limits. "What happens," she asked one day, "if the dearths come for me with pitchforks and torches?"

"Why, you run, my dear," I said. "As fast as you can."

"Won't the Fluence help me fight?"

"No, Elan. The Fluence will not empower you to cause direct physical harm to another person."

"So there's nothing I can do?"

"I didn't say that. Some sorcerers have learned spells that freeze people in place or shift them to another location or the like. A handful have even learned to transport themselves. But those spells are exceedingly difficult to master. Few sorcerers succeed in doing so. And even then, the spells are unreliable. Sometimes they work. Other times they don't."

"So what do I do if I'm attacked?"

"As I said, you run."

"And if I can't run?"

For some weeks, Elan and I experimented with various spells and incantations, both with and without her crystals. We pored through tome after tome, but nothing seemed to take. Alaric had been the same way. His power over weather patterns was breathtaking. But ask him to light a candle or open a door, and he would stand there fuming while one spell after another failed.

Simple spells are never simple. They are spoken, but the words you speak, whether out loud or in your head, must slot precisely into your power. How quickly you speak, your intonation, your pronunciation, your focus on each syllable – everything must fit precisely with your power. Like a key to a lock. Even one tiny variance causes the spell to fail.

And if one is under attack, well, the ability to recite the spell perfectly is quite difficult. A simple spell, indeed!

Elan and I were about to cease our efforts to find her a suitable defensive spell when we happened on the simplest spell of all. The born-and-bred call it the upside-down spell. Very small children do it instinctively. Without thinking. Without even knowing they are doing it. And of course they outgrow it almost immediately. But it is not uncommon to find a one-year-old sorcerer turning pets and dishes and furniture upside-down. A few have the strength to impose the spell on larger objects. But in the end, the power vanishes before they turn two, three at the latest.

I don't recall Elan using the upside-down spell as a child, but we found a grown-up version of that spell in a book, and it worked beautifully. Elan started with small objects, then moved to larger ones, such as, I found out unexpectedly one day, myself. I was reading Master Eusebius in the garden, when suddenly the world turned upside-down. Of course, the world hadn't changed; it was me.

"Put me down, Elan," I said without removing my eyes from the book.

"I'm a naughty witch!" she said from behind the jimberry tree, laughing merrily.

"We are not a witch!" I said. "We are a sorceress. The term 'witch' is coarse and shan't be used by a proper young lady such as yourself."

"I'm a naughty witch!" Elan sang out, dancing around the garden while I tried to read my book, floating in the air upside-down. Ultimately, when she got hungry enough for dinner, she set me down. She didn't know how to cook.

We practiced the upside-down spell every week for five years. It was important that she learn to execute the spell by rote. That she said the spell by instinct precisely the same way each time. And that she could do so if someone was punching her face or swinging a sword at her head or stringing her up on a gallows. Or, worse yet, if a loud mob was approaching at high speed with pitchforks and torches. She learned to control her breathing, her emotions, her heartbeat, everything – at least long enough to say the bloody spell!

After which she should run.

None of that solved the problem of Amelia. One which I did not, of course, raise with Elan. As I said, the Fluence does not permit itself to be used as a weapon. At least not bluntly. Indirectly, on certain occasions, perhaps. So how did Amelia wreak havoc on the Riege over such a short period? Especially if she used cloth and crystal. It is, as I witnessed for ten years with Elan, a surgical power. Hardly the kind of talent that enables one to lay waste to villages and the like. Sorcerers can go bad, of course, or dabble in black powers beyond the Fluence, but none of that explained Amelia.

And how did the rubystone fit into it?

Through my ten years training Elan, the problem of Amelia never ceased to vex me. How could I ensure that Elan did not turn into Amelia if I did not understand how *Amelia* became Amelia? I never did figure it out. In the meantime, if Elan ever needed to defend herself, she would have at her disposal the small child's upside-down spell.

12

Elan

"Why have we stopped?" I ask.

"We're here," Stille says.

I swivel my head. It is early evening. Our ride passed first in smalltalk, then long hours in tired silence. We are both exhausted. I've barely slept since I hopped into the back of the Vorstadts' wagon.

To the left are rolling fields, and to the right, a dense gently-upsloping forest. A tame forest, mind you. Flatlands forests are not like anything in the Reaches. There, the trees are hard-barked and gnarled. What life they have, they've earned. In the flatlands, trees are mellow and straight and soft. They take the sun and rain for granted. I feel like a good strong breeze could uproot the lot of them.

"I don't see anything," I say.

Stille chuckles. "Look closer."

I squint, and there, tucked in the trees, is a slouching two-story house. And off to the side is a small store and another unmarked building or two further along. If we had not stopped, I would never have noticed there were structures and people here.

"This is Heedle?" I ask.

"It is," he says. "Centuries ago, they called it Hayneedle. Because it was like a needle in a haystack to find. Then it was shortened to Heedle. I do two things in my spare time. One, I read. I think I've read every book in Master Depsik's library at least twice. Two, I come here. The farmers in this region need a scribe on occasion, and I needed income. I stayed at a spare room in that house there. The owner is Mister Weathersby, Mister being his actual first name. He'll put us up for tonight."

"So he's Mr. Mister Weathersby?" I ask, delighted.

"He is," Stille says, "although I wouldn't recommend calling him that."

The smile drops off my face when I meet Weathersby. He's an unshaven middle-aged man in greasy coveralls with dirt under every fingernail. Without expression, he eyes me top to bottom and side to side. He reminds me of the men my black fabrics have shown me in women's buried memories. Bad men. Unhappy angry ready-to-strike men.

The first floor of Weathersby's house is dimly lit with low beamed ceilings. The walls are a strange mixture of stones, bricks and wood. The air is smoky, and it smells of lamp oil and tobacco. The slanted floor creaks with nearly every step. The small curtainless windows are opaque with years of grime.

I do believe, I think, *that I'm the first woman who's ever stepped inside.*

The heavy air gags me. The Keep was always cold, but it surrounded me with fresh mountain air. I don't know how people can stand to breathe these dark stultifying smoky odors.

I've long since changed out of Master Depsik's white dress. The road spit and sprayed mud, so it didn't stay white very long. The hat flew off in the wind. And the shoes? Well, I don't know where they got to. I'm more comfortable wearing men's clothing – the white pullover and dark workpants with old walking shoes– under my coat of many colors.

But I like my new hair. Dark brown. I catch reflections of it now and then. And much as I hate to admit it, Stille's work with the shears has evened me out. Of course, soon enough my hair will be red again, my favorite color. But I am surprised to admit that, except for my clothes, I now look like a proper young Riegian woman.

I know Stille has stayed in this house before, but I do not trust Weathersby. Slowly I reach with my left hand for a dark fabric and with my right for a crystal. I need to read this man. I'm not taking any more chances. Not like I did with the Vorstadts. If I'm staying in his house, I need to know what he's done. What he's *capable* of doing. All I need is an opening. Just a second or two, and I'll be inside his head. I'm willing to bet he doesn't have a trained mind. Not like Praelat Ortun. He'll never know I was there.

"Elan, what are you doing?" Stille whispers, looking at my hands.

"I don't trust Weathersby," I whisper back.

"Don't do it," he says.

"He's a man, and I don't trust men," I say, my jaw clenched. I have vowed never to be burned again, and I mean it.

"Well, I'm a man," Stille says.

"That's different," I say. I'm struggling with that, but I don't want him to see it. "I mean, I know you."

"Not for that long," Stille says.

"I've seen what men can do," I say under my breath.

"And I've seen what witches can do," he says. "They killed my family. How is this any different?"

I pause. "Give me one reason to trust him."

"I trust him," Stille says, tapping his own chest. "I'll vouch for him."

I search Stille's eyes. This is a crossroads moment. If I go against Stille's wishes, I could lose him forever. My *Anaiah* will be lost. But if I don't, I'll be doing something I vowed never to do again.

"I've known him for over a year now," Stille says, taking my arm gently. "He doesn't say much, but he won't harm you. He's not that kind of man."

I breathe deeply. If I don't trust Stille, then nothing I've embarked upon is going to work out, so I take the leap. "Fine," I mutter, slipping the fabric and crystal back inside my coat.

"We're in this together, remember?" Stille says. "Criminals."

I offer a tight smile. "Yes, horse thieves."

"Among other things," he says.

Weathersby serves us a cold but tasty dinner on an ancient oaken table in the corner of his tiny kitchen. The plates are chipped and cracked, the tableware well-used. My chair has one leg shorter than the rest. Stille opens the shutters, so finally, some fresh air. Together we witness the sun setting against the cartpath we traveled all day. The orange and red hues are gorgeous.

Suddenly my stomach sinks. We traveled *into* the sunset. Which means we're headed west. But Kimbar is due south. I turn to Stille and lean into him.

"So, young man, where exactly are you taking me?"

He frowns. "I thought we agreed on Kimbar."

"Kimbar is west?"

"No, Kimbar is south."

"But we're going west," I say, pointing with my head at the sunset. "What aren't you telling me?"

He laughs, and that lock of hair falls into his face again. And again I resist the urge to put it back in place. I think the Fluence did that to his hair. Just to tempt me.

"Our pursuers know or can guess we are headed to Kimbar," Stille says. "They will assume we're taking the most direct route. Which is the king's road heading due south. Master Depsik's carriage is first-rate, but we can't outrun them."

"So where are we going?"

"Two days west to the seaport of Darine on the Tablas river. From there we'll catch a ship west and then due south to the bronze arms of Elden, then head east overland to Kimbar. That's my plan anyway."

"Fine," I say. "I just wish you'd told me."

"So now I've told you."

"Is there anything else you haven't told me?" I ask.

"One thing," he says sheepishly. "But I thought I'd wait until later."

"Now is good," I say.

"Weathersby only has one room. With one bed."

I raise my eyebrows.

"I'll sleep on the floor," he says. "You can have the bed."

"No," I say. "You planned your escape for one person, so you should get the bed. This won't be the first time I've slept on the floor. And probably not the last either."

"We can argue about that later," he says. Weathersby takes away our plates, and I realize he has not said a word in my presence. Nor has he once looked me in the eyes.

"Are you sure we can trust Weathersby?" I say. "He seems strange."

"He's not very social," Stille says. "He's lived alone his entire life. Never married, no children.

And in case you haven't noticed, Heedle isn't exactly in the thick of things. But that doesn't make him a bad person."

"If you say so," I say. *I'm going to trust Stille*, I repeat to myself.

I catch Stille staring at me, and I blush. "What?" I say, pursing my lips. "You're staring at me."

"I like your hair," Stille says, then reaches out to touch it. My instinct is to back off, but I fight it as our eyes meet.

"But red is definitely your color," he says. "Your complexion is too fair for dark brown. We'll have to change you back the next chance we get."

I think about the last time Stille washed my hair. And massaged my scalp. "I'll look forward to it," I say, then laugh because I'm blushing again. Flirting is new to me, but I'm starting to like it.

Then something Stille said tugs at me. His reference to Elden's bronze arms. I remember Bishop Fiske's memory and the bronze statue with the river in the background. The tall thin man with outstretched arms.

"So tell me about the bronze arms of Elden," I ask.

"There's an enormous statue of Mordecai, the Order's first brother, by the river there," he says. "Holding out his arms. Mordecai runs the Order like a fiefdom. Elden is the compound where they train the brothers."

"And there's a grassy hill behind the statue," I say.

"Yes," he says. "So you've been to Elden then?"

"No, but I've seen it in a memory." I tell him about Bishop Fiske and how the long-buried memory of fifty sleepy boys in nightshirts at dawn drove him to take his own life.

"Kimbar is always rife with rumors of sacred blood rituals inside the Order," Stille says. "You know, cleansing sin with sacrifice. They have an orphanage on the compound there, but I never heard anything about boys in nightshirts at dawn."

Our room in Weathersby's house is small but clean, and the bed has a real mattress. The sheets are fresh, and there is a pitcher of water on the nightstand. Three paraffin lamps throw flickering lights against the ceiling and walls.

I pluck the extra blanket from a spindly three-legged chair and sit roughly on the floor, my back to the wall. I am *not* taking the bed. I have my pride.

"You're being awful," Stille says.

"How so?" I say, pretending not to know what he's talking about.

"You're not letting me feel good about myself."

I laugh out loud. A big throaty laugh. "So that's what this is about? You feeling good about yourself?"

He grins. "Absolutely. Which is why you need to take the bed. It's the only kind thing for you to do. I can't feel good about myself as a man if I let you take the floor."

"Let's compromise," I say smartly. "You start on the bed, then halfway through the night, we'll switch places. Deal?"

He scowls at me. "You promise to wake me?"

"I'll shove you over onto the floor if I can't."

"Deal," he says, settling on the bed. He groans in relief as he sinks into the mattress. Neither of us has slept in a long time.

"So," he says, "Elan Montescue of the Northern Reaches, memory witch extraordinaire, tell me everything about you. Who you were, who you are, what you want, and how I fit into any of it."

"Seriously?" I say. "How much time have you got?"

"All night," he says.

Well, I think, *he asked.*

My head against the wall, I set down a paraffin lamp on the floor and start talking. My hand movements toss vigorous animated shadows around the room as I tell Stille the abbreviated story of my life. How I was a happy child until I was five, and how my life changed when Catherine left and then I witnessed Father's and Willem's deaths a year later. How Gregor and I escaped to the family Keep in the mountains. How we lived in near utter isolation while Gregor trained me for ten years to be a memory witch with cloth and crystal. How we traveled to flatlands villages so I could perfect my powers on the dearths, and the awful memories I unearthed in the people there, especially the women. How my sole purpose in life has always been, and still is, to hunt down and kill, one at a time, the hooded men who murdered Father and Willem.

Except I cried like a baby when Bishop Fiske hanged himself, I think. *I don't have any experience killing people.*

And then, I don't know why, I start telling Stille things I've never told anyone. The words pour out like they've been waiting patiently in queue. How my mother, whom everyone said was so beautiful, abandoned the family – how she abandoned me! – without reason or explanation. How for years Gregor refused to share his memories of Catherine or even talk about her. How I kept wishing and hoping and praying for her return. Until that day I realized she was never coming back, and then how much I hated her. And how much I hated myself for hating her. How I rehearsed a thousand times what I would say to Catherine if she ever did come back. How lonely I was there at the Keep, and how I transformed an entire family, the Vorstadts, into my own fantasy family, and how the Vorstadts betrayed me in Montauk.

And, finally, how scared I've been every minute since I worked up the courage to leave the Keep, to leave Gregor, to fulfill my mission. How none of my plans have worked as I intended. How Gregor told me about this preposterous crazy unbelievable folk tale that the Fluence had created a boy my own age to be my human crystal, my *Anaiah*, so I could perfect my powers and do what I was supposed to do. How I never believed him until there in Montauk I saw those beautiful tiny blue birds fly away in unison, and then the tingling all over, and how this boy walked into the night like it was a destiny that had been decided a thousand years ago. And how our merest touch turned into lightning.

I pause. I've talked so much and so long, my throat is sore and my voice raspy. "This must all sound crazy to you, huh?" I say.

There is no response.

"Stille?"

Soundlessly, I rise and step to the bed where Stille snores softly. I cover him with a blanket, then lean over. I study his face. His lips, his eyes, the texture of his skin. It's almost like I'm evaluating a fabric. He is not beautiful, but he is perfect. The way angels are. Except this is a boy, and the Fluence has placed him here in the Riege as my crystal. If I can keep him, that is. And I have no idea if I can do that. Or what the cost might be.

Suddenly I have an urge to kiss him on the mouth. I catch myself, and instead lightly press my lips to his forehead. There are no sparks. I detect, in response, the hint of a smile on his face.

"Sleep well, Stan," I murmur.

13

Elan

The next morning after breakfast, Stille brings an open-welled wagon and two horses to the front of Weathersby's house. The wagon is rickety and rundown, the seatbox a splintered gray board. The horses seem old and tired, and there is no cover to shield the sun.

"What happened to Master Depsik's carriage?" I ask.

"I traded it for this and some food and water," Stille says brightly.

"I think you've been cheated," I say.

"We can't take the carriage to Darine," he says. "It's too recognizable. We'll stick out like a sore thumb."

"It was more comfortable than this contraption," I say.

"This contraption, as you call it, is less risky.

And we can leave it behind with no worries when we board our ship to Elden."

"Fine," I sigh. It's only two days to Darine. After riding in the Vorstadts' wagon and then sleeping in a fireplace and on Weathersby's floor, what's a few more days of pain and inconvenience?

"And you're sure this is the road to Darine?" I ask.

"Positive," he says.

We throw our bags in the back, and Stille takes the reins. The day is cool, but by noon the sun will prevail. We'll be sweaty and dog-tired by nighttime. I remove my leathers to use as a seat cushion.

"So how much of my little speech last night did you stay awake for?" I ask. I'm half wondering if I said too much, half hoping he heard it all. I try not to sound too eager. Or sarcastic.

"Nearly all of it, I think," he says in a serious thoughtful way. "It's quite a story, and I'm sorry for all you've gone through. You've endured more in sixteen years than many people do in a lifetime."

"Thanks," I say. "But then I haven't had a drunkard punch me in the face every day. You've absorbed your share as well."

He shrugs. "I'm alive; that's what counts." Then he laughs and flips the reins. "And I'm a fast healer."

"And the part about my human crystal?"

Stille takes a deep breath. "I know you believe it, Elan, but I'm not there yet. It's fantastic and incredible and awesome but way too much to accept. I mean, birds flying at night. Pins and needles in your arms. That's a long way from proving that some boy who walks around the corner is predestined to be your helpmate for life."

"There's also our handshake," I say quickly. "Don't forget what happened when our hands touched."

"How could I?" he says, chagrined. "The back of my head still hurts. But maybe that's because you're a memory witch. The first one in, like, a million years."

"That's never happened when I've touched anyone else," I say.

"Let's do this," he says. "Let's get ourselves to Kimbar. Then you can go hunt the men who murdered your father and brother, and I can see about my uncle's estate. And investigate what happened to my parents and grandparents. The official explanation how witches destroyed our village has always been sketchy."

"So we get to Kimbar . . .," I say.

"And we go our separate ways," Stille says.

I can't let him get away, I think.

"No, we reevaluate," I say, kneading the air with my fingers. I try to keep the desperation out of my voice. "If by the time we arrive in Kimbar, you still don't believe you're my *Anaiah*, then we'll part. Friends and comrades forever. You fulfill your mission, and I fulfill mine. But I'll have until then to persuade you."

The horses canter, and I hold my breath.

"I can live with that," Stille says at last.

"Shake on it?" I say, holding out my hand.

Stille starts to reach, then quickly pulls back his hand. "It's a deal," he says gamely. "As long as you keep your promise not to touch me."

I think about last night. About kissing him while he slept. There were no sparks, but then he wasn't awake, and that wasn't a touch. I mean, not exactly. "I'll try my best," I say winsomely.

I have to touch Stille somewhere, so I grab his arm. There's no explosion, but then he's wearing a shirt. I guess sparks require skin-to-skin contact. I hold onto him for a few moments before letting him go.

He needs to know I'm serious, I think. *I'm playing the long game.*

Our wagon moves even more slowly than the Vorstadts', which I didn't think possible. I replay the conversation with Stille in my head. It didn't go as well as I'd wanted, but it went better than I'd feared. I have time. I'm still in the game. And when we get to Kimbar . . .

"Wait!" I say out loud. "What's this about me being the first memory witch in a million years?"

"I'm sorry?" Stille says.

"You said I was the first memory witch in a million years."

"So?"

"That can't be true."

"Why not?"

"Because Gregor knows everything there is to know about memory witches. That's how he was able to train me. He would have said something if there hasn't been another memory witch in, you know, like, forever."

"Guess it slipped his mind," Stille says.

"Gregor is not the type to let things slip," I say.

"And I suppose he didn't tell you how destructive the memory witches have been. And how they all died horribly. And how everyone hated them. Even the born-and-bred. Especially that last one."

I stare at him openmouthed. "No," I say.

He pulls tight the reins. "Seriously?"

"You're making this up," I say, my hands and fingers gesticulating wildly, which always happens when I'm upset. "Please tell me this is a joke."

He snaps the reins, and the horses obligingly start up again. "No joke. I told you, I read a lot. Including every book in Master Depsik's library about the Fluence and the great sorcerers, both good and bad. The last memory witch was the worst, but I forget her name."

"I don't believe you."

"Suit yourself," he shrugs. "It's all the same to me."

I spend the rest of our ride having loud conversations inside my head. First with Gregor, then with Stille, then with Gregor again. My hands move like those of the conductor of a large orchestra. Slowly it dawns on me that Stille may be right. It would explain Gregor's incessant attempts to hold me at the Keep year after year. And to teach me how to wield cloth and crystal with maximum speed. His fear of mobs with pitchforks and torches. And that stupid upside-down spell. Gregor knew what awaited me in the Riege. He just didn't tell me. Suddenly the last ten years of my life seem quite different.

I don't notice the landscape changing. The pleasant rolling fields, now stuffed with barren stalks after harvesting, give way to woodlands and then to thicker forests with thinner trees. As dusk approaches, we move with agonizing languor on a single-wagon road with tree limbs snatching at our shoulders.

I'm glad I'm not claustrophobic, I think. *It's like the trees want to suffocate us.*

"This is still the road to Darine?" I say.

"It is, my lady," Stille says warily. "But now we must stop for the night."

"And what strange untalkative man will host us this fine evening?" I ask. I am cross and wallowing in self-pity and barely fit for civilized company. Stille's revelation about memory witches beats at me like fisted knuckles.

"No host," he says simply. "No house. No dinner on the table. No bed. No nothing."

"Then what?" I ask.

"This region has many abandoned barns and sheds," Stille says. "My plan was to find one and bed down for the night. I haven't seen a live person for an hour, and here is a shack about to fall down. I suggest we sleep here. We can tether the horses and wagon behind it."

He points to a small building that was once painted red with a stucco roof. The paint is nearly gone, the roof mostly intact. It leans hard to the right but has not fallen over.

"Such a romantic," I say.

"Sorry," he replies. "I thought I'd be traveling alone. Why don't you go inside and settle down? I'm going to check the road ahead. I'll be back before you've missed me."

I raise my eyebrows, but I take our bags and Weathersby's food and head into the shed. Every muscle and tendon screams. I remove my leathers and fling them into a corner. Closing my eyes, I lie down on the hard-packed dirt floor. The air smells ancient and dusty. I wonder how many years it's been since another living person has been inside. I promise myself I'll set wards as soon as I rest my eyes for a moment. I doze, but I don't fall asleep.

"Well, hello, little lady," a voice rings out.

It's a young man, no older than Stille, but taller. His clothes and face are dirty, his teeth yellow and crooked. His hair is uncombed, and dirty toes thrust out of his sole-flapping shoes. Two more young men enter, similarly dressed but slightly shorter than the first. Their identical grins tell me that what's about to happen is not good.

"My husband is outside," I say, drawing myself into a tight ball.

"Didn't see no husband," the first one says.

"Me neither," says the second. Their grinning mouths remain wide open. When I smell their breaths and the stink from their bodies and clothes, I know my worst fears are about to come true. I have seen this happen before, just never to me. Never live and in person.

I quickly surveil the room and spy my leathers in the corner. I need a crystal. Any crystal. I know what I must do. I have to launch myself across the floor to grab a crystal from my coat. With that I can defend myself. I pause one second to gather my strength and wits and resolve, but it is one second too many.

The boys' attack comes without further words. The shorter ones grab my legs and try to pull me out of my fetal position. The first one lunges at me, trying to kiss me and grabbing at my shirt. I punch him to no effect, and his hands paw at me like I'm a milk cow. His stink gags me. I strike out viciously with my feet while I whip my head away. The tall one grabs my chin with his hand and squeezes tight, sticking his face into mine. I smash his nose with my forehead, like I did with Praelat Ortun. He rears back in surprise as blood breaks from his left nostril. He shakes his head and screams something I can't understand, then places his left hand over my mouth. I bite it for all I'm worth as he viciously drops his right knee onto my ribcage. Suddenly I can't breathe.

I try to roll over, but the taller one connects with a brutal right cross to my chin. Everything slows down, and the room begins spinning. I can't move, and I wonder if he's broken my jaw. Suddenly I am cold all over. I feel my pullover yanked toward my shoulders, and the night forest air is chilly on my torso. My arms flop at my sides. In a few seconds, I'll be completely exposed on the hard dirt floor of this godforsaken shed on the one-wagon road to Darine.

Out of the corner of my eye, I see another pair of feet. As the room tumbles around me, I catch a glimpse of Stille. He's returned, and he's holding something. A piece of wood, or maybe a board. Swinging with all his might, Stille smacks one of the smaller boys in the back of the head. Snot and blood explode from the boy's startled face while his eyes roll back. The boy falls like a limp rag onto my left leg.

The other two turn on Stille like animals. Each one is bigger and heavier than Stille, and together they overwhelm him. They shove him roughly against the wall of the shed, then they twist him face-first into the black dirt floor. The taller one lifts Stille by his neck, then turns and drops him. I try to stand up, but I am dizzy and fall onto my side. I try another time, and again I fall down. I hear the blows landing. So many blows. The stomach-wrenching sounds of fists on flesh. They are beating Stille to a pulp. Even in my haze, I understand he will not survive much longer.

I no longer know where my leathers are. Now I am on all fours, and I see Stille's left hand fall onto the floor. Like it's beckoning to me. Like it's an invitation. *Come on*, his lifeless hand seems to say. *You can do it.*

With whatever energy I have left, I lunge for Stille, stretching to my arm's full length. My nose scrapes the dirt, so I don't see it happen. Our touch. But my aim is true, and I grab his hand in mine. It is cold and unresponsive.

Just hold it tight and say the damn spell, I think. *Like you trained every week for five years.*

Instantly I am enveloped in all-consuming white. Like I've been buried inside the world's densest newfallen snowdrift.

Then everything goes black.

14

Gregor's Journal

I shouldn't say I never liked Catherine. Rather, it's that I never approved of her. Of course, I didn't like her either.

And why should I have? She stole my pupil. My pride and joy. Alaric. When an Ebb rolls around, the born-and-bred immediately militate to designate one sorcerer as the last great one of the era. This time it was slim pickings, but it didn't take people long to settle on Alaric. He was the only sorcerer of real talent whose powers were not dimmed by the accelerating Ebb. So he was the One. He had to be. If not him, then whom? And I took pride in that. Some of his luster rubbed off on me. I was the tutor who trained the last great sorcerer of the tenth era.

Catherine had the most beautiful face I've seen on a woman. And she knew her face was perfect.

She spent hours every day applying and retouching and removing her makeup. And she was careful. I never saw her once without her "face" on. If you live in the same house with a woman over a period of years, there comes a day, a time – at least once, anyway – when you see her at less than her best. Not Catherine. She was magnificently disciplined. Whenever anyone saw her, she was perfectly dolled up. I'm not even convinced Alaric saw her without makeup. Perhaps they always made love in the dark.

And the rest of Catherine complemented her face. I mean her hairstyles. Her flirtations. Her immaculate taste in clothes. Her conversation. She was a slender woman, not voluptuous. She radiated an aura of delicacy and finesse. Even fragility. In part, it was an act. Alaric loved helping others, and Catherine was expert at giving him opportunities to do so. Part of the act was portraying herself as weak and easily overtaxed. Alaric was solicitous in the way that only a besotted lover can be.

Catherine was reckless in one regard. She behaved a certain way in Alaric's presence, yet dropped pretenses when Alaric was gone. She didn't care that friends and staff and, yes, even the tutor would see that she was playing Alaric. She treated us with overt disdain. Such was her confidence that her hold over Alaric was absolute. Who would dare tell him that his beloved Catherine was less than she seemed?

Elan inherited her mother's looks and overall

physique. She certainly had her face. But growing up in the harsh forests of the Northern Reaches, Elan became hard and lean and athletic, not diminutive and demure. And Elan paid no attention to her looks. It's not merely that there weren't boys around, although that was true enough. It's that Elan had a mission. I cringed every time she talked about it. How she didn't expect she would come back. How she never wanted to marry or have children. No one enjoys hearing such an outlook from a girl whose life is still before her.

I took solace that Elan did have one indulgence. Her red hair. She grew it long and lustrous and spent hours combing it. Maybe someday, I told myself, she will permit herself to live a normal life.

Alaric met Catherine on a trip to Kimbar to visit distant Montescue relations on the coast. Her story was sketchy. She came from a born-and-bred family that had left the Riege several cycles earlier and migrated south. I say "her family," but in reality all we saw was a brother, one aunt, and two distant cousins.

The Riege hears only rumors and tawdry generalizations about the southern civilization on the other side of the ocean. "Down there," we say. We hear it is unbearably hot, teeming with small look-alike people, and riven with bizarre cultures and practices. Catherine and her family had returned to Kimbar six months prior to Alaric's trip, and her relations vanished back south as soon as the echoes of the wedding vows died away. Given Alaric's ascension to the top of his profession, I had assumed her family would do the opposite. They would desire to bask in his glow and influence, and, hence, they would always be underfoot. There was money to be made if they played their cards correctly. So imagine my shock when they departed the Riege quickly after the wedding and no one heard from them again.

Catherine didn't seem to mind. She adapted quickly to Alaric's isolated flatlands villa and never talked of her own family. She enjoyed telling people her name was Catherine Montescue. She also loved having servants to instruct and direct. She would have hired more if Alaric hadn't said no. It was one of the few times he didn't give her what she wanted. There wasn't the money. She pouted for a time but discerned, wisely, that on this matter Alaric would stand firm.

Catherine quickly delivered Alaric a son, Willem, and then Elan after a suitable interval. Giving birth did not generate any obvious maternal instincts in Catherine. After each birth, she handed the baby to the nannies and returned her attentions to Alaric. And to running the villa as a fiefdom. Now that I think of it, I never once heard her call the children by their given names. It was always "the boy," or "the girl," or if she spoke to them directly, "child." The way you would when speaking to neighbor children. She didn't shower them with hugs and kisses, play with them in the pasture, help dress them, or read bedtime stories. She rarely touched them at all.

Catherine's departure was a shock. I certainly didn't see it coming. Alaric had left late one afternoon for Montauk to arrange materials and hire laborers for the villa. Catherine never accompanied him on these trips, but that next morning she was absent. Initially we assumed she was with Alaric. Perhaps she felt cooped up in the villa and went to shop in Montauk. But something didn't feel right. Later that day, I ventured with bated breath into Alaric's and Catherine's bedroom. Everything was where it should have been, although a travelbag was missing. And then I saw it. The handkerchief on the dresser with a large rubystone in it. "For my daughter," the note said in her beautiful cursive strokes. And I knew she had run.

Alaric was beyond distraught. He was devastated. He dispatched men to chase ghosts in all different directions. Alaric even had his men stop several king's carriages headed to Kimbar, thinking she might be inside. She wasn't. He questioned everyone he thought might know anything, then questioned them again. Several people reported an unfamiliar carriage traveling backroads at a certain speed on the day she left, but descriptions of the vehicle and its location varied sufficiently that the reports were deemed not credible.

I noticed one strange fact that Alaric dismissed with a handwave. A month prior he and Catherine had hosted a diverse group from Kimbar and Elden. Their accents were perfect, but something seemed off. Their clothes. Their silences. Their teeth. The glances they exchanged. I didn't know what to make of them. The leader of the group was a small man with an enormous (and obviously dyed) black mustache and a heavy limp. The group left just as a new lot, this one comprised of Alaric's friends, arrived. When asked about the departing guests, Alaric said they were Catherine's comrades, but separately, Catherine said they were Alaric's. I mentioned the odd discrepancy to Alaric, but he paid it no attention.

I still go back to the day Catherine arrived at the villa after the wedding. She had an enormous amount of luggage, including several boxes. One box fell and split open, spilling various papers, some yellow with age. Catherine dropped to the floor – on all fours, believe it or not – and insisted on cleaning up the mess herself. It was the first and last time she did housework. She overlooked one brittle paper that had wafted under a chair. I retrieved it and handed it to her. It was a small cursive note written in a heavy black ink. I did not read it, except to note that it was addressed to "Katrin." I expected thanks when I handed it to her gracefully, but instead received a short vicious lecture on prying eyes and ears. The next day I noticed fresh ashes in the bedroom fireplace. Someone had spent the night burning things.

I never told Alaric about the incident. I considered it minor and, at the time, I still cherished hopes of developing a civilized relationship with his bride. I did not want to spoil my chances by tattling on a strange occurrence of possibly no significance. Catherine is a name with many spellings. In the Riege, it is usually spelled with a "C" and sometimes with a "K." But Katrin, pronounced to rhyme with spleen, is a version I'd rarely encountered. To my knowledge, the only exception was our western red-skinned Karator neighbors across the Impassable River. A nation with which we have been intermittently at war since the dawn of time. The Karators always have spelled this name "Katrin."

After Alaric's death, I determined not to share my memories of Catherine with Elan. In part, it was because I had grown to detest Catherine, and I knew Elan would wish to view the memories time and again. But the primary reason was Elan's well-being. In my memories, she would have seen Catherine as she was – beautiful, haughty, distant, cold, selfish and mean-spirited. And, most important, a mother whose children mattered nothing to her.

I suspect nothing compensates for the pain of abandonment, but I reasoned it would offset that pain somewhat if Elan could develop an idealized image of who and what her mother was. I did not expect Catherine to return, so that was what Elan would live with the rest of her life. This was one time I did not want reality to intrude on fantasy.

And I still harbor guilt that I never told Alaric about the "Katrin" note. He would have done nothing, of course. Not even inquired. But as his tutor, I should have provided him the information. That was my duty, and I failed.

15

Elan

Dawn glimmers through cracks in the weathered wooden slats of the shed. I've put my clothes back on, and then Master Depsik's muddy white dress on top of that, and then my coat of many colors over that. It is cold, but I don't mind. I sit cross-legged, my back against the wall, and I am humming a low tune with no melody. I do not move except for my right hand stroking Stille's forehead in my lap. I have covered him with a heavy blanket.

He moans briefly. It comes from deep inside, the way wild animals mewl when their pain is too much to bear. My jaw throbs, but I don't think it's broken.

I glance down and see Stille's eyes blinking. His face is swollen and covered in multicolored bruises, and his lips are split open in two places.

His hair is matted, and bloodstains spatter his shirt.

"Amelia," Stille says in a small tremulous voice.

"What?" I say.

"Her name was Amelia," he says, pronouncing each syllable distinctly. "You know, the last memory witch."

"It's a pretty name," I say.

"Yes," he agrees.

"You just thought of it now?"

"No, on my way back to the shed."

We sit in silence a few minutes more. I find something comfortable to rest my eyes on – a large ugly knot in a wooden plank on the far wall – and I stare at it.

"You're touching me," he says, then tries to laugh, which ends up in a cough and a moan.

"Yes," I say quietly, continuing to stroke his brow. "No more explosions or sparks. I guess our auras have gotten used to each other."

"I hurt all over," he says.

"I bet," I say. "I've tried using healing spells while you slept. Gregor once broke his right leg, and we concocted spells all that night. But I don't think they've helped you."

"My right leg feels great," he says, and I smile.

"I guess we're going to see if you were telling the truth," I say.

"About what?"

"That you're a fast healer."

I am numb, and my heart is empty and full at the same time. Gregor was right, as he usually is.

Seeing someone's memory of being harmed is one thing. Seeing it happen to someone in real time is another. Having it happen to you is the worst. I was, I know, fortunate. My virginity is intact. They were going to take turns with me, but we fought them off. Stille and me. Together. Hand in hand. A team.

A memory witch and her *Anaiah*.

"What happened to me?" he asks.

"You mean, you don't remember?"

"I remember leaving you at the shed to check the road ahead, and then I wake up here in your lap. Hurting like I've been run over by a carriage. By several carriages."

"Three boys tried to rape me. You came back and stopped it."

"I beat up three boys?"

"No, you took down one, and the other two turned on you. It ended when I crawled over, took your hand in mine, and said a spell. When I woke up, we were on the ground, and the three boys were gone."

"Are they dead?"

"I don't know. But I won't be sorry if they are."

"Don't say that, Elan. They should be punished, but killing someone is a heavy load. Even if they deserve it."

I shrug. "If you say so."

"What spell?"

"I'm sorry?"

"You said you used a spell. Which one?"

"Gregor calls it the upside-down spell."

"But you made the boys vanish," Stille says.

"I know," I respond. "I was rather stressed. I may have said the spell differently than usual. I'm not entirely sure what happened."

"Well, whatever you said, it worked. The shed is still here, and we're alive inside."

"Yes, we're inside."

"What did the boys do to you?"

I sigh and hold my elbows close, shivering. "They were tearing my clothes off when you arrived, and I've got an aching jaw from a wicked right hand, but that's as far as they got."

"I should never have left you to check on the road."

"Stop it, Stille!" I say more loudly than I intended. "Do not, I repeat, do not blame yourself. You did nothing wrong. There was no way to know they were lurking. When you travel in the flatlands, something like this is always a risk. We were unlucky, that's all."

But I know it wasn't bad luck. I was to blame. I let my guard down; there's no other way to say it. I should have had my leathers nearby. A crystal in my hand. Gregor beat into my head that exhaustion is no excuse for negligence. But this time I was negligent. I should have set wards immediately. Those three boys should have seen an empty shed when they walked inside. But we were so far away from civilization. From people. We were more at risk from wildlife than humans, or so it seemed. It boils down to one thing: I was lazy. And it nearly got Stille and me killed.

I can't put my finger on why, but one thing unnerves me more than anything else. More than all the anything-elses put together. I couldn't bear it if Stille remembered seeing me sprawled there on the floor. I felt so violated lying there. So ashamed. If he had seen me, I don't know what I would do.

"Are you sure you don't remember what happened after you came back?" I ask nervously.

"Not a thing."

"I mean, you didn't see me, you know, the way I was."

"No," he says weakly. "I never forget a beautiful girl. However difficult the circumstances."

"Thank you for saying I'm beautiful."

"You are, but then you know that, right?"

"I do?"

"Stop it. The pretty girl hasn't been born who doesn't know she's pretty."

"You forget," I say, "that I grew up in my family's Keep in the Reaches with only an old man for company. An old man who forgot to tell me I'm the first memory witch in a long time. There were no boys around."

"Was your mother pretty?" Stille asks.

"Catherine?"

"Yes."

"I'm told she was."

"So that explains it then."

"Well, thank you, Stille Vespers, for thinking I'm pretty. And thank you for not remembering."

"You are most welcome, Elan Montescue. Thank you for making my right leg feel better."

I laugh and fight the urge to bend down and kiss him. As shaken as I am, my attraction to Stille is powerful. This is the second time I've had that urge. I think it's the Fluence. But then I lean back and reality hits me. At this moment, my mission to avenge Father and Willem is further from my grasp than ever. I am only a few days from leaving the Keep, and I'm fortunate to be alive. I keep making mistakes. And if those boys had killed Stille and me, it would have been months, if ever, before our bodies were found. But Gregor would have known immediately. He wouldn't have known where or how, but his fluential powers would have vanished. And the last ten years would have been wasted.

Stille struggles to rise from the floor.

"You're too weak yet!" I scold.

"I need to see to our wagon and horses. At least make sure they haven't run off."

"Well, suit yourself," I say. I rub my jaw, which has settled into a dull ache.

Stille rises with enormous effort to his knees, then, one hand on the floor to steady himself, he rises to his feet. He walks like an eighty-year-old man, then throws open the door and sunlight floods in. He steps through like he's entering another realm.

"Elan," he says from outside. "You need to come see this."

"Are the horses still there?" I shout.

"Yes, but you really need to see this."

I don't realize how battered my body is until I

try to stand up. It takes almost every ounce of energy I've got left. I trudge to the door and step outside. It's not merely my jaw that hurts. I ache all over. I see Stille a few steps ahead.

"Yes, what is it?" I say.

"Look around, Elan."

The sun is incredibly bright, so I shield my eyes. At first, I don't comprehend any of it. It's all around us. In every direction as far as I can see. The forest is gone and replaced by, well, I don't know what.

"I don't understand," I say to Stille.

His eyes are wide. "It's your upside-down spell. You've uprooted every tree for miles in all directions." And then he points behind the shed to our wagon. "Except for the copse there where our horses are enjoying the morning."

We stand there for some minutes, turning round and round, gawking at the vast ocean of tree roots pointing skyward. Small animals cavort amidst the elevated turf, while masses of birds, squawking and chirping, fly in puzzled circles. The air is filled with clods of earth plucked from the tree roots by a stiff wind.

It's raining dirt, I think.

"This was you," he says, amazed.

"No, Stille, this was you," I respond. "I've done the upside-down spell thousands of times at the Keep. I can overturn small objects located close to me. That's all my crystals permit me to do. But I had a different crystal this time. A human crystal. I had you, and it magnified the power of my spell.

All this happened because I had you."

Without seeming to think about it, he pulls me closer. His arm around my shoulders. I gently slide mine around his waist, and it feels good. Like we belong together. It helps restore me so I can put last night's ordeal behind us. For several long minutes, we stare at the incredible sight of a forest turned on its head.

"I think I've changed my mind about Kimbar," Stille says softly.

"What in particular?" I say.

"About parting ways when we get there," he says. "I'm still not entirely sure, but I think there may be something to this crystal theory of yours."

"That's good to hear, Stille," I say.

"I keep feeling this strange powerful attraction to you," he says, shaking his head ruefully. "And it's not just because you're beautiful and funny and grab my arm."

"It's the Fluence," I say. "We were born to be together."

"I guess it is," he says. "But if I'm to be your human crystal, you have to promise me one thing. No secrets. This won't work if we keep secrets from each other."

"I promise," I say.

Tired as I am, my heart jumps for joy in my chest. My mission is now back on track. Maybe there was a reason we came out here to the middle of nowhere. A reason those three boys showed up. Maybe this is how the Fluence works its own special brand of magic. We needed a personal tragedy to bring us closer together. What doesn't kill us, the old saying goes, makes us stronger. Especially together.

"I pledge to help you locate and hunt down the men who killed your family," he says solemnly.

"And I pledge to help you find out what happened to your village," I say.

"Shake on it?" he says.

"With pleasure."

We take each other's hands – this time without sparks – not knowing what, if anything, will ever be the same again.

16

Elan

We reach Darine that evening as the sun sets. I took the reins when we left the shed, and by now the horses know my touch like an old friend. Stille has alternately slept in the back or huddled miserably up front. We had to reattach the wooden slat we use as a seatbox. The one Stille used to down one of my attackers. I've covered him in my leathers to keep him warm.

I can't imagine a city larger than Montauk, but then we arrive on our cartpath at the crest of the hill overlooking Darine. Relatively little traffic approaches, as we have, from the northeast. The busy roads are the ones entering Darine from the south and southeast. The view from our hill is breathtaking. Darine is a busy port on the eastern side of the freshwater Tablas River. Dusk hides the far shore. At least fifty boats of various sizes are docked at piers, wide as streets, jutting into the water. The city itself blossoms inland like a flower. Ten of Montauk could fit easily within the city walls, and Darine is already spreading far beyond that.

Stille sits next to me, wrapped in my leathers, listing to his right. His rhythmic breaths tell me he has been dozing.

"Stille, you should see this," I say. "It's spectacular."

"I've seen it," he mumbles, then yawns. "I've been here before."

"You never said anything," I scold.

"You never asked," he responds.

"So where are we going?" I say.

"The stables just up the street from the master scribe," he says. "Master Depsik dispatched me to Darine several times on business. My counterpart, a local boy named Dwumfour, owes me a favor. Several favors, in fact. He'll let us use his room for a night or two without telling anyone."

Stille points, and I guide the horses. We enter the city and, holding my nose, I am hit by the overpowering odor of fish. We find the stables, and they remind me of those in Montauk. I guess if you've seen one set of stables, you've seen them all. Involuntarily, I scan the street for Adam Vorstadt or his friend Anse. But they aren't here in Darine, of course. Stille gingerly steps down and talks animatedly with the stableboy about selling our rig. Their hands move, then their fingers. The boy shrugs, and Stille pats him on the shoulder.

"We should take our things now," Stille says upon returning. "The boy there knows a likely buyer. We won't get much, but it's better than nothing. He'll conclude the deal tonight, and we'll get our share in the morning."

Travelbags in hand, Stille leads me a few doors down. Creaking in the wind, a sign hangs by rusted chains from a short pole extending over the walk. The letters glint in the moonlight, yet I can't read them in the dark.

"The master scribe?" I ask.

Stille nods and pushes through the door. He takes a candlestick, then searches for the flint to light it.

"Here, let me," I say. I focus on the wick, say a simple spell in my head, and the candle lights.

"Well done," he says. "However, might I suggest in the future, you tone down your witchcraft . . ."

"Sorcery," I correct.

"Yes, whatever, but you don't want people knowing you're a witch, so best to keep that sort of thing under wraps as much as you can. At least until we're away."

"Fine," I grumble.

He leads the way up several flights of steep narrow stairs, and then we are in a library. I can tell by the smell. A rank combination of leather and dust and mold. It reminds me of the Keep's library. I spent many hours there reading books since I had so little else to do. But there were no volumes on memory witches. Gregor must have removed them.

A light flickers in the distance. Stille leads us toward it. There, in a small room, is a roly-poly young man I assume to be Dwumfour. He's younger than Stille, maybe fourteen or fifteen. He wears a rough soiled brown robe, which I suspect has been worn by more than one assistant scribe before him. By the light of a single candle on a cracked slanted table, Dwumfour laboriously copies a manuscript from a torn and faded original.

Stille steps into the light. "Hello, Dwumfour," he says.

Startled, the boy looks up, and immediately a smile lights his face as he stands. "Stille! My old friend! How wonderful to see you again!"

"Yes, and this time I've brought something."

"A book?" he asks, his eyes still on fire with excitement.

"Well, not exactly," Stille says, and then I step into the light.

"It's a, well, it's a . . . a girl," Dwumfour says incredulously. "A really pretty one." The smile drops from his face. Like he's never seen a girl before.

I laugh. "Hello," I say.

"This is my cousin from Kimbar," Stille says, putting his arm into mine.

"Well then," Dwumfour says, recovering quickly, "you are both welcome in my humble abode." He bows and throws out one arm with a flourish.

"And where is Master Jedders this fine evening?" Stille asks, looking around.

Dwumfour sucks in his breath and frowns. "Where he always is, Stille. Where he's been for the last fifteen years. In his office. Drinking."

"Well, he need not know that we're here," Stille says.

"And I shan't tell him," Dwumfour says, smiling broadly.

"We are in desperate need of a place to sleep for the night," Stille says.

"Found one, you have!" Dwumfour says lightly. "You can sleep in my room. It's cramped, and one of you will have to use the floor. But it's all yours for as long as you need it."

"I'll be the one to use the floor," Stille says, eyeing me. That evening at Weathersby's I failed to wake him, and he slept in the bed all night. He hasn't mentioned my lapse, but neither has he forgiven me.

"And where will you sleep?" I ask Dwumfour.

"In the stacks," he says. "Don't you worry about me. I have an extra blanket and pillow. I'll be fine. I've done it before."

Dwumfour peers at Stille more closely. "What happened to you?" he asks. "Your face looks terrible."

"Robbers," I say quickly. "We met robbers on the way here."

Dwumfour sighs. "The Riege is a vicious place. Now that the Order has taken over, you'd think that, well, there would be more order. But there isn't. They focus on the cities and towns. The countryside is more lawless than ever."

"Is it that bad?" Stille asks.

The boy lowers his voice. "They're everywhere in Darine, Stille. And the last few days, the sky has been filled with pigeons. You know, carrying messages here, there, and everywhere."

"What's happened?" I ask.

"A witch," he says. "That's what's happened. They spotted her in Montauk a few days ago. And then three boys dropped from the sky into some godforsaken hamlet. Claimed they fought ten witches in the forest and were lucky to escape with their lives."

"Three boys?" I ask.

"Yes."

"And they fought ten witches?"

"That's their story," he says. "I overhead the brothers talking about it to Master Jedders. That and some storm that wiped out half a forest."

"Sounds like a lot of tall tales to me," Stille says, throwing a cautionary glance my way.

"Tall tales or not," he says, "the Order is looking for this witch everywhere. Darine included. They're offering a big reward. Personally, I hope they don't find her."

"You couldn't use the money?" Stille asks, grinning.

"Of course," he says. "But everything the Order touches gets worse. So whomever they're looking to find, witch or not, I hope they escape."

"Well, best not to be too vocal with views like that," Stille whispers.

"Yes, yes," Dwumfour says, "but here I know

I'm among friends."

"You are," I say sincerely.

Dwumfour leads us on tip-toes through several stacks to a corner room. The floor groans underneath us. His room is barely the size of a closet. A narrow bed with a wafer-thin mattress takes up most of the floorspace, and there is a sink under a stained broken mirror. Stille will have to sleep on his side. I think about offering him the bed, then decide against it. I have Weathersby's to atone for, and I'm exhausted besides.

I wait to hear Stille's rhythmic breathing. I don my leathers and carefully step over him, moving quietly into the stacks where Dwumfour sleeps. The master scribe's office is easy to find. It contains the window overlooking the street. I push open the door, and it creaks miserably. An older disheveled man in stocking feet, who I assume can only be Master Jedders, sits upright in a high-backed leather chair. His head jiggles to the sound of his stop-and-start snores. The room smells of alcohol, some of which has puddled on his desk.

"So, you've been master scribe for fifteen years, have you?" I murmur softly. "Let's see what you remember."

A crystal between my right thumb and forefinger, I remove my special red fabric and place it against his neck. Instantly, I see that he knows nothing about the attack on our villa ten years ago, other than the memory of hearing that it happened. A memory I've encountered at least a hundred times. So Master Jedders can't help me iden-

THE MEMORY WITCH

tify the men who killed Father and Willem.

But then I try another fabric, and the crystal pulls my attention to other memory shards. From seven months before the attack. A much younger and thinner Master Jedders speaks to a small man with a large black mustache and a gimpy right leg.

"It will only be for one night, my old friend," the man with the mustache says.

"It's not much of a room," Jedders says.

"It will be enough. She has endured worse."

The memory breaks and starts up again. Master Jedders carries a tray down the hall. The hall that I just traversed moments earlier. He arrives at the door of Dwumfour's room. He looks around to make sure no one is watching. The room is nearly the same as it is now. Except the mirror is not broken, and the blanket is dark green. The mattress looks like it could be the same one.

A woman stands by the window, glaring into the back alley and smoking a cigarette. Quick hard impatient puffs. Her lips compressing the butt like she wants to explode it. She is sweaty, her hair askew. The man with the mustache sits on the bed, and she turns to Jedders when he arrives with the tray. This woman has a beautiful face. My face.

Hello, Mother, I think.

She takes in the tray and its glass of water, glances at Jedders with angry eyes, then waves it away. As if to say, *I am in no mood to be placated.*

"And you did what we instructed," the man on the bed says to her.

"Yes," she says. "I left the stone for the girl."

The girl, I think. *In other words, me.*

"Excellent," the man says.

"Which is not to say she'll get it. I wouldn't put it past the servants, or that awful prying prissy tutor, to steal it."

"We'll just have to take that risk, Katrin," the man says.

"And that assumes the girl somehow survives," Mother says.

"It does," the man says.

My mother takes her cigarette butt and crushes it into the wall, leaving a stain.

The memory ends as Jedders, having set down the tray, leaves. A new memory starts immediately. In this one, Jedders returns for the tray. Now the man stands by the window, smoking, and Mother lies on the bed, her bare ankles crossed, the fingers of both hands on her temples. Her eyes are shut.

"Are you sure Mother and Father are all right," she says.

"Our Master has always kept his word before, hasn't he?" the man says.

Mother says nothing.

"I say, hasn't he?" the man demands.

"Yes," she whispers.

"Well, then," he says.

"So what time tomorrow do we leave for home?" she asks.

"Ten o'clock at night. The belowdecks on Pier Four. Slipriders from upriver sneak in for travelers paying cash."

"I hope you have cash," she says.

"Of course," he says.

And then the memory ends as Jedders leaves the room, and there are no more shards for me to retrieve. I regard Jedders, sleeping fitfully in his chair. He is disgusting in his filthy sloppy drunkenness. *The things men do to themselves*, I think. But then I replay the memory shards, and I realize it's not just men.

I steal back into Dwumfour's room. By the light of the moon, I put one hand out for balance so I can peer at the wall. The place where Mother stubbed out her cigarette. And there it is. All these years later. A black stain. Other than the rubystone, the only tangible evidence I have that my mother existed.

I slide back onto the mattress. *What are the odds*, I think, *that I am here now sleeping in the same bed my mother slept in after she abandoned me?*

For the next hour, perhaps more, I can't sleep. I see and hear the memory shards over and over. Who is the short man with the mustache, and why did he call her Katrin? Who is their master? Where is home?

Just before I finally fall off, I realize something important. Something about my mother. *This is a woman*, I think, *who hates herself.*

17

Gregor's Journal

Elan ran away when she was twelve. It came without warning during midwinter. Sorcery lessons were a slog, but Elan was progressing. Her other studies advanced more quickly. She was whip smart, and her reading comprehension was superb. I even began teaching her Karator, a difficult guttural language unlike anything spoken in the Riege. Were she not a memory witch (and were it not the tail-end of the tenth Ebb), I would have pushed her to consider becoming a tutor. She had raw natural talent.

We had just returned a few weeks earlier from a two-day downhill trek to the crossroads for supplies. I noticed a change in her demeanor on our return. Less talkative. And keenly interested in learning the route. Before, she had always followed my lead. This time, she said almost nothing except to make sure she understood how to get from the crossroads to the Keep. Or, as I was to learn, from the Keep to the crossroads. And she began to practice a wider range of simple spells. Like building a campfire, or injecting warmth into a warded area. Spells she had previously been content to let me handle.

She retired to her room early after dinner one evening. I thought nothing of it. She was not unwell or, I thought, unhappy. The next morning, she did not appear for lessons. When I went to fetch her, she was gone. Out the window to her bedroom. She didn't need to tie sheets together or steal a rope, as you so often read in children's stories. She climbed down using her hands and feet. Unlike Alaric, she was a natural athlete. Even with grappling hooks, Alaric couldn't scale the Keep's walls. Elan could do it without material assistance by the time she was ten. Of course, she could have walked out the Keep's front door, but I suppose she didn't want to take the risk that I would see or hear her.

I waited until noon to panic. Elan was known to take long walks without prior notice, and her losing track of time had occurred more than once. I searched the Keep and the grounds. I knew she was not dead because my fluential abilities were undiminished. As I scolded her later, it would have helped if she had left a note, but she did not. I had nothing to go on. So I did what any tutor would do in such circumstances. I found the library, closed the door, and consulted my texts. What to do when your pupil runs away?

And it was my old friend Eusebius of the Second Ebb, of course, who had the answer. There are infinitesimal variations in the strength of a tutor's fluential abilities based on changes in physical distance from the pupil. Put in simpler terms, if Elan walks away from me, my powers will diminish ever so slightly. If I then follow her and close the distance, my powers will recover. Again, ever so slightly. Normally, the changes are so insignificant the tutor does not notice them.

Eusebius fabricated a spell that amplified the tutor's sensitivity to any change in his powers based on his distance from the student. In effect, I could follow Elan by walking in the direction that hurt me the least. It took more than one try to master this spell, which I attribute to my distress at Elan's departure, but finally I managed to harness my nerves and execute it.

I bundled myself for a long chase, and of course, a hard snow began falling that night. A once-in-a-generation blizzard was underway. Why, I asked myself, couldn't she run away in summer?

I also rather suspect Master Eusebius did not actually use his spell to chase down a wayward student. It was far more difficult in practice than his theory suggested. Elan may have been walking down a carthpath, but if I am two miles back in dense underbrush, it is not nearly so easy to walk a straight line. Or Elan may be moving down a hillside in switchback fashion. If I am on a narrow road, following her zigs and zags may present severe logistical issues. I am only glad not to have encountered onlookers. It must have seemed strange, this panicked old man, laden down with supplies and dressed for maximum warmth, changing direction every few steps based on how much or little he hurt.

And the howling nighttime blizzard, of course, made any travel problematic. Fortunately, it slowed Elan sufficiently that I was able to deduce her destination. After several hours, and thinking long and hard about our most recent journey, I became convinced, correctly as it turns out, that she was headed to the crossroads. Why, I did not know. So I terminated Master Eusebius' uncomfortable spell and headed directly there. Things became easier still when I discovered her tracks. At that point, I relaxed somewhat and began practicing the lecture I would deliver to her when I finally caught up.

Until she took a wrong turn. It was about a mile from the crossroads. I knew the way like the back of my hand. There is a sharp left turn onto the final path down. But of course, the return route requires a sharp right back to the Keep. Elan became confused and turned away from the crossroads. Following that path for more than a few hundred feet, she would encounter a steep ravine. In that terrible weather, she could find herself at the bottom, or dead, before she realized her mistake.

By this time, the snowfall was so thick, I could barely follow her tracks. And just as I'd feared, when I reached the edge of the ravine, I saw her tracks disappear down. My heart rose into my throat. Elan was my ward. I, her guardian. Was this how it ended? In the fierce backwoods of the Northern Reaches during the worst blizzard in a century?

I began yelling at the top of my lungs. I slid as far down into the ravine as I could without falling. I was steeling myself to drop to the bottom when I heard a small voice. I fought through treelimbs and underbrush, nearly losing my footing more than once, and there she was on a jagged rocky outcropping. She had managed to stop her fall before reaching the bottom, then she zig-zagged back toward the top – much like scaling the Keep, I would imagine – until she reached a rocky platform and collapsed from exhaustion. I was so happy to see her, I nearly overslid the rock. Which would have dropped me straight to the bottom of the ravine.

Elan, red-faced and freezing, was hysterical. She had tried repeatedly, and failed each time, to execute even the simplest spells for fire and warmth. Of course, as I had instructed her, those spells are surprisingly difficult under duress. So imagine my embarrassment when I, there with my pupil in challenging terrain under dire circumstances, also failed in my first two attempts at the same spells! Well, I finally collected my wits and set the strongest wards I have ever set anywhere, anytime, followed by a fire and real warmth.

Elan's story came out in a weepy torrent. I had to ask her to start over twice. As best I could decipher, during our recent trip to the crossroads, she had overheard the storekeeper talking to another patron. One of them had mentioned that a woman named Catherine would be coming by in two weeks. Elan's hopes and dreams and fears transformed that lone conversation into an unshakeable belief that her mother was returning to the Reaches. Looking for Elan, of course. Elan knew I would dismiss her conclusions as rubbish, so she determined to travel back to the crossroads to meet her mother. Alone.

I realized instantly that my approach to Catherine – refusing to share memories with Elan – had been a mistake. When a mother abandons a daughter, it tears a hole in the girl's soul. Ignoring it doesn't cauterize or heal the wound. If anything, it invites the girl to invent a fantasy world. One which, as I had now learned, could have dangerous repercussions.

As I reunited with Elan on that rocky outcrop in the ravine, we hugged for what seemed like the longest time. I vowed at that moment to hold onto her, to protect her, for as long as I could.

"Why did Mother leave me?" she asked there in the bitter snow.

"I don't know," I said, not loosening my grip.

"I drove her away," she wailed.

"You most certainly did not," I said. Our faces were inches apart. "I was there. I know. You were a wonderful child. Happy, charming, funny, lovable. And no bother at all. I don't know why Catherine left, but it wasn't because of you."

"If I'd been better, she'd have stayed," Elan said.

"No," I scolded. "Elan, sometimes grownups are not up to the responsibilities they undertake. And so they run away from them. As difficult as it may be for you to accept, it is not anyone's fault but their own."

"She's not coming back, is she?"

"No, dear child, she's not."

Elan buried her head in my chest, a signal, I think, that she finally understood. Not that she had necessarily made peace with it. Just that she had reached some form of closure.

We rested in our warded cocoon all night. The following morning, I led her to the crossroads. And, yes, a patron there was a woman named Catherine. She was my age and quite large. It took us five days – more than twice the normal traveling time – to return to the Keep.

I offered to share my memories of Catherine with Elan. Not all of them, but some. Those showing Catherine in her most favorable light. To my surprise, Elan declined. She said she knew what Catherine looked like. She had caught glimpses in certain memories I had shared before. She no longer, she said, needed more.

18

Elan

I sit upright in Dwumfour's bed even before I come awake. My forehead and armpits are damp. My heartbeat races. It's that dream again. One of the fifty nightshirt boys from Fiske's dream comes to me. We're there on that hillside at dawn. He wants to tell me something, but he can't get the words out. Can't even make a noise. The mist rises around us. Finally, his mouth opens, and bright red blood gushes out. Like it's coming from a hose. Then he takes off his nightshirt, sopping red, and hands it to me.

And I wake up.

"So, how was Master Jedders?" comes a sleepy voice from the floor.

"Who?"

"Master Jedders. Don't deny you visited him last night."

"Oh, all right," I say. "If you're going to scold me, get on with it."

He pauses. "That depends on what you found out."

"Hah!" I say. Being a memory witch does have its uses. I tell Stille what the memory shards showed me about my mother.

"You're sure he called her Katrin?" he asks.

"Yes."

"That's the Karator version of the name," he says flatly.

"I know," I say. "I speak the language."

"When did that happen?" Stille asks.

"In my spare time," I say lightly.

"Did anyone in the memory shard speak Karator?"

"No," I say, "although the man with the mustache had a Kimbarian accent that sounded a little too perfect."

"Like he didn't learn it as a child," Stille says.

"Exactly," I say.

"That changes everything if your mother was a Karator," he says. "It means she was a spy."

I sigh. It makes no sense that the Karators would want a spy in my father's villa. One who married Alaric and bore him two children. But I don't want to think about that now. I want to stay focused on the nineteen hooded soldiers in red uniforms.

I think back to Montauk and the small armory hidden in the walled courtyard. In the middle of the chall. Where no bystanders will chance upon it.

And now the Order is hunting me like their very existence depends upon killing me. Killing all sorcerers. Since when did the Order declare war on the Fluence, and why? It's like the Order wants all the born-and-bred families out of the way before they launch some kind of attack. Suddenly I know there is something I need to do.

Stille washes himself with water from a pitcher in front of the broken mirror. He has his shirt off. Red and black bruises snake across his back. I change my mind about him. He's not skinny. He's wiry. I can see the sinews in his upper arms and shoulders. He's stronger than he looks.

"So what's the plan?" I say.

"I'm working on it," he says, drying himself with a small thin hand towel.

"I have a suggestion," I say. I raise my hand and wave it. He sees it in the mirror and fights off a smile.

"Yes, Miss Witch," he says. "What do you have in mind?"

"Pier Four after dark. The way my mother escaped."

"That was ten years ago," he says. "And I don't have a lot of money. I wasn't counting on still being chased this far west, to be honest. I thought I'd be free and clear by now."

"Things don't change quickly in the flatlands," I say. "One year, ten years, fifty years, what's the difference? It's worth a shot anyway."

"And the money?"

"I've sewn some into my leathers. On the inside. The coins are old, but they should still be good. Some are gold."

His arms are splayed on the sink, and he whips his head around. "Gold? Seriously?"

I beam at him.

"Sold to the young lady in the white pullover!" he says cheerfully. "Pier Four it is. Belowdecks late tonight. Of course, that assumes we can get there without being caught and executed."

"I know the perfect hiding place until then," I say. "The chall."

"That's a terrible idea," he says. "The chall is the last place I want to be."

"It's the last place they'll look," I say.

"And . . ."

"And what?"

"What's your other reason for wanting to visit the chall?" he says, raising an eyebrow. "Your real reason."

I bite my lower lip. Stille already knows me too well!

"Tell me something?" I ask. "These new challs the Order has been building. They all look the same, right?"

"Yes," he says. "In theory, they are all modeled after the first chall they built a century ago. Somewhere near Elden."

"So if one chall has an interior courtyard, they all do."

"Sure, I guess so."

I tell Stille about the courtyard at the chall in Montauk and the armory I saw there. If every chall is built to the same blueprint, they all have that courtyard. One nobody gets to see except the brothers. And if one courtyard is being used as an armory, I wonder if they all are. That would explain why they want to kill me. And maybe establish a motive for killing Father and Willem.

"So what you're suggesting," Stille says, "is that all those challs they've been building are not for worship. They're preparing to overthrow the king."

"Precisely," I say.

Stille cocks his head, considering the matter. "You may be onto something. But how do you plan to access the courtyard in Darine? You can't just waltz through the chall's front door."

"I'm going to scale the back wall and sneak over the rooftop."

Stille's jaw drops.

"I've already done it once," I say. "Back in Montauk. The challs use the same materials as our Keep. Which I've climbed my whole life. Gregor says I could be an acrobat in my next life."

Stille takes a deep breath. "Fine," he says at last. "You're sure about this?"

"Easy as one-two-three," I say, chopping three times with my right hand. "There's only one thing I need."

"And that would be . . ."

"Directions to the chall."

Stille laughs at me. "I'm going to conquer the capital city of Kimbar in the space of one hour," he says in a playful mocking high-pitched voice. "If only I knew where it was."

I squeal and tag Stille on the shoulder for being mean. I kind of want him to tag me back, but instead he returns a level gaze. "I can get you there, Miss Witch," he says. "I've helped Dwumfour cart books to and from the chall. We always use alleyways and back streets. If you're truly certain you want to."

"I'm sure," I say. "This is something I need to know."

We say good-bye to Dwumfour, who is just coming awake in the stacks, then Stille leads me onto the roof of the master scribe's library. Stille reaches for my hand, and I let him take it. He guides me to the edge, and we both kneel. The air has that early morning bite. The rooftop offers a splendid view of Darine's large public park, known as Monument Square. A cobblestone walk cuts through it, and rows of tall trees, now barren as winter approaches, line the perimeter. The day is overcast and breezy. A team of black-clad brothers is already busy pounding boards into some kind of platform.

"A cold day for a hanging," Stille whispers.

"Who are they planning on hanging?" I ask.

"Us, I presume," he says, and I shiver.

"That fat man with a large white bandage in the middle of his face is Praelat Ortun," Stille says.

"We've met," I say.

"And the short disagreeable-looking man next to him is Master Depsik."

"Master Depsik? Are you sure?"

"Pretty sure," he says. "My eye stings just

looking at him."

I reach out and rub his shoulder in sympathy, but his eyes stay locked fiercely on the square.

"There's only one reason they brought Master Depsik all the way here from Montauk. And it can't be his cheery disposition. They want to execute us on the spot. If they catch us, I mean. But only one of us is a witch. So they need a crime we both committed. That's why Master Depsik is here. To testify."

"And our crime?"

"You said it yourself, Elan. We're horse thieves. In the flatlands, the punishment is severe."

"Death," I say.

"Yes, they'll hang us right there," he says softly. "As soon as they can find a judge to bang the gavel."

Stille turns to me. "Do you still want to visit the chall?"

"More than ever," I say grimly. For a moment, I wonder what Darine's public square would look like turned upside-down. But then I banish the thought. That spell is a last resort, and we aren't that desperate yet. And I could kill someone if I'm not careful. I think of Bishop Fiske's feet, one shoe on and one off, swaying in the air. For a memory witch, unintended consequences are always a risk.

After Stille collects money for our wagon from the stableboy, we find the alley behind the library. It smells of urine and sawdust and stale beer. And fish. The remains of dead fish are everywhere, and rattails appear and disappear as we move stealthily along. I hold my nose, and Stille takes my hand again. I like it when he does that. "Welcome to Darine," he says. "By the time we reach the chall, you'll be used to the smell."

Finally, we slide sideways between two buildings and poke our heads into the street. Across and down is the chall. Two brothers, their robes bulging with weapons, stand guard. The chall is enormous. Twice the size, and twice as tall, as the one in Montauk.

"You said you could climb, right?" Stille asks.

"That's what I said," I say, staring in disbelief at the massive structure.

A wall is a wall, I tell myself. *If I can climb it – and I can – it doesn't matter how far up it goes.*

"Okay," he says. "Here's what we'll do. I'll distract the guards, and you slip into the alleyway on the far side of the chall. I'll wait and watch for you to come out. If for some reason we get separated, let's meet at the pier. Take a fabric and crystal with you, but leave your leathers here. I'll come back for them once you're in."

I nod and take a deep breath. It's a sound plan, and I already have cloth and crystal in my pants pocket.

"Good luck, Elan," he whispers into my ear.

Impetuously, I grab his head with both hands and kiss him once on the forehead. *I don't know if I'm ever going to see him again*, I think. *Yes, I do. No, I don't.* Without looking back, I slip onto the street. Up ahead are two old women, bent over, shuffling forward on unresponsive feet. I fall in behind them, then gesticulate with my hands as if I'm talking to them. People watching me will think I'm with the old women.

I hear Stille behind me and peek back. He's staggering toward the guards, a bottle in his hand, pretending to be drunk. I hear him tell the brothers in a loud slurred voice that he's had a vision from god telling him to join the Order. As soon as he finishes the bottle, he wants to take off his shoes and wear one of those awful dirty smelly black robes. The guards wave him away, and then he breaks the bottle between them. To get their attention, he says. The guards converge on Stille, and he resists, and I know it's my time to slide across the street and into the alleyway. Stille's belligerent protests become faint as I scurry to the rear of the chall.

The surface is perfect for scaling. The structure is new, the mortar fresh, the stones strong. But the chall is so high. Higher than anything I've ever climbed. The key, I know, is to flatten my body against the wall. Become one with it. And going up is easier than coming down. The way to the top is stone by stone. Rhythmically, hand by foot by hand by foot. Fast, then faster. I take a deep breath, then launch myself. Minutes later, when I haul myself over the gutter, I fall on my back and catch my breath. The rooftop is wet with dew.

Crouching, I scamper across the slippery shingles until I spy an opening where the courtyard should be. I hear voices, so I fall to my stomach and crawl like a lizard to the lip of the overhang.

Ever so slowly, so quietly, one eye closed, I peer down.

The courtyard is twice the size of Montauk's, and it is filled to overflowing with weaponry of all kinds. Below me two brothers kneel before a tall slender man with a face older than Gregor's. He wears a white robe with a black belt and purple velvet slippers and gloves. His hair is a grating gray stubble. I have a feeling I've seen this face before – in a memory, I'm sure of it – but I can't place it. One brother addresses the man as Your Grace, and the other calls him Brother Mordecai. The man's voice and diction radiate supreme power and control.

I lean to hear. They are discussing a weapons shipment due the following week. Brother Mordecai begins inspecting the armory. He stops and cocks his head in front of the crossbows and one-man catapults. It is hard to hear what he is saying. And then he raises his voice.

"Well, well, well," he says to the brothers. "Here is something one does not find every day of the week. Nor every week of the month. No indeed."

The brothers, still kneeling, raise their faces to him expectantly.

Then Brother Mordecai turns, cranes his head, and looks me squarely in the eye. "A witch," he snarls. "Here in our temple."

19

Elan

I remember Gregor's simple instructions for responding to a threat – Run! So I run. Across the rooftop. As fast as I can go. Behind me, I hear Brother Mordecai in the courtyard roaring instructions to the brothers. The chall has many outer walls, he says, and the witch has to climb down one of them.

Then my feet slip out from under me on the dew-laden shingles, and I fly forward onto my face. Gamely, I rise to my haunches and reach for my nose. I don't think it's broken, but there is blood on my fingers. I try blinking away the dizziness, and after a few seconds, I regain my nerves. But I have lost the advantage – my head start! – on the brothers. And climbing down a wall is always slower and riskier than climbing up. They will be waiting for me no matter which wall I choose. Unless . . . unless . . .

I sneak back over the rooftop to the courtyard, and, as I suspected, it is empty, the door ajar. In their haste to cut off my escape route, Brother Mordecai and his two helpers created a new one. I shinny down the gutter, then jump onto the gravel pathway. I dash through the opening into a murky interior hallway. Shouting and footsteps lead outside. I duck into the nearest chamber, looking for a robe. Nothing. Then the next room. Nothing. Then another, and there's a large shapeless black rag on a hook. I snatch the robe and drop it over my head. *Walk*, I think, *like you have given your life to god. Like you belong here.* The robe's body odor gags me, so I breathe through my mouth, lean forward, and fold my hands in prayer as I shuffle slowly to the main entryway.

I consider bluffing my way out of the chall. Maybe the guards won't inquire who's wearing the robe. Or I could just race onto the avenue and hope to outrun them into the alleyways and backstreets. As a last resort, perhaps I could hide in the chall until later in the day and then slip out when no one is looking. I could set wards so no one would see me. It would work on dearths, but on Brother Mordecai? He felt my presence with his mind in the courtyard, so I'm not so sure.

Fearfully, I enter the main sanctuary. To my surprise, the front gates are wide open. The unconscious guards, their hands tied behind their backs, slump against the thick oaken columns supporting the chall's main façade. Could Stille have done this?

"This sweet visage is a glory unto mine eyes," a man's voice says from the pews.

Startled, I wheel to face the voice, my hands fingering the cloth and crystal in my pocket. For some reason, I did not see him sitting there in the pews. I shake off my hood. The man stands and places a hand over his heart. He is tall and wears a plain black suit with a red corsage pinned to his lapel and sports an ornate waxed white mustache. His hair, also white, is neatly combed.

"As fair Amelia slays the unjust forever with her sighs," he continues.

"Who are you?" I say.

He bows low, his right hand sweeping to his side. "I am Allamonde de Brigandi Sorti della Borda," he says. "But you, my lady, may call me Allamonde."

"What were those words?"

"Lines to a poem about the last memory witch in recorded history. Until yourself, that is."

"How do you know about me?"

"I was so informed yesterday. The skies are filled with pigeons. Such beautiful little creatures. I, of course, was dubious. We, the Patrons of Paul, have waited patiently for a thousand years. So many generations of patrons have been disappointed. I did not expect that my lifetime would witness such joy."

I've never heard of any patrons, and now I'm nervous. Here is a strange crazy awe-struck man reciting poetry to me, and I should be anywhere but lingering in the chall.

"But of course," he says apologetically. "I am remiss in not showing you my credentials straightaway. Please forgive. I am, to say the least, out of practice."

As he fishes in his pocket, I grip my crystal more tightly. I begin reciting the upside-down spell. It will give me time to escape.

But then Allamonde produces a lustrous red crystal. "Every one of us," he says, "every Patron of Paul, has such a crystal as a proof of devotion."

"Is that real?" I ask. I think of the rubystone Catherine gifted me. I knew when I saw it that the gem was authentic. I feel for it in my pocket. Safe in Gregor's handkerchief.

"Alas, no," he says. "I am a mere shoemaker and cannot afford a true rubystone. This is costume jewelry. But Amelia Martón wielded her power, and ultimately met her tragic end, with such a crystal. It is our calling card."

I walk up to him, and his stance stiffens. Like he's a soldier standing at attention. "Please sit down," I say, and we both sit in the pew.

"I need to leave here," I say quietly.

"I know a hidden exit," he whispers.

I recall that night in the stable near the inn at Montauk. I vowed never to trust a man again. But I trusted Stille and then Weathersby and Dwumfour. And there is something about Allamonde that appeals to me. Like Gregor, he seems to believe in me. I need help, and I cannot wait much longer to decide.

"You said you are with the Patrons of Paul," I say. "Who is Paul?"

"Paul Guiscard," he replies. "He was Amelia Martön's helpmate, her crystal, how do you call it – her *Anaiah*. It was his murder that led Amelia down the path to her ultimate destruction. After her death, our society was formed to pave the way for the next Amelia. To help her harness and perfect her powers for the good of all. We could not openly declare ourselves for Amelia, so we formed a society in honor of her crystal. A boy who nobly and freely sacrificed all he had."

"How many of you are there?"

He sighs. "Once upon a time, my lady, we were thousands! Tens of thousands! Now, we are perhaps a hundred throughout the Riege. Perhaps less. But know this! We are few but fierce. And loyal. We have pledged our lives to your service, and we will do our duty when and as called upon."

We regard each other there in the musty pew of Darine's chall. Footsteps coming nearer ring out in the hallways. The brothers have figured out I am no longer outside. And this awful smelly robe is suffocating me. I decide to trust this strange endearing man.

"Allamonde, please get me out of here," I say.

"With pleasure, my lady," he says. Taking my hand, he pulls me behind a high mahogany lectern. He knocks twice against the wood, and a shoulder-high panel pops. He pries it open with both hands, and we duck down an unlit stairs. He closes the panel tightly behind us. It is pitch-dark on the winding steps.

"Please be still, my lady, until I can find a candle," he says softly.

"No need, Allamonde," I say, and I speak in my mind the spell for light. The one Gregor taught me. Suddenly our tight space is illuminated, and his eyebrows shoot up.

"I can do more than read memories," I say archly, and smiling, he bows again.

The stairway leads to a narrow corridor with wide ancient boards for walls and dripping water the only sound. It smells like the river. Like scales. I bend low and wriggle out of my robe. Inhaling brine is better than a moment longer in an unwashed brother's clothing.

"The brothers built this as an escape?" I ask.

"No, to bring in prostitutes," he responds.

"So, piety and poverty?" I ask.

"Alas," he says balefully.

"Where does it lead?"

"I shall show you. We can emerge undetected. I live not far from here. It is safest to take you there. Until we can decide next steps."

"I need to find Stille," I say fiercely. I am not going anywhere alone. Not anymore.

"He is safe, my lady," Allamonde says, patting my arm. "Spry and lithe, your *Anaiah* is. He escaped the brothers in splendid fashion. We will endeavor to look after him. I am sure you two will meet again."

"We agreed to meet at Pier Four," I say. "The underdecks. We are traveling south."

"The same route, I am told, as your mother," he says. That stops me in my tracks. How does he know about my mother? I just found out last night from Master Jedders.

"No, I mean, that wasn't my plan," I say. "But I hooked up with Stille . . ."

He raises one eyebrow, and I realize my choice of words is unfortunate.

"What I mean to say is, I joined with Stille . . ."

His other eyebrow raises, and I sigh.

"Stille and I met in Montauk and ran away together," I finally manage to say. That isn't much better, but Allamonde smiles and nods.

"I understand," he says. "It was the same with Amelia. I am an old man, a grandfather, if you can believe it, so permit me a small liberty to speak candidly. Your connection with this young man is uniquely intense. It is nearly impossible for you not to fall in love with him. And he with you. So it was with Amelia. With all memory witches. But do not rush the process. Let nature take its course, as it will. Trust the Fluence. It has created all of this for a reason. And if he is taken, if your boy suffers the fate of Paul Guiscard, you must remain balanced. You must not succumb to rage. Please always remember that."

Instinctively, I reach up and hug Allamonde around his neck. At last, an ally. "Let's get out of here," I say.

"As you command, my lady," he says gallantly.

He takes me to his home, where I meet his wife, Elisabeth, and their three daughters. They say little, but their eyes are wide, and their hands cover their mouths. I don't think this is the day they expected to meet the first memory witch since Amelia. Allamonde has three sons, but they are deployed in Darine. Helping Stille escape and gathering intelligence.

In the meantime, I enjoy my first home-cooked meal since I left the Keep, and then a bath. In a real bathtub. With actual hot water. And an unused bar of soap. I emerge clean as a whistle and red-haired for the first time since Montauk. Elisabeth has even washed and dried my clothes while I bathed. But my rapture is short-lived.

"I sadly must inform you," Allamonde says somberly, "that several unfortunate tragedies have occurred in Darine this day."

"Stille!" I say.

"Not him, thank the Fluence," Allamonde says. "But others have suffered a grievous fate. The Order was displeased you both slipped through their fingers today. They exacted punishment on those they could find. I urge you to remain in hiding until it is time to take you to the river."

I tremble uncontrollably. If people have died because of me, or for me, or in defense of me, I need to see it myself. I kiss the mark of Saint Dezzie on my wrist and tell myself I am done witnessing the world solely through the eyes of others. Through memories. "No," I say, "I need to see."

"Are you certain?" he asks.

"I am."

Allamonde and his sons, now returned from

their errands, carefully lead me through buildings and basements and back staircases and secret doors and unmarked corridors. I see the Darine that even Darinians rarely experience. I am bundled in a warm cloak and hood, and I feel like royalty. Yesterday I didn't even know these people, and today they are placing their lives and the lives of their loved ones on the line. For me. A girl they only just met and may never see again.

Finally, we enter a portico with an angled corner view of Monument Square. It is early evening, but there is enough light. I catch my breath. *Oh no, no, no,* I think. The gallows are massive, and six nude bodies twist and sway. Their heads are uncovered. On the left are four bodies. Adam Vorstadt and his sons. And Molley! They killed her, too.

And two more on the right. I recognize Weathersby. We stayed there one night. I never exchanged a word with him. And then I fall to my knees when I see the sixth body. Dwumfour. Just a boy. Doing a favor for Stille. Something one person does for a friend without a second thought. And like Mother, I slept in his bed.

And there is Brother Mordecai in his fancy white robe. A look of intense piety on his face. The brothers poke the bodies with long poles. Just to keep them moving in the dead autumn air. The first brother struts and preens and scans the buildings around the square with an intense gaze. He is looking for something.

Suddenly the rage boils up in me, and I clench

my fists. I want to kill the brothers. Kill Brother Mordecai. Kill the Order. If Stille were here, I could eliminate Monument Square with an upside-down spell.

"My lady," Allamonde breaks in, "the Order has done this for one purpose and one purpose only."

"To punish innocent people," I say.

"No," he says gently. "To enrage you. To provoke you into a reaction. A mistake. It worked oh so long ago with the fair Amelia. Pray let it not work with you. Some of these six were good people. Some were not. None deserved to die. Not today, anyway. Not for their contact with you. There will be a day and time to repay this debt. But today is not that day. You must learn from this and become stronger."

Allamonde is correct, and I unclench my fists. I shall avenge them, but I have another mission to fulfill first. Father and Willem. I must not lose sight of my primary mission. The one I trained on for over ten years.

"What will they do with the bodies?" I ask.

"Take them down at dusk," Allamonde says. "About an hour from now. And then dump them in the river. At least, that's my hope!"

"Your hope?"

"Yes, that's how we'll transport you to Pier Four. In the horse-drawn cart with the bodies."

"You can't be serious!"

"Deadly serious, my lady," Allamonde says, his face intensely sincere. "Security will be impossibly tight getting to the river. Riding with the dead is the only way."

"And Stille?"

"He'll be with you, my lady. Everything is arranged. Just remember to breathe through your mouth. We can't have a corpse coughing or retching, now can we?"

As night falls, Allamonde and his sons squeeze me into as narrow an alleyway as exists in Darine. My instructions are simple. Wait for the mortuary cart to stop, then slip into the back, throw a blanket over my body, and act dead.

"Will I see you again?" I ask Allamonde.

He shakes his head. "Hard to say. We must assume my service to you ends this day."

"They will come for you as well."

"We have covered our tracks. The others were unprepared."

"Can you stay with me until I board the wagon?"

"I am afraid not, my lady. It would attract attention. But you are tiny. No one will see you there. You must do this alone."

"Then I guess this is goodbye," I say.

"Yes," he says, touching two fingers to his lips. "Goodbye, sweet visage."

And then Allamonde is gone. I crouch in the heavy gloom of Darine so a death wagon can set me free. It approaches slowly. The horses are old, and it is late. As the cart pulls alongside, the clouds open, and the rain pelts the wagon. The noise startles me. For a moment I think the cart will drive by, but then it stops. I lurch to the doors, fling them open, jump in, and pull them shut.

Inside are more than six bodies. Perhaps as many as twenty, but I don't count. Tossed into a careless heap. I jump to one side and burrow in, pulling a blanket roughly over my head. I shudder as I turn to see Dwumfour's dead eyes, still open, next to me.

I'm so sorry, I think.

I don't know if I can go through with Allamonde's plan. The stench covers me, and I breathe hard through my mouth. I need to jump out. To escape. To scream. To run and run. Just like Gregor taught me. The rain on the roof of the cart sounds like cannons going off. I must leave now or explode!

And then a strong sure hand slides itself into mine and squeezes. Stille! He is there somewhere amidst the dried blood and terrible odors and rotting flesh. I squeeze back, and then, as instructed, I pretend to be dead.

I'm never letting him go, I think.

20

Gregor's Journal

If Karators did not exist, I suppose they would have had to be invented. How else to persuade Riegian boys and girls to eat their vegetables, do their chores, or go to sleep at night? Thanks to my older brother, with whom I shared a room, I believed until the age of ten that a red-skinned Karator warrior lurking under my bed would jab his sword through the mattress and into my soft squeamish body if I made the slightest noise at night.

Karator has been a warlike nation since before time. All that saved the Riege was the wild Kangor river dividing the continent in two. Karator in the west, the Riege in the east. When the Karators finally developed sufficient capability to cross the river in force, the Fluence came to the rescue. Opinions are divided whether the Fluence always existed and chose that precipitous moment to reveal itself or whether the advent of the first Flow in advance of those vicious Karator attacks was mere happy coincidence. Either way, sorcerers provided the edge that, time and again, enabled the Riege to foil Karator landings or throw the dreadful creatures back across the channel.

Despite our victories, casualties were enormous and the property damage crippling. The Riege could not have withstood more invasions, and so it was during the Second Ebb that Marcus d'Uberville, perhaps the greatest Riegian sorcerer, rendered the Kangor virtually impossible to cross. Renamed the Impassable River, at least from our side, that channel has prevented fatal Karator incursions ever since.

Which is not to say that the Karators have relinquished their hopes of conquering the Riege. Or, as they view it, reuniting the continent under Karator leadership, as once occurred in the distant mists of time. While Karator's massive southern reefs withhold from it nearly all ocean trade, limited if indirect commercial intercourse between Karator and the Riege has occurred. Over the centuries, the Karator nation, like the Riege, has bled slowly south. As a result, it is not unusual, I am told, to see the occasional Karator walking the streets of Elden, our largest seaport, or even the tranquil vistas of Kimbar.

Rumor has it that thousands of Karators, perhaps even tens of thousands, have waded ashore into the Riege in recent decades. Presumably they arrive in the Riege via "down there," much the same way Catherine did. Oddly, I have yet to see a single Karator in all my years in the Riege. Not in Kimbar. Not in Elden. And certainly not in the flatlands. Whichever geography these alleged Karator refugees may favor, it apparently is not one in which any god-fearing Riegians deign to live.

According to an old acquaintance of mine who visited the villa when Alaric and Catherine were newly married, Karators had arrived on commercial ships from "beneath the ocean" and, given their peculiar talents, congregated in filthy dense ghettoes near the docks in river towns, even as far north as Darine. Catherine dismissed this speculation with a roll of her pretty eyes. And my friend freely conceded, upon her close questioning, that he had traveled the Tablas many times without seeing a single Karator.

My exposure to the typical Karator physique came in the form of illustrations in various history books, which offer detailed if unflattering portraits. Compared to Riegians, Karators are short and squat with enormous physical strength and, their most obvious telltale signs, red-tinted skin and fierce black hair. Of course, Karators come in all shapes and sizes, as do Riegians. Men dominate Karator society to a greater extent than in the Riege, and women are rarely seen in public. The fierce demeanor of the Karator warriors – stony-faced and lacking normal human cognition – has birthed speculation that Karators are less intelligent than Riegians. Whatever the truth of these musings, the ruling Karator elites, from all reports, are an intellectual match for anything Elden or Kimbar might offer.

It is difficult to verify sightings of Riegians inside Karator, but from time to time, world travelers have reported seeing tall, fair-skinned people there. During the invasions, the Karators took hostages as they retreated, or were pushed back, across the Kangor. On one occasion, they demanded significant tribute in exchange for returning their Riegian prisoners, but this proposal was dismissed as a ruse. Karator is always short of hard currency given their paucity of true international trade. It has always been assumed that what Riegian prisoners they did take were either killed quickly or assimilated into Karator stock. One shudders for the women, of course, but such are the tides of war.

As a land, Karator is hot and harsh. Fertile regions are scarce, and the majority of Karators huddle in their three largest cities. I use the term "largest" cautiously, as, according to reports, three cities are all they have. Two facing the Kangor, and a third on the southeast tip of their landmass. Karator is a theocracy ruled by a man known only as Our Master. They pretend the same individual has been Our Master for centuries, but no sensible person believes this. More likely, there is an ongoing bitter struggle for the throne, with many Karator deaths and casualties, and they paper over the carnage with the fiction of a single enduring human presence as Our Master. As to their religious rites and beliefs, little is known.

When Elan was twelve, I decided learning a new language would be good for her. Her sorcery lessons were progressing apace, yet she had too much idle time. There were, of course, various Riegian dialects to choose from, but none impressed me as repaying close study. The Karator language, on the other hand, is known for its difficulty. Like a dog cutting its teeth on a bone, I thought letting Elan chew on such a language would sharpen her mind. And they say, correctly I believe, that speaking a language helps you understand the people. The mindset.

Over the years, I keep coming back to that note I discovered at the villa addressed to Katrin. In the back of my mind, I wondered if, sooner or later, Elan would find knowing this rough language a useful skill. And, of course, I had selfish reasons. As I was Elan's tutor, the Fluence installed in my head the entire language from the first day. A tutor's fluential capabilities are a wondrous thing. One day I speak Riegian and its many dialects, and the next I am fluent, no pun intended, in Karator. Simply because I am teaching it to my pupil.

I have learned less about the Karator character than I thought I might, with the exception that the guttural quality of the language elevates tone of voice as a control mechanism. If you speak with a certain inflection and diction and can do so without raising your voice, you can assume a commanding presence. However, given the remote likelihood that I will ever have a need to speak Karator, the value of this observation is slight indeed.

21

Elan

I am a wreck. I told myself I wouldn't cry, but that's all I seem to do. I keep wiping my face. Stille hands me a dry towel from time to time. You'd think I'd empty out at some point. I guess I'm too well hydrated. The tears keep coming and coming.

We are on a candy red sliprider called THE COURTESAN. Sleek and long and low in the water, it glides south in the powerful currents of the Tablas. There are three passenger cabins. Each with passengers. I can hear them through our open window. Stille and I paid cash for the fourth cabin. Smaller than the others. This is where the Riegian captain sleeps, and for two gold coins he is willing to live in the wheelhouse until we reach Elden.

Belowdecks are four red-skinned Karators dressed in rough burlap shirts and pants with ropes for belts. They handle the maintenance and rigging. And they'll row if the ship gets stuck. The Karators do not show their faces, and the other passengers do not even know they are there. But when Stille signaled the sliprider last night by flashing a gold coin in the dim moonlight, it was the Karators, not the Riegian captain, who pulled the ship over and negotiated our passage.

And I stood there beneath Pier Four like an icicle. Not moving. Afraid to move. They pulled me from the mortuary cart like I was one of the stiffs. I didn't say a word. The stench of the cart had seeped into my clothes. Into my soul. Stille held my hand, stroking it with his thumb. But it was all I could do to blink. To breathe. To pretend to be alive.

Six people had died because of me. Seven, if you counted Bishop Fiske. And what about Allamonde and his family? If their contact with me were discovered, I'd have eight more deaths on my conscience. Like Amelia, I was leaving a trail of death behind me. Every heartbeat, every breath, was an effort.

And then my haunted reverie was broken when one Karator sailor whispered to the other in their own tongue. "We should consider whether these passengers are safe," he said. "At all costs we must avoid reprisals from the locals."

I arched my back. "What you will do with these passengers," I whispered fiercely in Karator, "is precisely what you have agreed to do. Deliver us to Elden. My master – Our Master! – expects no less." As Gregor taught me, I spat out the words but did not raise my voice.

The Karator sailors stared at me like they'd seen a ghost. I may have been the first Riegian they'd met who spoke their language.

"Did you hear what I said?" I demanded in my best guttural rasp.

Instinctively, they bowed their heads, one of them several times, and responded in submissive murmurs. *We were just talking. We meant no harm.*

I sniffed and turned my gaze away from them. *Now, somebody, get me on board,* I thought, *before I keel over.*

As they brought a dinghy roundabout so we could board the sliprider, I peered back at Darine's docks in amazement. It wasn't just Pier Four. It was all the piers. Underneath them was an interconnected series of smaller piers stretching nearly a mile, none visible from Darine itself and all manned in the candlelight by Karator dock workers. Behind and under the piers was a Karator community built into the Tablas riverbank. An underground city! I caught glimpses of Karator children and even, I think, the women, a candle's flame catching and releasing their large darting eyes through open windows. I sniffed and thought I smelled unfamiliar but intriguing flavors of food. But then, anything would smell good compared to a mortuary wagon.

I did not sleep, but today is a new day. On the sliprider, two Karators bring us fresh sheets and a pitcher of water. They bow so low their heads touch the decking. My eyes meet theirs for an instant, then I raise my chin slightly, dismissing them. They do not know how to treat a Riegian who speaks Karator, so they treat us well.

"You must have had a lot of spare time at the Keep," Stille says, trying to start a conversation for the umpteenth time. He lies on the bed while I crouch and stare out the porthole. "Karator is a hard language to learn."

"Yes, I had time," I say. "And a good teacher."

Stille is suffering almost as much as me. Dwumfour was his friend. And Weathersby. He blames himself for their deaths. He shouldn't. How could he have known when he met that witch with the bad haircut back in Montauk that anything she touched – anything *we* touched together – would end up dead.

"What did you say to the Karator sailors?" he asks.

"They were debating whether the price was worth the risk," I say.

"And you said what?"

"I convinced them to honor their end of the deal."

"Well, I'm glad you told them we were headed to Elden."

"Why?"

"Because we're not going there," he says. "At least, not on this boat."

"But we paid for Elden," I complain.

"The docks have ears, Elan," he says. "The Order will learn that we bought passage on a sliprider to Elden and paid with gold coins. They'll be waiting for us there. If they get impatient, they may even try tracking this ship on the river."

"So where are we going?"

"To Agnes."

"Is that a port?"

"A woman."

I turn and stare at him. His eyes lock with mine.

"Allamonde's oldest son, Stefano, told me about her," Stille says. "She's a retired patron who lives in a river town called Durande. It's about two days downstream. They have one dock. Agnes has a memory you'll be interested in."

"I'm listening."

"Some years ago, twenty riders on twenty horses were killed near an abandoned chall, and then everything was burned. She didn't see it happen, but she saw the aftermath. And then one day, it was all gone. The charred remains, I mean. Transported somewhere else."

"She'll let me read her?"

"She's a patron, so, I mean, yes."

There weren't twenty riders that awful day. There were nineteen. I saw them over and over in Gregor's memory. But this is the first decent lead we've had on Father and Willem's murders. It's progress.

"How will we get our sliprider to pull over?"

"This," he says, producing a gold coin.

"And where, may I ask, did you get that?"

"Where I got the others," he said. "Your coat."

I almost laugh, but then I remember I'm in a bad mood, so I pretend to frown at him. I'm not yet ready to feel better. Unless he wants to wash my hair again.

~~~

The Tablas river currents are two to three times stronger than the fastest carriage. For two days, I peer out our porthole at the western shoreline racing past. The trees, stark and barren, are enormous. In the spring and summer, they must be beautiful. That side of the Tablas is the Finger region. It's fifty miles to the Impassable River. Centuries ago, this is where the Karators invaded. Most of the local Riegians were killed, and those who survived left. After the invasions stopped, the enormous defenses erected along the Kangor were abandoned. By now, nature has reclaimed most of what it lost. All these centuries later, the Finger region is still underpopulated. Bad memories die hard in people who work the land.

Gradually I emerge from my shell. That night at Weathersby's, I gave Stille the outline of my life. On these two days, I fill in details. I start haltingly. Slowly. But like THE COURTESAN, I quickly pick up speed. Collapsing sixteen years into two days is not as difficult as it might seem. Especially for a girl who's never had an audience before. And Stille is perfect. He listens to every word. Asks the right questions. Makes appropriate comments. And embraces the silence when the deaths I've caused overwhelm my ability to speak.

"You are not responsible for the evil other people do," he whispers, his arm around my shoulders.

"A memory witch," I say bitterly, wiping my tears, "is responsible for everything she causes."

Several times I begin to tell Stille about the rubystone. I can feel it there in my pocket, seemingly inert like a lump of coal. But something always happens. A distraction. An interruption. Our sliprider bumping on the river. And then the moment passes, and I tell him nothing. I know we promised each other there would be no secrets. We would tell each other everything.

I'll tell him about the rubystone, I think. *But later, now not. I need to find the perfect time to do it.*

Late the second day, THE COURTESAN slows and then begins veering toward the eastern bank. Stille talks in low tones to the Karator sailors. I can't make out what they are saying. The transaction happens in seconds. A nod and the flash of a gold coin changing hands. Then Stille and I are ushered out the rear to a dingy pier, rocking hard with every wave. A Karator sailor stares at me as the ship heads back into the current. I glare back, and at last he averts his gaze.

I wonder if my powers work on Karators? I think. *Or can I only read Riegians?*

Stille clears his throat loudly, and I realize a tiny woman is now standing on the pier. Her white hair is shorter than Weathersby's, and she smokes a well-bitten pipe from the left side of her mouth. It has an odd smell, something other than tobacco. The woman wears an ill-fitting black suit with a red corsage pinned to the lapel.

"Elan," Stille says. "This is Agnes Antoine."

"Hello," I say.

Agnes snorts. "I thought you would be *taller*," she says, then chuckles. Wisps of smoke burst from the pipe.

"Oh, I nearly forgot," Agnes says. "My credentials." She reaches into her suitcoat and withdraws a red crystal, smaller than Allamonde's.

"Thank you," I say. "The Patrons of Paul have been good to me. Allamonde saved me at the chall in Darine."

"When Allamonde's not trying to repopulate the flatlands with more children," she says loudly, "he's quite capable. I don't receive many pigeons, so the one two days ago was a surprise. Like Allamonde, I expected never to be in this position. But better late than never. I took a solemn oath, and today I shall keep it."

Agnes walks briskly off the dock. Stille and I rush to catch her.

Durande sports a single dirt road and five or six low dwellings. Huts more than houses. Smoke trickles from chimneys, a sure sign people live here. Chickens wander between buildings, and Agnes has a goat tied to a bent oak tree. We drop our bags on her porch.

"We aren't a *one-horse* town," Agnes says. "But

unfortunately, we are a *two-horse* town, and I don't share. So you two will have to ride together."

"I don't know how," I say.

"I do," Stille says. "Uncle Martin taught me in Kimbar. You can sit behind me."

Agnes walks out a white Etruscan with a shaggy brown mane. Stille climbs onto it without any effort at all. Like he's showing off. I stand on a stump and try to swing my legs over, but I can't get enough leverage to climb up.

"Try it again," Agnes directs.

I grit my teeth and swing up again. This time Agnes puts her hand on my bottom and shoves hard. It's enough for me to pull over, and I grab Stille for balance. I worry I've knocked us both to the ground, but Stille recovers, and then I nestle in. My thighs behind his. I tell myself not to blush, but I do anyway.

We're just riding a horse, I think. *And this is how you do it.*

Agnes mounts a brown-and-beige-spotted Etruscan. She holds the reins negligently with her left hand, her pipe with her right. She rides like she's done it her whole life. Which she probably has. She glances over and grins at me with to-bacco-stained teeth. "Comfortable?" she asks.

I force a smile. "Almost," I say, but then Stille moves the horse forward and I start bouncing. I can't figure out where to hold him. Is his chest too high? His stomach? Do I grab his hips? Any lower would be chancy and possibly inappropriate. And where do I put my head? Do I hold it erect or nestle it into his back?

"You're squirming," Stille complains, turning his head.

"I can't figure out where to put my head," I confess.

"Anywhere is fine," he says.

So I jam my chin into the middle of his back, and he arches like he's been shot with an arrow.

"How's that?" I say in a challenging voice.

"If that's where you're most comfortable, I'll make do," Stille says, then he flips the reins, and the horse trots forward. I decide to rest my hands on his hips and my cheek on his shirt. Slowly the tension drains away. Everything that built up begins to fade. Darine seems like a million miles away. The horse knows the route, and it's a pleasant ride. Agnes tosses a few glances back, chuckling each time.

Once away from the river, the land quickly becomes forested and hilly. Paths are well-marked, but the underbrush on either side is dense. We arrive at a clearing and a decrepit one-story building. The roof has largely dropped in, and one wall has tumbled outward. Grass and flowering weeds decorate the inside. Agnes dismounts and beckons.

"It's back behind here," she says, tromping through the grass.

I drop off the Etruscan to the ground, and the sudden aches in my thighs and bottom and lower back make me stop to stretch. I focus on breathing, and each step hurts.

Agnes points to a large rectangular patch where

nothing grows. A few coarse weeds perhaps, but little else. The ground is tarry black and covered with pebbles and twigs.

"Here's where I found it," she says, her face a mask of dismay. "We'd heard rumors that something terrible had occurred by the old chall. Which surprised us since this chall had been abandoned for decades. It wasn't even habitable. Word came down to stay away, but I'm a contrarian by nature. Tell me not to look, and I want to look. Tell me to stay away, and I'm saddling my horse."

Agnes takes a deep breath, then another. Her voice cracks. "It was the worst I've ever seen. Horses and people all thrown into a ditch here – this was a ditch back then – all burnt to a crisp. The smell was enough to make you retch. Even now, I think I catch a drift or two of that stench. It looked like about twenty of each. I mean animal and human skulls. But then I was not myself so my counting might have been off."

I walk up next to her. I have fabric in my left and a crystal in my right.

"Can you really do it?" she asks, fear written on her face. "I've heard the stories, but somehow I've never really believed it was possible."

"Yes, I can do it," I say.

"Will it hurt?"

"Not the intrusion, but you'll relive the memory. Memories can hurt."

"Damn straight," she says, sniffling.

Suddenly she holds out her arm. "Do it, girl!"

I brush her arm with fabric, and time freezes as

I enter her mind. It's late afternoon. It feels like autumn. Like the Equinox. Only a few leaves remain on the trees. I filter out her reactions – her little yips and cries, her heavy breathing, her staggered steps – to focus on the horrific scene. I slow everything down to a crawl. Agnes spent a few seconds examining the corpses before she had to look away. Slowing down her memory, I spend longer than that. Counting. Horse heads and human heads.

They died in a hellish agony. But then skulls always look that way. The eye and nose holes. The open mouth and damaged teeth. Like they screamed and screamed until all their flesh was gone.

And then I see something out of the corner of Agnes' eye. A piece of cloth. I push to see it better. Red cloth. Like a uniform. I push harder. Instinctively, I reach down to pick it up. I want to feel the fabric. But I can't quite get to it. I need to feel it . . .

"ELAN!" Stille shouts, and I startle back to the present moment.

Moaning, Agnes thrashes on the ground, her arms and legs churning wildly. Stille leans down to calm her, and gradually she resumes breathing normally.

"What happened to her?" I ask.

"You happened to her," Stille says. "I told you to stop, and then I told you again, and you didn't. So finally I yelled at you."

Agnes sits up with difficulty. I drop to my knees and hug her tight from behind. "I'm so sorry,

Agnes. I didn't know I was hurting you. I didn't hear Stille shouting."

"You pushed into my memory," Agnes gasps.

"I just wanted to see the red cloth and pick it up."

"Elan, that wasn't in my memory."

"Then how could I see it? I can only see what you witnessed."

"I never saw any cloth," Agnes says. "That was you. You looked for it, then you saw it, then you tried to make me bend down to pick it up. But I couldn't do it. It wasn't in my memory. I felt like my brain was going to explode."

"Shh," I say, as Agnes starts to cry. I hold her more tightly and caress her brow, then I look up to Stille. His eyes are wide as saucers.

"And the horses and riders?" he asks gently.

"There were eighteen," I say decisively. "Eighteen horses, eighteen riders."

"So number nineteen is still out there somewhere," Stille says.

"If there's a number nineteen," Agnes says, her sobs subsiding, "he probably did all this. Tying up loose ends. Eliminating witnesses."

"Dead men tell no tales," Stille says.

"But the horses?" Agnes says. "That was just cruelty."

Suddenly, I notice something that's been there for a minute or two. A hot pain on my right thigh. The ache grows with each breath. I reach down and discover a hole in my pants pocket. I shake my leg, and my rubystone falls to the ground. It sits there, pulsing like a beating heart before it slowly cools. It burned through Gregor's handkerchief and then my pants. Through the hole, I see a large red welt on my upper thigh.

Before I can tell him not to, Stille picks it up. He holds it up to the sun.

"How long have you had this?" he asks.

"Since I left the Keep," I say sheepishly.

"It's a rubystone," he says.

"I've been meaning to tell you . . ."

He glares at me. "Guess you forgot."

We stare at the brilliant gem in the late afternoon sunlight. The pulses have vanished, but the rubystone radiates unrivaled crimson splendor. Finally, Agnes breaks the silence. "Well, mine eyes have seen the glory," she says under her breath.

22

Elan

"I said I'm sorry," I whisper.

"I heard you the first ten times," Stille mutters, looking out the coach window.

We had escorted Agnes back to her hut, then continued our journey by flagging down a commercial coach headed south. The local, not a king's coach. At least we didn't have to pay in gold coins! The cushions are worn through to the bare wood, and they've crammed eleven people inside a six-person carriage. The coach stops every mile or two, and people pour out and then pour in. At each stop, Stille steps out to make sure nobody nicks our travelbags stowed up top. The coach smells, but, I remind myself with a rueful smile, I've recently endured worse. The good news is no locals seem to notice two traveling companions who aren't speaking to each other. Not much anyway.

"It's not like I intended not to tell you," I say.

"You tell me your life's story in intimate detail," Stille grouses. "Even the time Gregor forgot your eleventh birthday. But this you forget?"

"For some reason, it always slipped my mind," I say. "You have to believe me."

"Maybe the gem was enchanted," he says sarcastically. "It instructed you not to tell me."

I snap my fingers and sit straight up. "That's exactly what it did!" I say. "Gregor told me never to use it. Said it could be enchanted. He used that word."

"Oh, come on, Elan," Stille murmurs.

"No, really. That's how wards work. They make you invisible, yes, but they also emanate a spell to discourage others from coming nearer. The closer they get, the stronger the compulsion to walk away. The rubystone doesn't want anyone but me to know it exists. So it creates a compulsion in me not to say anything."

I feel for the rubystone in my pocket. It now resides in a thick burlap pouch Stille constructed from materials in Agnes's cottage. If the gem wants to burn through my clothes again, it's going to have to work harder. And my right thigh has nearly healed. Agnes dabbed salve on it. But I have this feeling something more was at work. It's like the burn mark wanted to disappear.

"I wonder if all the memory witches had this issue," I say.

"No," Stille responds.

"No, what?"

"All the other memory witches didn't have this issue."

"How do you know?"

"They didn't have rubystones."

"But the patrons use a red crystal as their calling card?"

"Amelia had a rubystone. According to the books, she was the only one."

Stille resumes staring out the coach window, resting his chin on his elbow. I think about reaching for his other hand, but he's pulled it all the way across his lap.

"I'm trying to apologize," I whisper.

"I'm not ready to stop being mad," he says.

"And what's so interesting out there anyway," I say, leaning across, attempting to peer out. I softly lay my hand on his shoulder to steady myself. My face is inches from his, my body nearly brushing against his. I need to distract him from being angry. "All I see are trees and dirt."

"I think we're being followed," he says.

"What?"

"I've noticed things for the last few hours."

"What kind of things?"

"Horsemen in the woods. Trying not to be seen. And some behind us keeping their distance. And lots of pigeons overhead. I think we've been spotted."

I haven't paid any attention at all. I've been focused on mending relations with Stille. I can't afford to lose him. After years of dismissing the idea of a human crystal and planning to fulfill my mission alone, now I can't imagine doing it without him by my side. For the first time, I think I might be able to understand how devastated Amelia felt when her *Anaiah* was murdered.

"So what are they waiting for?" I ask.

"The countryside is too risky," he says. "And they don't know what you're capable of. Maybe that rubystone scares them. Remember, you overturned half a forest. We're almost to Elden. They'll feel more comfortable there."

"So we're walking right into a trap?"

"Not exactly. I thought we might get off at the next to last stop. Cowardston."

Cocking my head, I detect the glimmer of a smile, Stille's first in hours. "It's named for the young men who agree to become brothers," he says, "but change their minds at the last moment. If you're coming south by boat or coach, it's the last stop before Elden. Lots of conscripts head for the hills."

"I get it," I say. "A town for cowards. So, Cowardston."

"Exactly. Agnes told me there's a patron there. Arlene Delacroix. We can figure out next steps, and she can put us up for the night. And . . ."

He pauses, like he's unsure how much to share with me.

"And what?"

"There's someone in Cowardston I need to see. Anselm Grist. I sent him a letter a few weeks back. He's the constable who investigated the destruction of my parents' village by witches. Filed a report with King Marcellus. Which no one has laid eyes on. He's retired now. Lives up by the old mill. I need to find out what he knows. If he'll tell me."

"I'll go with you," I say too quickly.

"Elan, I'd like to do this by myself," he says.

"You're pushing me away, Stille."

"No, I'm not. I'll honor my vow. The one I made to help you avenge your father and brother. But this is something I need to do alone. You go find Arlene Delacroix, and we'll meet up later."

I know instantly Stille's plan is a bad idea. Extraordinarily bad. Splitting up is the worst thing we can do. We are stronger together. By myself I can turn a tree upside-down. With Stille, I can ransack a forest. But I am in no position to argue.

"Fine," I say.

Cowardston is a small dirty village, comprised mostly of taverns and inns, on the eastern bank of the Tablas. Most people who arrive don't stay. They travel on to Elden, flee back home, or wander the Riege. The buildings are mostly wood and sandbags, and prices for everything are high. Repeat business is obviously not a priority. One building, a former river guardhouse, is made of ancient bluestone. Mortar pieces litter the ground, and it looks like no repairs have been made for years.

I shrug into my leathers as we step off the coach. On the corner is a fidgety middle-aged woman wearing a long-sleeved black dress with black gloves and a red corsage. Her bonnet is tied so tightly it slices her neck. She reminds me of the choirgirls in Montauk. Stille takes our travelbags inside the Cowardston depot and hands the steward a coin to watch them overnight. He disappears quickly on a backroad uphill. Presumably towards the old mill.

I walk to the woman. She tries to smile, but it comes across more as a frown. I guess she's not someone who smiles often. Her eyes are wary. She's playing a part, I think. My right hand goes to a crystal, my left to a fabric. Black. I can't help myself. It's my training.

"Hello, Elan," she says. "The pigeons said to expect you."

"Hello," I say. "You must be Arlene."

"Yes," she says.

"And of course you have a calling card," I say.

"Of course," she responds, leaning towards me, and she unpins the corsage from her dress and holds it up. "Ta-da," she says. "As per protocol."

I wait for her to show me a red crystal. Her costume jewelry. Like Allamonde and Agnes. And then it's clear she hasn't one – that my instincts are correct – but my pause is a moment too long.

They have killed the real Arlene Delacroix, I think, *and sent an imposter.*

The woman grabs my wrist with a wicked sneer, but I am faster. I sneak my fabric up her left sleeve onto her colorless skin, and instantly I am inside her head. I twirl the crystal in my right hand. The memories I seek aren't buried. They're on the surface. There for the taking. Never more than a moment away from tormenting her. It's why she can't smile. She wants to bury them, but she can't. They won't let her.

I blast her with the memories. They start when she is a girl. Her mother beating her. Kicking her. Berating her. Her mother tying her to a bannister and spanking her until her bottom bleeds. Nearly putting her hand into a red hot fire. I flash the images one after the other until I realize she is no longer holding my wrist. She is on the ground, writhing and moaning. I should feel sorry for her, but I don't. She's trying to hurt me, and I'm trying to survive. So I do what Gregor wants me to do.

I run.

Instantly, I sense footsteps behind and glance back. Two large barefooted brothers, their coarse black robes flying, chase me. I have no idea where they came from. One, I recognize. The brother from Montauk. The one who herded the choirgirls into the chall. Why is he this far south? There's only one explanation. He came by boat. The Order has mobilized every available resource in the Riege to catch Stille and me. The realization chills me.

I swerve toward the large stone guardhouse. I wheel around the corner, my breaths coming fast and hard, and then – it's instinct now! – I latch onto the wall and climb straight up. Two stories. The crumbling mortar gives me ample foot- and hand-holds. I scramble to the top in seconds, then roll over on the roof and lie perfectly still. Like I practiced in the mortuary wagon. A moment later, the brothers charge by underneath and then out into the streets of Cowardston. But I am gone, and one of them curses.

"It's like she vanished," the other one says, hands on his knees.

"Well, she's a witch, after all."

"Brother Mordecai will be most displeased."

"Well, we should have the boy at least. I'll look forward to punishing the whelp for his insolence. That'll get the girl's attention."

They've captured Stille!

The other one belches, and they jog back toward the Cowardston depot.

I lie prostrate, there on the ancient rooftop, and close my eyes. I knew splitting up was a bad idea. There's a chall in Cowardston. That's where they'll take Stille first. Then probably to Elden tonight when it's dark. And Arlene Delacroix is almost certainly captured or even dead. She didn't hand over her red crystal to the Order. She didn't betray the calling card. Protecting me to the end. Honoring the oath she'd sworn. And we'd never even met! Silently, I thank her. The Patrons of Paul are magnificent. I owe them my life.

I crawl slowly on all fours across the roof, trying not to make a sound, and peer low into a narrow alleyway on the other side. It holds garbage bins and an orange cat. There are no brothers in sight. The bluestone wall, with its crumbling mortar, makes for an easy descent. I am on the ground in no time. There is only one thing to do. Find Anselm Grist. He's a man, and I don't trust men. But Weathersby was a man. Allamonde was a man. Stille trusts this Anselm Grist, and so shall I.

I retrace Stille's path as he left the depot. I know the brothers are searching for me, but the last place they'll look is the last place they looked. I'm safe for a while. I see a jagged stripe of lightning in the sky, then hear thunder a moment later. The rain, as if on cue, pelts down seconds after that. I pull the hood up on my leathers and quicken my pace. Stille's steps will be erased in short order.

The cartpath Stille took leads away from Cowardston into forested hills. Shortly I arrive at a fork, and a hand-painted sign, now fallen into the weeds, points to the left for the Old Mill. I catch its dim silhouette on the ridge. But Stille turned away here. That makes no sense. That leads him back to the village. Then I kneel in the misting dust and see why. This is where he starts running. I can tell by the depth and distance of his steps. Which means this is when he realized he was being followed. He turned right to avoid betraying his destination, which led him back toward Cowardston. Back to where more brothers awaited him.

He never once called out to me. I'm sure I would have heard him. Was he still angry with me? Or was he protecting me? Probably both. I guess boys like Stille are like that.

Now the rain is hard and slanted. I see where the tracks come together in a scrum. This is where the brothers caught him. And hurt him. And then something in the dirt. I reach down with a finger, and my heart skips a beat. Blood. Stille's blood. By the side of the cartpath is a torn piece of Stille's shirt. With red stains.

Stille is not being hunted because of his quest. He's being hunted because of mine. Because he has the awful misfortune of being born my human crystal. My perfect helpmate. This is the second beating he's suffered because of me. I hold his shirt to my face. A strange emotion sweeps over me. I pull away and stare at the shirt. Then I caress the shirt, the red stain, with my fingers. The fabric is alive to my touch! I have one other fabric like that. My special red cloth that directs me to memories of that awful day. The cloth it took Gregor and me so long to find. And now I know why. And it's not due to the cloth's peculiar shade of red.

That fabric must have blood on it. Like Stille's shirt. I have a thousand fabrics in my coat of many colors, but only one has blood diluting the dye.

I am struck with a terrible intuition about the boys in white nightshirts on the Elden hillside at dawn. At long last, I think I know what the boy in my recurring dream is trying to tell me. And how Bishop Fiske's memory relates to my father's and Willem's murders. It is too awful to be true, but something inside me knows that it is.

The torrential rains have turned the cartpath to mud, and the wild winds shake and rattle the treelimbs. Lightning and thunder detonate the skies. I kneel there on the cartpath, Stille's torn bloodied shirt in my hands, and I retch my guts out.

23

Elan

From the back, Anselm Grist's small house is nearly invisible. He built it into a hillside, and its roof is groundcover. Dirt and twigs and pebbles and a smattering of grass, weeds, and brush. The telltale sign is a thin curl of smoke rising contentedly from behind a stunted jimberry tree. A chimney! The rain has not let up, and the mud reminds me of the tunnel Gregor and I escaped through at the villa. Each step makes a disgusting noise. The mud covers my shoes, and my leathers and legs are spattered brown.

I don't know why, but I clutch Stille's shirt. I want to cry, but I can't. I want to scream, but that would call attention to myself. I want to destroy something, but Allamonde's words ring in my ears. I must not succumb to rage. That's what the Order wants. What Brother Mordecai wants. So I will hold off on rage until I find the man who murdered Father and Willem. At that point, all bets are off.

I bang on the door, a four-slat pine construction that does not fit the opening. I peek through a crack and spy a foot. So he's there. I bang on the door again. Nothing. Silence. I peek through again, and the foot is gone. I bang on the door a third time.

"Open the door or else!" I shout. I am so angry I am trembling. I realize Grist has done nothing to offend me. Except not answering this stupid misshapen door.

"I'm not going to open my door," an old man's voice replies. "And you can't make me."

"I can cover your chimney," I yell back, and then, stuffing Stille's shirt in my pocket, I march around the house and onto the roof. I stomp to let him know I'm there. I find the opening, then I kneel down and grab two handfuls of mud. It won't take much.

"You've made your point," his voice says, now closer. I turn and there he is. He's a mess. He's grown a scraggly white beard, which he does not trim, and his silver hair cascades below his shoulders. His stained clothes hang on him, smelling of smoke layered over tobacco. He puffs on a pipe with an elongated stem. His face is ancient, but his eyes are fierce and utterly clear.

"You sleep in those clothes, don't you?" I say.

Sizing me up, he puffs twice. "Maybe," he says. "Sometimes. What's it to you?"

"And you don't want me to come in because you're ashamed of your house," I say.

He puffs four times. "How much did you see?"

"Enough," I say.

"You're going to come in anyway, aren't you?" he says.

"Yes," I say, the mud still in my hands.

"You're the one who should be ashamed," he says, poking and shaking his pipe at me. "Smoking an old man out of his home."

The rain increases in intensity. I can hear it striking the limbs of the trees.

"I could have done worse," I say. "Like change you into a turnip!"

The corner of his mouth twitches. For the first time, I see the hint of a smile on his face. "I think not," he says. "You're not that kind of witch."

"You don't know that," I say.

"So the Order is chasing all over the Riege for a turnip witch?" he asks. Then, stuffing his pipe into his mouth, he chortles. His teeth are yellow and black.

"I can do other kinds of sorcery," I say defensively.

"Oh, I have no doubt of that, Miss Montescue," he says, turning sharply to retreat into his house. I wait a moment, then realize I'm to follow, so I run to catch up. There is a barrel outside his door, and the top is overflowing with rainwater. I wash the mud off my hands. The door is open, and I walk in, closing it behind me. The acrid smoke is so thick, I wave my hands to push it away.

"Give yourself a moment," he says. "You'll get used to it."

"This is unhealthy," I say.

"I certainly hope so," he responds acidly. "Now sit."

Grist has collapsed amiably into a large red overstuffed chair with three legs and a piece of wood for the fourth. I sit in a spindly dinner table chair with half its straw seat missing, except there is no dinner table anywhere. My leathers drip onto Grist's floor, but he doesn't seem to mind. A smoldering fire inside a blackened firepit warms me.

I don't wait to be asked. The words rush out of my mouth and fall over themselves. I tell him what's happened to the boy who wrote him a letter. And our joint missions. Stille, finding out what happened to his family's village. Me, killing the men who murdered my father and brother. Grist listens with his eyes closed. But at that last comment, one eye opens.

"How are you going to do it?" he says.

"Do what?"

"Kill the men who murdered your father."

"Well, I'm going to end their lives," I say.

"I heard that. I'm asking how."

Truth be told, I'd never thought about the details. I knew what I needed to do. What the required outcome was. I'd planned the journey to Kimbar, but frankly, I hadn't thought how I'd do the dirty work. The killing. So I sit there in front of Grist and say nothing.

"I mean, are you going to stick a knife in his

belly?" he asks.

I gape at him.

"Hit him over the head with a rock?"

I stammer.

"Perhaps poison his coffee."

"I'm keeping my options open," I say at last. Yes, that sounds good. The kind of plan a smart person would have. I'll wait until I catch the man, and then I'll figure how to kill him based on the circumstances.

"Killing a man is harder than it sounds," he says. His eyes bore into mine like he wants to see through to my soul. "And I don't mean merely the doing of it. I mean the living with having done it."

"Some people can," I say.

"Far too many, unfortunately," he says, sighing. "But I don't believe you are one of those people. Even if you are a memory witch."

"When the time comes," I say defiantly, "I will do what needs to be done."

"Of that I have no doubt," he laughs, smoke leaking out of both nostrils. "You have rare persistence and determination."

We regard each other through a circulating fog.

"Were you really going to block my chimney?" he asks.

"Yes," I say, jutting out my chin.

"Hmm," he responds.

"I'll go back up there," I threaten.

"Fine," he says. "So you've come to find out what happened to the boy's village?"

"I've come for that," I say, "and anyways I have

nowhere else to go. In Cowardston, Elden, or anywhere else. And I need to save Stille, but I don't
know how, and I can't do it alone."

"Well, let's start with the village," Grist says. "It
was a little one I'd never heard of. Bearwallow.
Fifty miles due north. I worked in Kimbar then.
For the Constabulary. It was my last job before
they kicked me out altogether. This wonderful retirement you see," and here he waves with his arm
amidst the drifting smoke, "was not voluntary."

"You can't hold a job?" I ask.

He pauses to select the right words, then raises
his chin. "I had difficulty accepting instruction
from people less intelligent than myself," he says
at last.

I let the matter drop.

"Anyway," he continues, "we received reports
that this little village had been destroyed. It was in
the middle of nowhere. No one else wanted to investigate. So I volunteered. The initial reports
from local busybodies said two elderly witches
were responsible."

"Sorcerers," I correct.

He nods affably. "As you wish. *Sorcerers*. The
reports made no sense. In general, as I'm sure you
know, the Fluence cannot be used to harm people.
Not directly, at least. Indirectly, of course. But destroy an entire village? This close to the next Dry?
Only an idiot would do that, and sorcerers aren't
idiots."

"Pitchforks and torches," I say.

"Yes. Indeed, yes," he says. "I had another theory. It was the Order. I'd had run-ins with the brothers before – and those black bonnets, the sisters, who can be equally vile – and destroying a village is certainly within their capabilities. What I didn't know was why this village? Why Bearwallow?"

He pauses to relight his pipe from a worn brown-leather switch he pulls from the firepit embers.

"So why did the Order do it?" I ask.

"They didn't," he says, then he turns his head in a fit of coughing.

"The king?"

"The Karators!" he bursts out between coughs. "The Fluence is sorcery, a power which resides in and operates through people. Through sorcerers. Free will is involved. The Karators also have magic, but it resides in one person – Our Master – and he operates by enchanting objects. A sword. A ring. A book. Even a person."

"A crystal?" I ask.

"Especially a crystal," Grist replies. My hand inadvertently goes to the burlap bag in my pocket.

"Anyway," he continues, "there are telltale marks from using enchanted objects. Striations. Burns and scrapes. That's how Bearwallow was destroyed. It was indiscriminate, not house by house. Not person by person. The entire village. Wiped away. Everyone suffered for the same mere instant, and then it was done."

"Why would the Karators want to destroy a Riegian village?" I ask.

"I had no idea. I looked high and low. Investigated for months. I vetted every family who lived there. Nothing. I finally filed my report, but it didn't reach the desired conclusion. Kimbar didn't want to deal with a new Karator menace. It was far more convenient to blame two old witches, both of whom had since died. So the bureaucrats buried my report. It took them some years, but ultimately, they forced me out altogether."

Grist pauses, blowing smoke rings absentmindedly, staring into the fire.

"And remember," he says, as if continuing a long-running conversation he's had inside his own head, "the Karators have little presence in the Riege. So importing an enchanted object with this much power, as well as a person capable of wielding it, was a major operation. It must have taken months or even years of planning. And for what? Why did Our Master need to eliminate this little village in the middle of nowhere?"

Anselm Grist's eyes burn like the embers in his firepit. Then he sighs like a tired old man.

"That was sixteen years ago," he says, "and not a day expired that I didn't agonize about Bearwallow. The people who lived and died there. I investigated them so thoroughly, they became my extended family. Every day I'd sort the evidence in my head, hoping for that flash of insight, a solution to the riddle. But I never was able to do so."

"I'm so sorry . . ."

"Until the letter from Stille Vespers arrived," he croaks hoarsely, his mouth twitching, smoke pouring through his nose. "Wanting to know about his parents. Followed, of course, by the pigeons informing everyone hither and yon that a memory witch and her *Anaiah* were cavorting about in the flatlands."

"We were not cavorting," I protest.

He holds up a hand. *Let me finish!*

"And then more pieces fell into place. All but two. I knew why Our Master wanted to destroy the village. And I knew, with equal certainty, that his plan had failed."

Grist stares into nothingness. Like he's speaking to someone not of this world.

"Well, are you going to keep me in suspense or . . ."

"Our Master destroyed Bearwallow to make certain Stille Vespers was never born," Grist says.

"Why would he care?"

"Because a memory witch deprived of her human crystal can do enormous harm."

"Amelia," I say.

"Exactly. The history books don't reflect how close the Riege came to losing all sorcerers – every born-and-bred family – in Amelia's aftermath. And all because Amelia had a rubystone but no human crystal."

"You mean, like Paul Guiscard," I say.

Grist ignores my comment. "And sorcerers are all that have stopped the Karators from conquering this continent. To this day, the Karators believe their destiny is to rule the Riege."

"But the Impassable River . . ."

"It can't hold forever," Grist says. "Who knows, maybe Our Master thinks he can tame the river. Or maybe he's found another way to take the Riege."

I think of the Karators I saw in the underbelly of Darine. If they're in other river towns along the Tablas, they've already invaded. Already secured a beachhold. They have an army in place awaiting orders.

"But whatever his plan," Grist says, "Our Master desired to weaken the Riege by eliminating the Fluence. Destroying the born-and-bred. Which required a memory witch . . ."

". . . without her *Anaiah*," I say, completing the thought.

The fire crackles, and an ember jumps from the firepit, landing at my feet. Startled, I watch the red turn to black.

"You said you're missing two pieces of the puzzle?" I ask.

"Yes," Grist says. "How did Our Master know a memory witch would be born to the Montescue family in the flatlands? It's been a thousand years. How did he know you were in the hopper?"

"And the other piece?"

"I looked into Hector and Annabelle Vespers. Their families. Where they came from. What they did. Their likes and dislikes. Which house was theirs. I knew everything about them."

"What's wrong with that?" I say.

"They were childless, Elan. No offspring."

"That's not true! Stille is their son."

"So Stille's letter informs me," Grist says. "But

there is no record in the Riege of a Stille Vespers being born. He didn't exist until some kindly unidentified stranger dropped him at his Uncle Martin's doorstep in Kimbar. Sixteen years and one week ago."

The same day I came into the world, I think. *The daughter of a Karator spy and the last great sorcerer of the tenth Ebb.*

"We need to save Stille," I say.

"Yes," Grist says, exhaling wearily. "But not tonight."

24

Gregor's Journal

I became a tutor to be let alone. And to escape my older brother. Both motives tied into an intricate knot that lodged permanently at the back of my throat. I came by the skillset naturally enough. My parents were that rare exception – tutors who married. Which is possible only in Kimbar, where a sufficient number of the born-and-bred lived near each other so Mother and Father could pursue their vocation while raising a family. Mother worked for the duchess of something-or-other inside the palace walls. Highly prestigious, but the wages were low and the duchess deliberately forgetful about paying. Father worked for a nouveau riche born-and-bred family in the seatrade business "down there." No prestige, but the pay was better and prompt.

The vast majority of tutors did not marry.

Could not marry. A tutor was just another servant, living with his pupil's family and receiving a meager stipend. Family members were off-limits for romance if you valued job security. And trysts with house staff were risky if they concluded in a row or a baby. So for practical purposes, a tutor lived a solitary life, and retirement depended upon saving what coins fell his way. Of course, a few tutors, and I count myself a member of this blessed fraternity, were taken in by their families. Treated like the husband's aunt who never married or the wife's favorite third cousin.

The Ebb is, of course, the worst time to be a tutor to the born-and-bred. You are out of work or soon will be. When I was born, the tenth Ebb had not yet begun, but the writing was on the wall. So I was to be apprenticed in a guild, and my younger sister, Sylvia, was to find a suitable husband or, barring that, secure a place on the payroll of Kimbar's purple palace. As to our older brother, there was never any doubt. He would join the Order. Sylvia and I rarely referred to him by name. He was always "our brother." Mother and Father did not appreciate the Order. No sense of nuance or subtlety. To the Order, there was right and wrong, and black and white, and up and down. Decisions were made and executed promptly and literally and with no room for error. Hierarchy ruled. But that was precisely what appealed to our brother.

To this day, I do not believe Mother and Father fully understood the brutality of my day-to-day existence. It started with verbal abuse, but that ended once I developed a thick skin. Sticks and stones, don't you know. So our brother moved on from mere wordplay to various iterations of physical pain. Beatings, and cruelty that verged on torture. As the victim, I received a steadily decreasing amount of sympathy and support from my parents. They were tired at the end of every day, particularly once Mother became ill, and did not want to police boys being boys. I was supposed to fend for myself. It was part of finding my place as a male in the Riege. Our brother's explanations for my injuries and ailments – I was clumsy again, or I didn't watch where I was going, or I was the one who started it – always had a modicum of credibility. He even gave himself the occasional black eye for emphasis. I didn't have the courage to run away, so I endured it.

As the only daughter, Sylvia had a room to herself, and at a young age she accompanied Mother to the purple palace. Mother needed a helper, and Sylvia was a perfect fit. Other days, Sylvia found an excuse – any excuse, truth be told – to be somewhere else. Which left me alone with our brother. Sylvia observed everything in our household with a keen eye. And over the years, she became quieter and quieter. To the point where days and weeks would go by without her saying a word. I thought about asking Sylvia to stay with us in the house. A witness, don't you know. But in the end, I couldn't do that. Our brother was my burden to bear. He did not have to be hers as well.

Things changed when I was fourteen. Our

brother, sixteen at the time, was set for his triumphant enlistment journey to Elden. The Order required its adherents to recruit, and I negotiated a moratorium on being tortured by promising to become our brother's recruit. He had no others, so this was the only real leverage I was ever to have. The Order performs an elaborate departure ceremony, which our entire family attended even though Mother was too ill to stand. Our brother was there, regal in his black robe and bare feet.

After the initiates recited the oath, they formed a block unit, much like soldiers on parade, their right arm on the shoulder of the person next over. The recruits were to stand on the podium and, one by one, pledge to follow in two years. A black brick, the Order's symbol of piety and poverty, was handed from recruit to recruit as each spoke his pledge.

All along, my plan had been to wait until this moment – when our brother was no longer in a position to inflict raw physical pain on me – before declining to offer my pledge to the Order. I thought about it constantly. Fantasized about it. Dreaded it. Even dreamed about it. But I never knew if I would have the guts to do it. Maybe the better course, I reasoned, was to take the pledge but back out later. The pledge was, as everyone knew, not legally binding.

But there on that podium, I knew I had to make my decision. In an odd sense, I felt like I owed it to our brother. Not for his sake, mind you, but for mine. I wanted to live by a different standard. Under that standard, he deserved to know what my final choice was. There, in public, in front of everyone.

So when the boy to my right handed me the brick, I took a deep breath and, my voice cracking, said as distinctly as I could without shouting: "I do not wish to follow." Then I handed the brick to the next recruit, his eyes wide in disbelief, and I descended the podium. I peeked once at our brother, whose face showed no emotion. Our eyes did not meet.

And I thought it was over. That I had done it. Sylvia stared open-mouthed like she didn't know who I was. Father breathed a sigh of relief and clapped me on the back. Mother sat there lost in her thoughts. I felt triumphant. I have no courage, but stepping off the podium felt like real bravery. Looking back now over the course of my life, it may have been the only truly courageous thing I ever did.

And then I felt a hand jerking my shoulder, pulling me aside. It was our brother. His face suffused with anger.

"Mark my words, you little two-faced traitor," he whispered. "One day I will be first brother. You'll see. You'll see."

I met his stare. "Of that I have no doubt, Mordecai. No doubt whatsoever."

25

Elan

This is a real bed. The first I have slept in since the Keep. Dwumfour's didn't count. That mattress was thin as parchment. I was amazed when Grist showed me this room. Scrubbed clean and well-appointed. His son's, Grist said, stone-faced. Joined the palace payroll decades ago and disappeared into the bureaucracy. The two stopped speaking, and the room hasn't been touched in years.

And I had the dream again. I am there on the grassy hill in Elden with the boys in heavy white nightshirts. Each dream, it's a different boy, but the outcome is the same. I'm relieved there's no bloodstains in the bedsheets when I wake up.

I feel a presence in the room. I do not know how long I've slept, but I am reluctant to rise. To even move. I lie there blinking, focusing on slow deliberate breathing.

We need to save Stille.

"It's been twelve hours," a genteel melodic but brittle voice says. A woman's voice. As if she knows the question I'm asking myself.

I sit up, and it's a face I've seen before. "I know you," I say.

She cries, big wet juicy tears streaming down both cheeks. A petite woman with long silver blond hair, she wears a gray travel dress and cloak. Her face is wrinkled and lined. I saw that face when she was a girl in Gregor's memories.

His sister.

"Is he alive?" Sylvia asks.

"Who?"

"Gregor."

"Yes," I say. "As of a week ago."

Her head bobs, and she smiles gamely. She makes no effort to wipe her tears.

And now I know why the first brother seemed so familiar in Darine. I know where I had seen his face before. In Gregor's childhood memories of his family! It all rushes back to me.

"You have another brother," I say, a bad taste in my mouth. "Mordecai. He's still alive, too."

"Yes," she says simply.

"And he's kidnapped Stille."

"Which is why I'm here," she says.

"You're with the patrons?" I ask.

"I am their leader," she says, squaring her shoulders. "I was on my way to Elden when I received Anselm's message last night, so here I am.

He is not formally a patron, but he is sympathetic to our cause. We can trust him. The patrons are not what we once were, but we are still a force. And we have allies in surprising places. We must plan carefully, but I believe we can ensure your Stille does not suffer our Paul's fate."

Sylvia sniffles and wipes her cheeks.

"Why are you crying?"

"For Gregor. He deserved better than the sister I was. I saw what Mordecai did to him, day after day, and I did nothing. Worse, I turned away. I left him to fend for himself. Mordecai's brutality was unquenchable. I was the witness who refused to testify."

"You were just a girl. Gregor survived."

"Yes, but with what scars? He never once criticized me. Never asked me to put myself on the line. He protected me from our brother, and I thanked him by withdrawing into myself. I let him absorb all the punishment alone. And the price I paid was losing him forever. When Gregor left home, I never saw him again. He never visited. Never wrote or sent word. And why should he? The relationship we once had was gone. Disintegrated. We were no longer anyone to each other anymore."

I don't know what to say, so I say nothing.

"I tried to repay Gregor, in my own way, by doing something useful, so I joined the patrons and over time I became their leader. When I heard the incredible news that a Montescue daughter was a memory witch, my heart leapt. I knew third-hand that Gregor had tutored Alaric. So I crossed my fingers and hoped Gregor had survived to tutor this new sorceress. I couldn't imagine anyone better suited to doing so, no thanks to me."

Sylvia drops her head into her hands, and I go to her. She is so tiny and thin. If I hug too hard, I'll break her.

"Grandmother, something's happened," a voice says from the door, now open a crack. There stands a gorgeous young woman, trim and lithe, a replica of Sylvia except sixty years younger and with glossy raven hair. She sports a wicked silver dagger against her left shoulder. She studies me, her expression not entirely friendly.

Sylvia draws herself up, sniffs once, and stops crying. "Yes, thank you, Marta." Sylvia pats my hand, then slips out the room past Marta. The girl remains an extra beat. "Are you worth this?" she asks me, biting off the words, her eyes boring into mine. "All this?"

I chew my lower lip. "I have no idea," I say.

I don't know what I'm worth, I think. *Or even if I'm worth anything at all. I've accomplished nothing except getting people killed.*

I take my time getting dressed. I realize I would pay a small fortune to have Stille here washing my hair and massaging my scalp. I am a bundle of nerves. People will be looking to me for leadership, and I don't know what to do.

I don my leathers and stride through the door. Grist sprawls in his chair, as if he slept there, chewing his pipe. Oblivious to the wafting smoke,

Sylvia and her granddaughter talk in hushed tones with several men, one of whom I know. Allamonde! He smiles and dips his head in greeting. Sylvia's mien is transformed. She is stern and decisive. She uses her hands to frame her words.

I reach into my leathers and remove Stille's blood-stained shirt. For a moment, I want to cry, but I push the tears back. There'll be time another day. I caress the bloodstain, and it's electric under my touch. And then I know what I have to do. Whether alone or with help, I don't know. But it's where my dreams have pointed. They've been talking to me. I just haven't been listening.

"Elan!" Sylvia says loudly. She's been talking to me.

I surface from my reverie. "Sorry," I say quickly.

"Elden is burning," Sylvia says. "A single Karator snuck into the Order to attack Stille. He didn't make it, and so far as we know, Stille is alive. But the Order has overreacted to being penetrated. They moved to cleanse the waterfront of all Karators. The fires are enormous. The entire city may burn to the ground."

So far as we know.

The words hang in the air like the smoke from Grist's pipe. Everyone looks at me.

"I need someone to take me into Elden," I say.

"Did you hear what I just said, child?" Sylvia says, trying not to be cross.

"I need to go to the grassy hillside behind the statue of Mordecai. The one overlooking the river."

"And what do you hope to find there?" Sylvia says.

"Answers," I say. "I've been receiving an invitation every night since Montauk. I need to go."

Everyone stares at me with their mouths open.

Grist breaks the silence. "I know the hillock. Under normal circumstances, getting Elan there would be impossible. It's in the heart of the beast. Far too well defended. But with the city on fire, and a Karator attack against Stille foiled mere hours ago, I can't imagine a better time to sneak Elan in and out. No one will be watching the hillock this day."

"Can it be done, Allamonde?" Sylvia asks.

Allamonde takes a deep breath before offering a toothy smile. "Of course," he says. "It will be – what is it the young people say? – a piece of pie."

On the cartpath outside Grist's house, three plain black carriages sit like crows. This is how the Order's elite travel. On each carriage, two men in black robes and dirty black feet perch on the box with reins in their hands. Another rides on the boot. There is room for six in the carriage itself.

"Patrons?" I ask nervously.

Sylvia nods and grabs my arm. "The plan was to speed you to Kimbar, but we can sneak you into Elden as well. And we've thrown yours and Stille's travelbags in the back. And there's room for your marvelous coat of colors, of course."

The air in Cowardston is gritty. You can taste it. Like a volcano exploded and spit lava into the skies. The roads are filled with people fleeing.

Every kind of vehicle vying for position. And people on foot, dragging bags or carrying them on their heads and pulling carts. Hauling the aged and infirm on tarps or two-wheeled hand-built wagons. And riders intently guiding their horses through the churning mobs. The bedlam is surreal. A constant undercurrent of moans and wails pierced by occasional shouts and cries and babies bawling.

It takes all day for our procession to fight upstream against the panicked refugees to the ridge overlooking Elden. The vista at dusk is apocalyptic. Our carriages empty, and everyone stands there aghast. The riverfront, ten times larger than Darine's, is a massive conflagration of ships, docks, and warehouses. It makes a sound I have never heard before. Like hell unleashed. The fire spreads patiently up the slope towards the city center. We hear an eerie pop in that awful moment when the flames reach out to grab and engulf a new structure.

The Order's walled compound, in the shape of a square, is enormous. Nearly as large as Darine. The main spired fortress, which functions as a chall, is the centerpiece, and it is surrounded by a sprawling tumult of smaller outbuildings and extensions. The raging fire is kept at a distance by the encircling greenery, which functions like a moat protecting a castle. Even from this distance, I spy the bronze statue with open arms and, behind it, the hillock I saw in Bishop Fiske's macabre memory.

I remember the Karator city underneath the piers of Darine. Burrowing deep into the shoreline. The Karator foothold in Elden must be so much larger. The underground city must contain thousands. Women and children. Families. Communities even.

The comment of the Karator bilgeman on the sliprider haunts me. His concern for reprisals. I dismissed it so easily. Stille and I were trying to escape. That was all that mattered. But now I see what reprisals look like, and I am stunned. The bilgeman was right to be terrified.

How many Karators have died today? I think. *Thousands? Tens of thousands? All because a Karator – one single Karator – snuck into the Order and tried to harm Stille. How many of the dead even knew what the reprisals were for?*

"Are you all right?" Marta asks me. She's constantly looking at me. Studying me. Now her normally sour look has given way to concern, perhaps because my cheeks are wet. Due to Catherine, I have more reason than most to dislike Karators. But this? It is butchery on a breathtaking scale.

"Do you still want to sneak into Elden?" Sylvia asks.

"More than ever," I say grimly.

By the time we reach the Order's main compound, it is nearly midnight, but the sky is bright as noontime. The fires push against the north and western perimeter, while the winds, now at gale force, sweep the flames like a broom along the Tablas into Cowardston. Our procession steers to the compound's south gate, which is lightly guarded by two older brothers with scarves wrapped around their faces to filter the smoke and grime. They wave us through, and the gates clank shut behind us.

My first thought is for Stille. I hop down from the carriage as the patrons subdue the unsuspecting guards. I don my leathers, and I do not ask permission. Fabric and crystal in hand, I read the first guard. He has a memory of Stille being hauled into the main fortress through the south gate a day earlier. Stille's face is bloody and swollen, his shirt ripped. He is barely able to stand. The brothers have liberally taken out their frustrations on him. But Stille is alive, and I breathe a jagged sigh of relief.

The second guard's memory is that morning. Stille being frog-marched into the stables, and then ten carriages speeding through the compound's east gate into Elden's sulfurous haze. Headed toward Kimbar. But something is off. Stille disappearing, then the carriages racing away. I watch the memory twice more. And then again before it hits me. This time I view the memory and count. From the moment Stille disappears through the door until the carriages speed away, four seconds elapse. That's not enough time to load Stille into a carriage, even if you throw him in headfirst.

I replay the memory again, and now I wait until after the procession leaves. Five minutes. Ten minutes, then fifteen. Finally, a lone carriage rumbles slowly out of the stables and through the gate.

The carriage is old, the horses tired. I catch the flash of an elbow in the carriage window. I focus on it. Suddenly I feel drawn to it. Like when I nearly kissed Stille on the lips that first night at Weathersby's. It's the Fluence telling me Stille is in that carriage. The elbow belongs to him, and he showed it in the window as a signal.

Thank the Fluence, I think. *We are still a team.*

Stille knew I would find a memory. That I would come for him. The ten carriages are a diversion. The Order is gambling everything on a single rickety carriage delivering Stille safely to Kimbar.

I tell Sylvia and the others, huddling in the shadows, what I've learned. They agree to get a message to patrons between Elden and Kimbar. Grist is certain Stille's carriage will take the back roads. It is, he says, what he would do in the circumstances. Sylvia agrees to focus their limited resources on the single carriage. The stakes could not be higher. If my guess is wrong, Stille will arrive in Kimbar in the possession of the Order.

"Why are they taking Stille to Kimbar?" I ask.

"The first brother is there now," Sylvia sighs. Always at her side, Marta tosses her glossy hair and scowls. "Presenting an ultimatum to King Marcellus. Mordecai can overthrow the king by force if necessary, but he would prefer a negotiated outcome."

"Why would the king agree?" I ask.

"He may feel he has no choice," Sylvia says. "He is old and tired. His son, Standish, is an Order sympathizer, and much of the bureaucracy already has sided with the first brother. The daughter, Presella, would make a fine ruler, but she is headstrong, and the Riege has never before had a queen. So Marcellus stands on thin ice."

"And Stille?" I say.

"Mordecai wants you dead," Marta says, fingering her dagger absentmindedly, "and Stille remains the bait. We've taken the bait so far, and he assumes we'll continue to do so."

"Which we will, of course," Grist says.

"My dear," Sylvia says to me, "I don't know how many brothers remain in the compound, or how much time we have. You wanted to see the hillock. There it is. Now is the time. Do what you came to do."

The Elden riverfront burns spectacularly in the background as I pace delicately onto the hillside. I find the precise spot, as near I can place it, where Bishop Fiske stood in his memory. I twirl a crystal in my right hand, and I play with fabrics in my left. I close my eyes and wait for something to happen. Anything. I did not ask the boys into my dreams, but they came. It was an invitation. Now I have come to them. So here I am, waiting for a sign.

I open my eyes, and there is nothing. I'm a sixteen-year-old girl standing on a grassy hill at midnight by the Tablas while Elden burns horribly to the ground. I have never felt less like a witch in my life.

26

Elan

It is mere noise. At first, I think it's from the in-ferno Elden has become. But the sound gets louder, and I realize it's voices. Many voices talking all at the same time. Saying the same thing, but not together. I twirl crystals in my pocket. The noise modulates, but it does not clarify. I feel like a conductor when musicians won't play together.

What am I even doing here? I think. *I read people's memories. There are no people here. Just grass and dirt. My powers don't apply.*

Or maybe I need a different tool. Stille is my human crystal. He's not here, but I have his shirt. It's stained with his blood. I retrieve the shirt, and sparks fly as I touch the stain. Now when I twirl the crystals, the voices meld. They are all speaking in unison. Saying the same thing.

Get closer.

Without thinking, I sit on the ground. The voices get louder, and still they entreat me.

You must get closer.

I lie on my back and stare at the sky. The voices now surround me. The stars are barely visible due to the smoke from the fire, but gradually they come into sharper focus. As if I can see through smoke. Then I realize there is no smoke. No fire. It is not autumn. It is springtime, and I am on the dew-laden grass. My hands, spread out at my sides, are wet. My hair is wet. Slowly I sink into the grass. Then I realize I am the grass.

The hillside has turned back time and absorbed me.

I turn my head and see Praelat Ortun and Bishop Fiske as younger men. The boys from the Order's orphanage march out in their nightshirts. I hear them muttering and complaining. Some yawn. Others blow into their hands. They stamp their feet in the cold grass. Some of them march over top of me.

Praelat Ortun barks at the boys, so they line up and drop their hands. On command, they turn around facing the river. Facing the statue with its outstretched arms. Ortun barks another order. *Eyes ahead!*

And then I see Brother Mordecai. His beard is longer and jet black, and he wears a velvet black robe with a red sash and a swordbelt. The boys stand, shivering, at attention. I see Bishop Fiske look up and down the ranks, and Praelat Ortun sports a wolfish grin. He holds up his arm, taunting Bishop Fiske with a make-believe sword.

I do not want to see what comes next, but the ground holds me and makes me watch. I am to witness. The first brother pulls his sword, and the atrocity is finished in seconds. Some boys cry out, some do not. One at a time in rapid succession, they fall where they stand. Their nightshirts are stained red. I am the dirt and grass, and the blood feels like rain on my face. I cannot wipe it off.

Bishop Fiske vomits by his side, and Praelat Ortun laughs at him.

Women in shapeless black dresses and tight black bonnets scurry to the scene. Eerily, they do not make a sound. They work feverishly, removing the sopping nightshirts and collecting them in baskets. They disappear as quickly as they arrived. They will make uniforms. Uniforms for the men – the brothers from the Order – who will attack and kill the Montescue family in the flatlands.

Listen!

The first brother speaks to Praelat Ortun and Bishop Fiske. He tells them the blood of orphan boys will consecrate the uniforms and bless the attack. All sins are washed in blood and forgiven in advance.

Listen closely!

The attack, Brother Mordecai emphasizes, will eliminate the last obstacle to the Order's assertion of dominion over the flatlands. The Montescue line will be terminated. The other born-and-bred are already scattering. The king is losing his grip. It will take years, and the timing must be precise, but the Riege will fall to the Order.

Here it comes!

The first brother's voice sounds like it's coming deep from a well. It echoes and rolls and bounces. But I can still understand it. Brother Mordecai stresses that he will lead the attack. And he will kill Alaric himself. Reputed as the last great sorcerer of the tenth Ebb. Mordecai will stab him through the heart. The son and daughter must be killed as well. Another born-and-bred family will be extinguished forever.

We died for your family's deaths!

Now everyone is gone except the bodies. Fifty boys. I try to rise, but the ground holds me fast.

Not yet.

A group of brothers, young and newly enlisted, emerge with picks and shovels. Muttering in the cold, they dig industriously. Some dig into me, but I do not feel pain. They dig and they dig. It lasts a long time. Finally, they pull and push and roll the naked boys into the ground, and they shovel the dirt back on top.

We gift you our pain, Rador-elan of House Montescue. Pray use it well.

The ground is solid beneath me again, and I see drifting smoke in the air. I hear the roar of the fire destroying Elden. I rise groggily, and I am sore and stiff all over. My vision dances before me. It is not merely that I have witnessed a murder. Many murders. But the atrocity happened on top of me. Inside me. I feel like I am covered in blood and dirt, but my skin looks normal.

I am so tired.

I stagger back to the patrons, still concealed in the shadows of the compound's south gate. I hold Stille's shirt in my hand, but it feels different. It is no longer electric to my touch. I examine both sides, then turn it inside out. The bloodstain is gone. Washed away.

"Yes, did you forget something?" Sylvia asks.

"No," I say.

"Well, then please do what you intend to do," she says. "Time is short."

"I've finished," I say.

"You were there barely a minute," Sylvia says.

"What are you talking about?" I say. "It felt like hours."

"Elan, you walked over there but sixty seconds ago."

"It seems longer than that to me."

The patrons exchange baffled glances.

"We can go now," I say. "My task is finished."

"Did you get the answers you seek?" Marta asks.

"I did, thank you," I say.

"What is that place anyway?" Marta asks.

"A cemetery," I say.

As we steal back to our carriages, two brothers leap from the gloom at Sylvia, armed with longswords. The compound is nearly empty, but our presence did not stay undetected. The Order will fight to the end. With catlike movements, Marta leaps into the fray, her dagger flashing in the firelight. She slits the throat of the first brother with casual elegance. I recognize the second brother. The one from Montauk who gathered the choirgirls and chased me into the chall's courtyard. Marta whirls and pivots behind him, twisting one arm behind his back, and positions her dagger underneath his chin. His eyes bulge as he drops his longsword, then he sees me. He knows I recognize him. I could save him if I give the word, but I don't. Marta waits for a long moment, then grins ferociously as she thrusts the dagger up to its hilt. Blood pours from the brother's mouth and nose as Marta, her eyes never leaving my face, drops him to the turf.

In the carriage leaving Elden, Sylvia sits with me. I think she talks to me. Something about taking the backroads to Kimbar. But I cannot listen. It sounds like babble, and after a few minutes she stops and we ride in silence. I am numb and heartsore. And angry. After all this time, I have finally identified the man who murdered my father. The man I saw so many times in Gregor's memory. Burning the villa, talking to the skies, and then casually piercing my father through the heart with a rapier. No wonder he was so nonchalant. He thought he had purchased forgiveness with the blood of fifty innocents.

So now the first brother must die, and I will do it myself. I don't know how, but I know it must be me. Some tasks you can delegate. Others require your own two hands. Yet Anselm Grist's questions linger in my thoughts. Am I seeking justice, or revenge?

But first we must save Stille. I miss him so much it hurts. Like there's a hole in my being. I cross my fingers that I interpreted the guard's memory correctly. That the Order is trying to sneak Stille into Kimbar through a single carriage on Riegian backroads. Well, we'll find out soon enough.

Silently I lean over and kiss the burn mark on my wrist. Saint Dezzie! She wore my clothes so I could escape. Her death ensured that I could live.

Girl, I need you to look over me now more than ever, I think. *The man I'm after is your murderer, too.*

Sylvia sits across from me in the carriage as we bump across the pitch-black Riegian countryside. The carnage of Elden is now a blurry fading memory. There are so many things Sylvia and I could discuss, but I can't talk. I am filled to overflowing with images and emotions. My rage burns and I douse it. Then it flares back up and I douse it again. This process will continue for a while. There's no room for spoken words.

Suddenly I awake. I am alone in the carriage, which is no longer moving. I must have dozed off. There is a glimmer of light on the horizon. Dawn breaking. Unsure of my balance, I step from the carriage like a wobbly old woman. The other patrons are off to the side, talking quietly in a grove of jimberry trees. The blossoms would be beautiful in springtime.

Sylvia sees I've awakened and splits from the group. She approaches me, a strange expression

on her face. Like something important has occurred that she doesn't fully comprehend.

"Congratulations, Elan. You were right. Our
people laid an ambush for the carriage, and we
have rescued Stille. Now we are devising a plan to
enter the purple palace. Getting into Kimbar will
be easy. The palace, well, that may require a bit of
skullduggery."

I should shout with joy. Leap into the air.
Dance a jig. Hug Sylvia until I break her in two.
Run over and pull hard on Anselm Grist's beard.

But what I actually do is collapse in a heap on
the sodden cold damp turf by the side of a foul
muddy road.

27

Gregor's Journal

"What kind of name is Elan?" Alaric asked me.

I shrugged.

"Have you ever known an Elan?" he said, obviously perturbed.

"No, Alaric."

"Have you even heard of anyone named Elan? Ever?"

I raised my eyebrows.

"Ever read a history book or a story where someone in it was named Elan?"

"It's an unusual name, Alaric."

It was the day after Catherine had given birth to a daughter. It was Alaric's most fervent wish to name the girl after his mother, Evellana. She had died birthing him, and Alaric had vowed all his life to name his daughter for her. Yet Catherine wanted a different name. An unusual name. In fact, I'm told her first words after learning her newborn child was female were that the baby should be named Elan.

It was the only major disagreement Catherine and Alaric ever had. Catherine nearly always had her way with Alaric on anything she really wanted. And the few instances where Alaric put his foot down – Catherine's desire for still more servants, for example – she quickly intuited Alaric's implacability and backed off. She could manipulate Alaric, but she was shrewd about when not to push her luck.

Except for Elan's name. It was a row of major proportions. Alaric was furious because it was one of the few items he had raised with Catherine before they married. If they had a daughter, he insisted at the time, she would be named Evellana after his mother. Catherine had agreed without hesitation. If only she could have met Evellana, Catherine purred. She's certain they would have become fast friends.

Yet from the moment a bawling baby girl emerged from her womb, Catherine demanded that she be named Elan. Catherine gave no reasons other than that she adored the name. And the enjoyable way it spilled from her lips. She claimed not to remember Alaric raising the issue or agreeing to the name Evellana. It was her fondest wish, Catherine said, for the girl to be named Elan. No, Alaric had responded. Her *very* fondest wish, Catherine said, batting her eyelashes. And still

Alaric had refused.

Alaric felt Catherine was being deliberately du-plicitous (imagine that, I thought) and that she was forcing him to choose between her and his mother, who wasn't alive to defend her interests. After one of their disagreements, with Alaric al-ways being near to shouting and Catherine speak-ing in a rigid whisper, Alaric would stomp off to vent his anger on me or some hapless servant while Catherine, expressionless, would retreat gracefully to another room.

Yet even Catherine was not immune to the stress. After one spat, she glided into the library, seemingly unperturbed. But through the cracked-open door, I saw her attempt to lift a teacup. Her hand shook so violently she could not hold it.

What I could never ascertain, and what to this day still mystifies me, is why Catherine cared so much. Alaric had strong reasons for his preferred name. Catherine, frankly, had none. Yet the woman who normally was so discerning about Alaric's malleability threw caution to the winds to have her way about the girl's name.

In the end, of course, Catherine prevailed. When it comes to naming children, mothers al-ways do. Alaric's acquiescence was never an-nounced or even publicly acknowledged. Privately, he told me the decisive moment came when he got down on his knees and asked his mother for guid-ance. He realized that Evellana would not wish for this disagreement to ruin his marriage. Or to fol-low the baby like a bad coin the rest of her life.

Alaric had honored Evellana sufficiently by his passionate efforts to bequeath the girl her name. It was time to let go.

But the damage had been done. The marriage now had fissures, and they did not heal with time. I do not know this for a fact, but I believe Alaric and Catherine never resumed normal marital relations. It wasn't long thereafter that Alaric began sleeping in his study. Nor was he as solicitous of Catherine as he once had been, and, interesting to me, Catherine no longer sought to manipulate him shamelessly for small favors. As if she knew she had cashed all her chips to secure his consent for their daughter's name.

With that said, Alaric's fondness for Catherine remained an active part of their life together. Alaric still laughed in spite of himself at Catherine's flirtatious repartee. His eyes brightened when she entered a room, and he continued to enjoy spoiling her as much as she enjoyed being spoiled. And when Catherine vanished that day, Alaric's devastation was gut-wrenching. All told, Alaric and Catherine were married for less than ten years. Speaking for myself and the staff, it seemed much longer than that. For Alaric, despite his anger at Catherine's recalcitrance over Elan's name, time never moved more quickly.

In the end, Catherine was a puzzle I never was able to solve. After risking her marriage to bestow a unique name on her daughter, she never used it. I had expected to hear "Elan this" and "Elan that" from Catherine as the girl grew older. But Catherine largely ignored both children and rarely called either by name. I thought perhaps she wished to avoid antagonizing Alaric by appearing to rub in her victory. But even when Alaric was away, sometimes for weeks at a time, Catherine would never address her daughter as Elan. Apparently she didn't enjoy the name spilling from her lips as much as she had once let on.

28

Elan

The carriage ride to Stille is a competition between my breathing and my heartbeat. Both are rapid. The bucolic countryside of the southern Riege is stunning, even in the autumn. I wonder why anyone voluntarily lives in the flatlands. Pastures and forests have their place. Mountains, too. But this landscape –the rolling hills, the rivers and streams, the flowering trees and bushes – is beyond gorgeous.

And it matches my mood. Since Stille was taken, I had pushed away worries that I would never see him again. That I would be another Amelia, trying to live life without her *Anaiah*. I assured myself I would survive. I would cope. I would grieve but I would move on. I would not succumb to rage and try to destroy the world.

I would be okay.

"You're smiling," Sylvia says.

"Am I?" I say, smiling.

She tosses me an indulgent glance. An older woman wishing she could be young again, and in love. Perched on the seat next to her grandmother, Marta wears an enigmatic expression. Absentmindedly, Marta strokes the silver dagger by her shoulder. Sylvia squeezes her granddaughter's hand, then draws it to her mouth for a kiss.

"Soon you shall be reunited with your *Anaiah*," Marta says to me softly, her eyes direct and gleaming. "Your joy shall be complete." I laugh because I don't know if she's being serious or trying to be funny. Her expression gives me no answer.

Our carriages slow, and I know we are almost there. I push my head out the window. I need to see ahead. Suddenly the landscape doesn't matter.

"Elan, please withdraw yourself back into the carriage," Sylvia instructs. "We don't know who's out there. That's not safe."

"I don't care," I say, searching the roadside for Stille. For his carriage. For anything that suggests he's here. It is midafternoon and the air smells sticky sweet.

"The latest message," Sylvia says, "informs me they've constructed a makeshift tent well off the cartpath. We should be quiet. He's had a rough time. I believe he's sleeping."

"Not for long," I say.

"He's been through an ordeal," Sylvia emphasizes.

"So have I," I say.

Our carriage lumbers along, but I bang open the door and jump out. Striding through the underbrush, I swat away branches, ignore the buzzing insects, and spy large off-color sheets flapping in the breeze. The tent! I start running, fight my way through the wind-splayed fabric, and there is Stille, large as life, sitting on an improvised wooden bed. His face and upper torso are even worse than before. Scrapes and cuts. Dried blood. Blue and red and yellow-black bruises. The brothers must have taken turns beating him.

His face lights when he sees me, and I skid down to my knees. I grab hold of both cheeks and kiss him on the lips. It's a fast hard forceful kiss. Not a long lingering let's-think-about-later kiss.

"Well, that was nice," he says.

Then I hug him, and he hugs me, and my eyes are closed so tight. I never want to lose him again. Never want to be anywhere if he's not with me. We came so close to losing each other. That can't happen again.

Then I pull back and punch him with two hands in his shoulders.

"Ouch!" he says.

"That's for leaving me in Cowardston without saying goodbye," I say, my eyes wide and my expression fierce. I shake him by his shoulders.

"I'm so sorry about that, Elan. I knew I should say something, but I was still angry at you, and I just stormed off, and then the brothers found me . . ."

"I know, I know," I say, hugging him again.

"And all the time the brothers had me, I thought, you know, this is the end. They're going to kill me. I'll never see Elan again. And we never got to say good-bye, and that's all my fault."

"No, it's all my fault," I say. "I should have told you about the rubystone. I was so stupid, and I'm so sorry."

"Well, we don't have to worry about saying good-bye ever again," Stille says. "You're here, and I'm here and, I mean, I'm still in one piece, and I'm a fast healer, and we can fulfill our missions. Like we promised each other."

I am dimly aware that others are watching our reunion with amusement from the tent flap. I don't care. All I know is I have Stille back in my life. Back by my side.

"Tell us about the Karator who tried to kill you," Sylvia says, her voice tender but firm.

"I only witnessed the tail-end of it," Stille says. "The brothers kept me bound and gagged in their detention area. This small squat red-skinned guy lurches into the room holding a knife. He has white hair, and his skin color is thinning, so I think he must have been old. And he protests loudly how he doesn't want to do this. He doesn't want to hurt anyone. But he can't help himself. Can't control his actions. He begs them to stop him before he goes too far."

"How did he get into your room?" Sylvia asks.

"I don't know," Stille says, "but the brothers descended on him like fire ants. They beat him down. One of them clubbed his head, and he went limp as a dishrag."

"Dead?" Sylvia asks.

"Maybe," Stille says. "The brothers dragged out the body. But Praelat Ortun panicked. He seemed to think all the Karators in Elden were a threat. That they were an army working for Our Master. Ortun said it was time to take care of the Karator menace once and for all."

"Did the attacker say anything about Our Master?" Sylvia says.

"No," Stille says. "But he acted strangely. Like he was possessed."

"Not possessed," Anselm Grist says, poking his head through the tent flap. "Enchanted. Probably from years ago. Maybe even twenty or thirty. The problem with Karator enchantments is they erode over time. The compulsion remains, but the subject partially reestablishes free will. This Karator's mission was to kill you, but he was sufficiently aware to fight it."

"So you're saying," Marta asks, "that Our Master was already preparing for Elan and Stille twenty or thirty years ago?"

"Yes," Grist says. "And I doubt this gentleman was the only Karator he enchanted. I'm sure there were others. They may still be out there."

"But Our Master didn't enchant the entire riverfront of Elden," I say.

"No," Grist agrees. "The vast majority of Karators who died in the Elden catastrophe, maybe even all of them, knew nothing of this. It was a senseless slaughter. Borne of fear and ignorance.

But the brothers are like that. They make snap decisions and execute them ruthlessly."

"If we want information on Our Master's efforts inside the Riege," Allamonde says, "there is someone we can question. Some years back, the palace imprisoned a Karator spy. They did not want him in the general prison population, so they caged him at the king's summer house in Magestor."

"Well, it's on the way to Kimbar," Sylvia says.

"Elan, do your powers work on Karators?" Stille asks.

"There's only one way to find out," I say.

Sylvia turns to Allamonde. "Can it be done? Quietly and quickly? We need to know the scope of the danger."

"Yes, Madame Leader," Allamonde says, bowing slightly. "I know someone who works there. Not a patron, but a friend. The house and grounds are empty – the king hasn't been there in years – and they have only one prisoner. This Karator. So it's a skeleton staff. I should be able to arrange something, well, quite clandestine."

"Then make it happen," Sylvia says, and Allamonde's ample mustache twitches merrily. Sylvia seems wary and weary. Marta, her granddaughter and protector, rarely leaves her side. But then, Sylvia is nearly as old as Gregor, and our greatest challenges are ahead. Magestor is another bump in a rough and rutted road.

I insist on riding in the carriage with Stille. He is so weak he can barely walk. He nestles into the corner and falls asleep under a blanket as the carriage rocks down narrow country lanes. The only healing spells I know work on right legs, and his seems fine.

I stare at him. I want to touch him. Smooth his hair. Stroke his cheek. His lips. Hug him tightly. I reach over, only to withdraw my hand. He needs rest. Lots of it. I already disturbed him once. Anything more would be selfish.

"I suppose we could find a straitjacket," Sylvia suggests, smiling. "That would ensure you keep your hands to yourself."

"I'll be good," I say, shoving my hands in my pockets and pretending to pout.

"The books say the connection between a memory witch and her human crystal is incredibly strong," Sylvia says. "Now I'm seeing the evidence firsthand. I think the only thing as strong as your feelings for Stille may be his feelings for you."

"We make a good team," I say.

"A powerful team," Sylvia says, raising her eyebrows.

Sylvia has no idea how powerful. I think back to the hillside in the compound. Stille wasn't even there in person. Just his shirt with a bloodstain. And I was able to read, well, what did I read? Not a living person. The dirt and grass, I guess. The horrible event. An atrocity occurred, and the location showed it to me. I bet there's nothing in the books about that.

And I am no longer seeking justice merely for Father and Willem. I now have fifty orphan boys to add to the list. Somewhere inside me, I carry their pain. Their gift to me. I don't feel different. Maybe more tired. But then it's been an exhausting week.

"So what's this about a rubystone?" Sylvia asks.

I say nothing.

"You know," she says gently, "the one you forgot to tell Stille about."

"I guess it's not a secret anymore," I say.

"No," she agrees.

"So I have this rubystone," I say at last. "A gift from my mother. Gregor warned me never to use it because it could be enchanted. Stille says Amelia had one."

"Catherine," she says.

"Yes, my mother," I say.

"Do you remember her?"

"No."

"From what I've heard, your father was the only one who ever cared for her."

"Gregor intimated the same."

"Did she leave a note when she left?"

"No," I say, then stare out the window.

"I'm sorry," Sylvia says. "It can't be enjoyable to discuss her."

"No," I agree. "It isn't."

I don't know why, but I pull out the burlap bag, untie the strings, and pour the rubystone into my hand. Sylvia gasps while Marta suppresses a wicked laugh.

"Put that away, child!" Sylvia says.

"Do you suppose it's Amelia's?" I ask.

"The mere possibility that gem is Amelia's is

reason enough never to use it," she says, holding her breath. I drop the stone in the bag, which I shove into my leathers. Our discussion of the rubystone has ended.

The rubystone doesn't like when I talk about it, I think. *It wants not to be seen.*

"What do you know about this Karator prisoner?" I ask, changing the subject.

Sylvia shrugs. "His name is Kortok. He's been a model prisoner. The purple palace believes he's waiting for something before he dies. What, they don't know. We've gotten remarkably little information from him over the years."

"Is he enchanted like the Karator who tried to harm Stille?"

"We must assume so, Elan."

Our convoy arrives at the rear of the property in the early evening. Even from the backside in late autumn, the king's summer home is magnificent. The orchards, the gardens, the statuary, the ponds – they are immaculate and stretch as far as I can see. The house is enormous and decorated with intricate frescoes of all colors. Like a skating rink, a blue-and-red marble patio extends the width of the house.

"For dancing," Sylvia says. "The king and his queen consort used to throw parties here. They danced all night."

"I thought he never comes here," I say.

"He hasn't since his wife died," Sylvia says. "I think it reminds him too much of her."

"You've been here, haven't you?" I ask.

Sylvia smiles. "A time or two. With my mother when she attended a duchess. It was quite a sensory experience for a young girl. Marcellus's father was king then. His name was Albert."

I point at the flags on the roof. "Why are the flags at half-mast?"

"For the queen consort, of course."

"How long has she been dead?"

"Ten years at least."

"And they're still at half-mast?"

"Marcellus still grieves."

Allamonde hustles to our carriage, gesticulating expansively. "Come, my ladies," he whispers. "We have an audience with the prisoner. We should do what we came to do, then be off before we are noticed."

I wake Stille, and our group marches to Allamonde's lead. We are ten. Stille and me. Sylvia and Marta. Allamonde and Anselm Grist. And four other patrons. Men and women who wear red corsages and smile at me and are prepared to die for me even though we've never said hello. People who took an oath but never expected they would be called upon to serve. But the call has come, and they have left their lives and loved ones to honor their oaths.

I don't know if I deserve all this.

Allamonde ushers us into a small courtyard. It is ringed by tall Fonteyns, sleek stylish evergreen trees with dense branches and soft needles. The pond in the middle has been emptied of water for the winter. A small man sits on an ornate black bench. His eyes search for me, and he smiles broadly.

Allamonde's unsmiling friend leans to him. "You have fifteen minutes, my old comrade, then I must return the prisoner."

Kortok stands as I approach. I know before he takes a step that he will limp. His mustache is white, but I know that once upon a time, it was jet black. His skin is now rued a sickly red, but in days past it was as white as any Riegian's. I know these things because I have seen this man before.

He extends his hand to me. "It is a pleasure, my lady, to meet you at last," he says amiably.

I don't take his hand. Instead, I stick my face into his.

"Where's my mother?" I demand.

29

Elan

Kortok is smaller than I remember from Darine. In that memory I snatched from Master Jedders. Kortok drops his hand, but his smile does not waver. He is genuinely pleased to see me.

"I do not know where your mother is, my lady," he says.

I glare at him, and he beams at me.

"Was it the scribe, or the butcher?" he says, a finger to his mouth.

"I'm sorry?"

"I'm trying to determine whose memory you read in Darine. You obviously saw Catherine and me together. I'm guessing it was the butcher, or that filthy drunken scribe, what was his name . . ."

"Master Jedders," I say.

"Yes, him."

"It was Master Jedders," I say. I don't know why I'm telling him this. I'm supposed to be the one asking the questions. He's supposed to be the one giving the answers.

"When one goes through life knowing a memory witch is to come along," he says cheerfully, "one becomes cognizant of the memories one creates in others. Memories that could be harvested years into the future. It's a strange sensation, but in some ways quite exhilarating."

"I'll ask again," I say. "Where is my mother?"

"I was not dissembling, my lady," he says. "I truly do not know. My job was to transport her to Darine and make sure she boarded a sliprider down the Tablas."

"Pier Four," I say. "The underdecks."

"Precisely!" he says.

"And you don't know where she went?"

"I do not. That is how Our Master operates. Everything is compartmentalized. I had a job. I did it. I never saw Catherine again."

I am disappointed, but I try not to show it.

"There is method to his madness," Kortok says. "It limits the number of useful memories inside a single person. The work of a memory witch becomes more arduous."

"I could read your memories to see if you're telling the truth," I say.

"Elan!" Sylvia exclaims.

"Please do," Kortok says, holding out his bare arm.

"He may be enchanted," Grist says dourly.

"I most certainly am enchanted," Kortok says. "As I was all those years ago in Darine. But as my captors can confirm, I am now fraying at the edges. Well, more than fraying, actually. I've been coming apart for some years now. I am going decidedly downhill, and the slope is getting steeper."

"So die," Marta says heartlessly.

"If only it were that easy," he says. "I have one last task. Then my service to Our Master is concluded and, mercifully, I can pass from this mortal coil."

"What task?"

"I need you to read me," he says, shaking his wrist.

"It's a trap," Grist says, swatting Kortok's wrist.

"I don't even know if I can read a Karator," I say.

"It's not a trap," Kortok says. "And, yes, you can read a Karator. After a fashion, that is."

"Meaning what?" Sylvia says.

"Meaning if I were not enchanted, you could read my memories the same as any Riegian. Really, you people amaze me sometimes. Karators are humans, too. We are a different ethnicity, but not a different species. Our lady here can read a Karator as easily as any Riegian."

"But you *are* enchanted," I say.

"Yes," he says expansively. "Which means you can only access the memories I am permitted to share. Our Master is capable of altering those memories. It's time-consuming and exhausting, but he can do it. In this case, I can assure you, he has not done so. The memories he wishes you to see – or, rather, the memory, singular, not plural – is quite accurate. I was there, obviously, so I know."

It is now evening, but the moonlight illumines the small elegant courtyard. Everything is motionless. Quiet. As if someone is trying hard to listen from thousands of miles away.

Kortok turns his gaze to Stille.

"Ah, the *Anaiah*. You have survived this far into the story. Good for you! I didn't know if I would get to see you. But I'm glad you are here."

Stille frowns and opens his mouth, but says nothing.

"So you haven't broken your crystal yet," Kortok says.

"I'm not going to break him," I say, clenching my teeth.

"It is not my task to harm you," Kortok says to Stille. "So be not afraid. My task is to live until I share a memory with the young lady. Nothing more is left on my to-do list."

"How long has this memory existed inside you?" Sylvia asks.

"Twenty-two years," he says.

"We should go," Grist says. "There can't be anything of value in a memory that old. The risks are too great."

"The only risk is learning information you may find disagreeable or not know what to do with," Kortok says.

"What kind of information?" Grist says, towering over Kortok.

"The memory is only for the young lady," he says. "No one else."

"I'll do it," I say. Is that me talking or the rubystone in my pocket? I think it's me, but I can't be sure.

"I'm here for you," Stille says. "If you need me, reach out with your hand."

"It is your decision, Elan," Sylvia says, wringing her hands, "but are you certain? Absolutely certain?"

I nod. It feels right. Our Master has something to say to me. And he knows things I want to know. I need to see what this funny little almost-red man has lurking inside of him. I may never have another opportunity.

I select a pure white fabric and a small crystal. If Kortok has a single memory, and it's intended for me alone, it shouldn't take much to access it.

Normally I enter the subject's head before accessing memories. Not this time. I enter directly into Kortok's memory, which disorients me. I see an old man in a rocking chair. His hair is gone, and his face is deathly pallid, but his eyes gleam. There is no trace of red I can see in his skin. His head is cocked, his demeanor pleasant, even affable. He wears simple white clothes the color of my fabric.

"Hello Elan," he says, rocking rhythmically. "This communication has been a long time coming. Permit me to introduce myself. My given name is not important. My people, the Karator people, the people of the red tint, call me Our

Master. They lovingly bestowed that name upon me centuries ago, and I cherish it more now than ever.

"You may have fair reason to bear me ill will, so let's get this out in the open. You are a memory witch because of me. I placed an enchantment on your mother. If she were to marry a born-and-bred with whom the Fluence was strong, any girl child would be a memory witch. The first, I believe, in quite a long time. The first since Rador-amelia of House Marton. That happened, and here you are.

"If you worry that you are now half Karator, let me put your concerns to rest. Not that Karator blood is anything to be ashamed or afraid of. We are people as much as Riegians. But there has been a robust Riegian community inside Karator since before the Kangor became, what do you call it, the Impassable River. They were refugees torn from the Riege by war. We offered to return the captives, but our offer was spurned. Your mother came from this community, and her blood is undiluted Riegian.

"If you dislike being a memory witch, Elan, then you have me and only me to blame. I apologize, although I have my reasons for what I have done, which you shall understand shortly. On the other hand, if you are pleased with your powers, then I suppose you owe me something more than thanks. After all, it took enormous preparation and effort over a long period of time to make my plans a reality. To give you the powers you have today.

"In addition to my powers of enchantment, I

also enjoy the gift of sight. It is not always as clear or comprehensive as I would like, but as I have grown older, my vision, when focused, has been on target. What more proof do you need than this memory, this communication, which comes to you across time. I foresaw your rise as a memory witch, and now it is a reality by my hand and my hand alone.

"The Riege is crumbling. Your king is weak and losing control of his bureaucracy. The Order is comprised of brutish authoritarians who can no more rule the Riege than honor whatever deity they pretend to worship. Chaos is at hand. Thousands of Riegians will die or be tyrannized unless action is taken.

"Elan, there are only two people who can restore just order in the Riege. You and me. I propose we work together to do so. That we form an alliance and rule Karator and the Riege as a single unified continent. As it once was. Before the Kangor was transformed into a barrier against commerce and travel and understanding. Before skin color became more important than our common humanity.

"It will not be easy. In fact, it will be more difficult than anything I have undertaken in my very long life. I need your help, and we are more alike than you know. I am prepared to work cooperatively with you to ensure that our actions serve a common humane purpose.

"There is nothing you need to do at this moment in response to my message. Other than think about it. You've seen what the Riege has become. The violence people inflict on each other. Vicious and untamed. It will only get worse unless we act together. I have seen the future. It is beautiful, but only if we make it so together.

"After a due period, I will present you with an opportunity to respond to this message. Trust me, you will know when that time has come."

At that moment in the memory, a Riegian woman sits next to Our Master and takes his hand. Catherine! My mother, so young and beautiful. And then Kortok's mind ejects me, and I land hard in my own body again.

I blink several times to orient myself. Before I can speak, Kortok coughs, and his eyes bulge. He smiles awkwardly. "Thank you," he says. "At last . . . I am freed . . . of the enchantment." Kortok falls to his knees, and puts his hands to his mouth. "I am finally . . . alone . . . in my own head . . . one last time."

I drop down onto my knees. I am face-to-face with the dying man. "Kortok, why was it necessary to come get my mother? Why did she leave?"

"Because, dear lady . . . Our Master learned . . . of Mordecai's plan to attack . . . the villa."

"He did not want Catherine to die?"

"Yes," he croaks.

"Is this something he knew in advance?" I ask. "Years in advance?"

Kortok smiles but does not answer.

I grab his shoulders and shake him. "Answer me!"

His eyes begin to roll back, but he fights against it for one last moment of clarity. "Beware the rubystone, my lady," he croaks. Then he keels backward, and his chest heaves once before he dies.

"What did Our Master say?" Grist says, ignoring Kortok's quivering corpse. Everyone tenses.

"He wants to rule the Riege together," I say. "The two of us."

"And you said . . .," Marta demands.

"I didn't say anything," I said. "It was a memory from twenty-some years ago."

"But he knew you would be here, today, with Kortok?" Allamonde asks, his eyes troubled.

"I don't know how much he knew about the logistics," I say, "but the message was for me."

"He knew you by name?" Sylvia asks.

"Yes," I say.

"Names are everything in the Karator world," Grist says urgently. "Did he tell you his?"

"He said it was not important."

They ask more questions, and I answer curtly. I know they want to be helpful, but I need to be alone with this new information.

I am struck by what Our Master did not say. He did not mention Stille. Or the rubystone. Which means he wasn't sure I would have either one when I received the memory. All he knew – all he *really* knew – was that I existed, and my name was Elan. And my existence was no feat of vision since the memory was targeted for me. If I had died or did not become a memory witch or had never been born, the memory would not have been accessed.

The only aspect of the memory that showed real foreknowledge was my name. Somehow he knew Alaric and Catherine would call me Elan.

I pity Kortok, whose body has shriveled horribly under the moonlight behind the king's summer house. It disappears almost before my eyes. I decide then and there that I will not accept Our Master's offer. This is a man to whom everyone else is an object. He uses them cruelly and, when he is done with them, tosses them away like garbage. Like Kortok.

And in the end, I suppose, like Catherine.

30

Elan

Stille is unnaturally quiet. He and I share a carriage by ourselves on the road to Kimbar. Privacy, at last. We can finally talk without being overheard. I have so much to tell him. What I've learned about Brother Mordecai, the atrocity on the hillside, and the murders of Father and Willem. But also what Anselm Grist told me about his family's village.

"What's bothering you?" I ask. I reach for his hand, and he lets me take it. I squeeze. He squeezes back.

"Kortok," he says after a pause.

"Yes, that was horrible," I say. "Our Master destroyed the man's life. All so he could share a memory with me."

"Not that," Stille says. "But yes, that was horrible. Our Master is a tyrant."

"Then what?"

"How he knew years ago that you would be born. A memory witch in the flatlands named Elan."

"Yes, very creepy," I say.

"Something like that happened to me as well," Stille says.

I say nothing. I discover that, without intending to do so, I am holding my breath. I am on information overload. I'm past the point of seeking new revelations.

Stille stares out the coach window. His hand searches for mine, and I take it emphatically.

"So tell me," I say at last.

"I never asked Uncle Martin about how I arrived in his household that morning. It never occurred to me. I was like most kids, I guess. I took for granted what was. But a neighbor asked him. Uncle Martin said a strange woman dressed in white was about to leave me in a basket on the step. He thought he heard something, so he opened the door. She smiled and handed me to him. He said she had the most beautiful smile he had ever seen."

"What's so unusual about that?"

"It's what happened next. The woman explained that I was his nephew, and my parents had died tragically with their entire village in a disaster. So he was the only family I had left. Uncle Martin said he asked her name, and she said it wasn't important. And then, according to Uncle Martin, she said something strange about my eyes."

And then she left."

"What was wrong with your eyes?" I ask.

"Uncle Martin said he took me to a healer, who found nothing wrong with them. So he just assumed it was a stray remark of no significance."

"Maybe it was," I say.

Stille turns to me, his face pinched. "Elan, the woman wasn't talking about my eyes. She must have told him I was an *Anaiah*. I'm certain of it. But Uncle Martin didn't know that word or what it meant. So all he heard was something about my eyes."

I say nothing. Like this strange woman, Our Master also declined to give his name. Said it wasn't important.

"I never figured it out until today," Stille said. "When Kortok delivered a memory to you by name from over twenty years ago."

"I doubt it means anything," I say.

"Are you sure, Elan? Really sure?"

"No," I admit.

"And who was the strange woman in white?"

"I don't know, Stille. We may never know."

For the next hour, I talk his ear off about what happened to me while he was a prisoner. This time he doesn't fall asleep! And then I tell him about my conversation with Anselm Grist. And Grist's claim that Stille's parents were childless.

"That's not true," Stille says, displaying himself with his hands. "Obviously, I was born. I mean, ta-da!"

I laugh.

"And Bearwallow was a small village in the middle of nowhere," he says. "I doubt they kept fastidious records like the bureaucrats in Kimbar. And I was a newborn, so maybe they just hadn't gotten around to the paperwork yet."

"That's probably it," I say.

"But Grist really believes Our Master destroyed the village in order to kill me?"

"He can't come up with another reason."

"So someone else knew I was an *Anaiah*. Like the woman in white. But how would they have known? How could anyone have known?"

"I don't know, Stille. More questions we can't answer."

"Well, I guess Our Master's vision was imprecise. He destroyed an entire village, which means he didn't know which family to target."

"Maybe," I say.

"And even then I survived," Stille says. "Somehow."

"Yes, somehow," I say.

At that moment, light pops over the horizon and into our carriage. Another dawn. Destiny is a day closer.

The nearer we get to Kimbar, the less we talk. Stille's face gleams, and he fidgets excitedly. His head is out the window. Basking in the sights and sounds and scents. Kimbar is his home. He has dreamed of this day for the entire time he spent in Montauk with Master Depsik. He is nearly home.

Kimbar lies on the land like a finely brocaded quilt. It has been constructed in concentric circles.

The inner circle is the palace, surrounded by the famous purple wall. Built of Paemok sandstone, the wall turns from dull tan to bright lavender when the temperature of the rock rises quickly. In summer, tourists gather before midday to witness the spectacular event. It rarely occurs in winter, and today, even from this distance, the wall is the color of dried mud.

The outer circles were built as the city expanded over the centuries. Status and prestige are higher, closest to the palace. The old-money families, including many born-and-bred, reside in the first ring. After five rings, growth was a sprawl. A free-for-all among those who had money or ambition. Even from these hills, I can see the parks and public buildings, and far to the south, the deep dark blue of the ocean. Somewhere in Kimbar are distant relations, although none with the Montescue family name. They say Catherine arrived in Kimbar from beneath the ocean, and maybe she did. But I know now where her journey originated. From Karator, where she sat at the right hand of Our Master.

"We lived just outside the fifth ring," Stille says in a low intense voice. "See that public park with cherry trees massed in the middle," he says, pointing. "You know, the one with the white marble statue of a young King Albert? Our street was two up towards the palace, and one over."

Kimbar is massive, and I have no idea where he's pointing. "Okay," I say, squinting. My head is next to his in the carriage window. I do not kiss him because it's his turn to kiss me. Or something. I shake my head slightly, and my red curls caress his left ear. He reaches up and scratches.

"You can't really see the house from here, but it's there," he says. "It's not big, but it's big enough."

"For one person," I say, remembering his previous description.

"Yes," he says, not taking his gaze from the panorama. "Although Uncle Martin and I managed to squeeze in together."

Our caravan pulls off the cartpath and into a grove of ten-point jaffur trees. The glossy green leaves will cut you wide open if you so much as brush by them. The leaves are sharper the more points they have.

As Stille and I step out to stretch our legs, Sylvia approaches. Like she's made up her mind about something. Head down, hands in her pockets, and a quick stride. Marta is two steps behind.

"We have a plan to enter the palace," she says. "It's risky, but I think it will work."

The others circle around. Sylvia explains that Brother Mordecai heads a large contingent from the Order housed inside the palace. They interrogated the brothers taking Stille and learned that the carriage was to be admitted through a small rear entrance. Praelat Ortun and his private staff would verify the prisoner and then escort Stille through back-palace corridors into the Order's main sanctum.

"Has Brother Mordecai delivered his ultimatum to the king?" I ask.

"Yes," Sylvia says. "Last night. Submit peacea-bly, or we'll tear the Riege apart."

"What did the king say?"

"He's mulling options," Sylvia says. "Mordecai insists that he abdicate and hand the crown to Prince Standish. Standish is an Order sympathizer from early on. He even sought to join the Order until Mordecai realized he would be more valuable inside the palace."

"What are they planning to do with Stille?" I ask. My hands tremble. I'm not certain I wish to hear the answer.

"He's a dead man walking," Sylvia says. "The Order wants you out of the way, Elan. If they be-lieve Stille can be used to that end, they'll keep him alive. Otherwise, they'll kill him now and be done with it. But they need him here at the palace. El-den is no longer secure."

"How do you know all this?" Stille asks, his brow furrowed.

"We have people inside the palace," Sylvia says, her eyes sparkling. "Some are, how shall I put this, quite well placed."

"How long does King Marcellus have to give Mordecai his answer?"

"Twenty-four hours," Sylvia says. "So, tonight."

"I'm assuming you have a plan," I say.

"Yes, but it involves using Stille as bait," she says.

"No," I say. I flash my hands outward. I don't even want to discuss it.

"I'll do it, Elan," Stille insists. "This is my fight, too. This is everyone's fight. If using me as bait will get us into the palace, then I'm game."

"Stille . . .," I plead.

He turns to me. "It'll be all right, Elan. You'll see."

Then he turns back to Sylvia. "What do I need to do?"

"We're going to bind you and gag you and put you back in that carriage. The one you left Elden in. We need them to believe their stratagem to sneak you into Kimbar has worked. Except, of course, we'll have our people under the black robes. Once Stille is verified, the guards will direct us to Praelat Ortun. Once that occurs, we'll pounce."

"I'm in the carriage," I say.

"No, Elan," Sylvia says. "It's too dangerous, and you're too valuable."

"This is not negotiable," I say. "If we're using Stille as bait, I want to be there with him. We're not splitting up again."

Sylvia purses her lips.

"Besides, if we find ourselves in a pinch, you'd be surprised what Stille and I can accomplish together. A memory witch and her *Anaiah*."

Sylvia sighs. "Yes, we heard about the forest in the flatlands. Did you really do that?"

I smile at her.

"Fine," she says wearily. "But you'll have to wear a black robe. It won't be fun."

"It can't smell as bad as the last one I wore," I

say, thinking of my disguise at the chall in Darine.

"Who else will go?" Stille asks.

"You have my sword," Allamonde says.

"And my dagger," Marta says.

"Well, I don't have a weapon on me," Anselm Grist grouses, "but I suppose I can find a stick somewhere. Anyway, I'm in. I know the palace grounds like the back of my hand. I can help us maneuver."

"So six of us on or inside the carriage," Sylvia says.

"How many brothers are now inside the palace?" Stille asks.

"Several hundred, I believe," Sylvia says.

"And how do we plan to reach Brother Mordecai?" I ask.

Sylvia takes a deep breath. "Let's just get inside first, shall we? One impossible task at a time."

Smiling ruefully, Marta holds up the gag and some twine. It is time to prepare the bait.

Suddenly Stille grabs my shoulders, and he kisses me on the lips. Our eyes open together, mine in surprise. "For good luck," he whispers. It all happens so fast, I don't think to kiss him back.

Then Sylvia applies the gag, and they lead Stille to the carriage.

31

Gregor's Journal

The day started earlier than most. I had promised Elan a lesson on edible plant roots. So before dawn I headed past the partially-built structures of Alaric's dream villa to the west pasture. No one was up when I left.

I felt good about myself. Events were conspiring, if indirectly, decidedly in my favor. Catherine had militated for long months to replace me with a young woman to attend her more closely. The children were without fluential abilities, or so we thought at the time, and a remedial tutor for the types of subjects the dearths studied – reading, writing and whatnot – came much more cheaply than a snooty prissy born-and-bred tutor from Kimbar. Mercifully, Catherine's flight ended all talk of replacing me with a less credentialed if younger dearth.

And then Alaric's and my discovery, literally days after Catherine vanished, that Elan was a memory witch removed any doubt that I would be gainfully employed to the end of my natural days. Ebbs may come and go, but sorcerers require careful instruction if they are to become useful. And the first memory witch in a thousand years, well, it would be full-time employment. I was even considering approaching Alaric for funds to hire an assistant tutor, whom I would oversee rigorously.

The greater concern, of course, was how to ensure that news of Elan's abilities did not leak before we were in a position to prevent reprisals and inquisitions. The dearths would be fearful, but the born-and-bred even more so. It was dangerous for all concerned to have a memory witch on premises. Given her age, it was a distinct possibility, as so often happened with young sorcerers, that her instinctive abilities would gradually subside. Like a strange allergy, her unwitting knack for entering heads and sorting memories – a magician plucking a rabbit from a hat! – might fade to nothing with a bit more time. We could certainly hope so, anyway.

When I returned from the west pasture that morning, Elan was up, and we headed for the cellar. There was stirring in the house, but I had no reason to pay further attention, so I did not. But when I heard strange noises outside, the hair on the back of my neck – my tutor's intuition – told me something was seriously amiss. It didn't help that Alaric and I had held a lengthy and detailed discussion the night before regarding which parties might wish to take matters into their own hands if they learned the Riege harbored another memory witch. But we were both certain, as I am today, that word had not leaked out. He and I were the only two to recognize the fluential implications of Elan's cerebral horseplay, so she was, we assumed, safe for the moment.

Upstairs, the house was filled with smoke, and a young girl, Dezzie, had struck her head on the fireplace hearth. I felt for a pulse and found none. Alaric had hurried the other staff out the back door, trusting that whomever was attacking did not wish to divert their attention and resources by targeting servants. He was correct about that, and it almost certainly saved lives.

"You must do something!" I wailed at him. By then, I had seen the attackers circling the house on their steeds. Their strange red uniforms and hoods did not inspire confidence that they would be reasonable.

And Alaric laughed! He actually laughed! He was minutes away from death, and he threw his head back and roared. He was, after all, a weather sorcerer. "Gregor, what would you have me do?" he said. "Make it rain and water them to death?"

He put his hand on my shoulder. "Elan is all that matters, Gregor. Willem and I are as good as dead. In a minute, I will dash out the side door and see if I can find him in one of the outbuildings. But we will not survive. There is a tunnel leading from the cellar out the east pasture. It's in the corner behind the corncribs. You must take Elan to safety. Be sure to take the crystals and rubystone with you."

Then he looked over at the dead girl. "But first I want you to bring up some of Elan's clothes. Anything that looks like it cost money. Dress that girl in them. I think her name is Dezzie. If she were alive, she'd forgive us. When all of this burns to the ground, they'll think the corpse is Elan. Which means they won't keep looking for her."

I followed my instructions to the letter, returning with Elan's garments. I hastily dressed Dezzie. Alaric had armed himself with sharp kitchen utensils and was preparing to sprint out the door.

"You can save yourself," I said. "We both love Willem, but there is nothing to be done for him."

"You are right, dear friend," he said, "as you almost always are. Except there is one thing I can do for Willem. Just one. I can die with him. He should not go alone, and I will not let him. Tell Elan I love her. She is now your responsibility."

I think he saw me pause. I had never been responsible for another living creature before.

"You can do this, Gregor," he said, hugging me. "After all," he whispered into my ear, "you are the last great tutor of the tenth Ebb."

And then he was gone.

I have thought back many times on our conversations over the years, especially those in the last few months about Elan. He never would tell me why, but he seemed confident that King Marcellus would not seek to harm her. I pressed him, and all I received back was Alaric's inscrutable smile. The one that said he knew something I didn't.

"Give me one good reason," I asked Alaric on an unseasonably warm evening as we sat in the courtyard with snifters of brandy, "why we shouldn't fear the wrath of King Marcellus." Alaric looked at me seriously, clapped me on the shoulder, and said, quite mysteriously, "Let's just say, Gregor, that I am willing to trust any man who is known for wearing a red corsage."

32

Elan

At least I'm riding on the inside of the carriage. If nothing else, Stille and I are together. I think about our hit-and-run kisses. We are skittish with each other. We don't know what we want today or if we'll continue wanting it tomorrow. All I know is I think about him constantly. I feel empty when he's gone, and the thought of people hurting him enrages me.

Amelia gave in to rage, I think. *Look where it got her.*

Stille is bound and gagged in his seat. I suggested we wait until reaching the back gate before tying him up. Sylvia decided otherwise. Our carriage, she said, could be stopped at any point. Even before we reach the palace walls. Stille needs to be exactly how the brothers expect to find him. And he needs to look like he's suffered. Of course, Stille didn't complain. He never does.

Allamonde and Marta ride outside on the front seatbox. They are the opposite sides of lethal. Allamonde, older and world-weary, seems so pleasant and patient. Like we have more time than we think. Marta, young and inexperienced, is so intense and humorless. Like everything is happening now. But each is capable of killing in a heartbeat. Anselm Grist rides with Sylvia in back. Grist isn't even a patron. Not formally, anyway. All he wants is to be back in Cowardston chewing his pipe and bathing in smoke. And Sylvia? She's mulling that debt she thinks she owes Gregor.

The carriage creeps along the byways of Kimbar, but then, that was Brother Mordecai's plan. He needed Stille at the purple palace, but he didn't need him there quickly. The carriage windows are curtained, so I catch mere glimpses of Kimbar. I've never been anywhere before where all the roads are wide and paved. Everything in Kimbar seems bigger. Clean and new and shiny. Even the brothers on the street seem fresh, their feet washed. And there is more of everything. More houses. More stores. More inns and taverns. More people.

And more danger. Despite its elegance, I have a feeling Kimbar is a city where you can get yourself killed easily. And if you're not careful, no one will miss you. Our carriage is spotted but not stopped. In Kimbar, there are eyes everywhere. Nothing goes by unnoticed. The city is tense. The people know momentous changes are brewing. The king weakens daily, while the Order strengthens and the Karators lurk. And Brother Mordecai is in town for a chat. The larger the house, the tighter the doors and windows are closed.

We reach the purple wall and turn left. We'll follow it around to the back. The side furthest from the ocean. Up close the wall isn't circular at all. There are long stretches of flat sandstone, and doors, some tiny, some large, are everywhere. The wall is a many-sided sieve.

"Getting through the wall is not the hard part," Sylvia says to me through the back opening. She always seems to know what I'm thinking. "There are a million ways to do it and just as many ways to be apprehended once inside. The kingsguard is experienced and efficient. What takes skill is penetrating the palace corridors."

The carriage comes to a creaking juddering halt, and then Grist jumps down from the carriage and pounds on a large wooden door.

"Showtime, everyone!" Sylvia says.

Two brothers, large and burly, lift the rusted metal latch on the inside, and the gate groans open. The expressions on the brothers' faces are dubious, and I reach for my cloth and crystal. I spy Stille's hand across from me on the seat. I wonder idly what an upside-down spell would do to the palace with Stille as my crystal. I'm not as concerned about the king as I once was, but I don't trust him yet either.

"You're late!" one brother accuses Grist.

Grist shrugs. "We were told there was no hurry."

The second brother swings our carriage door open and dips his head inside. My hood is up. He glances quickly at me but focuses on Stille, his eyes wide and in pain from the gag. Sylvia tied it tightly, and it has sliced into his face.

The brother chucks Stille hard in the chest. "You doing all right there, little brother?" Stille's rude response is muffled by the gag, and the brother chortles.

"And how is Brother Harold doing?" the first brother asks Grist. "You know, the one who runs the stables."

"I come from Cowardston," Grist mutters. "I don't know any Brother Harold."

"Good answer, my friend," the man says. "Because there is no Brother Harold at the Elden stables."

"There may not even be an Elden stables anymore," Grist says sourly. "The fire was yet gaining strength as we departed."

"The compound stands," the brother says, "but it may be all in Elden that does. The city is destroyed."

"As long as all the bloody Karators are dead," Grist spits out, "that's fine with me. We can rebuild the city. This time without those little red barbarians."

"Amen to that, Brother."

The second brother signals with his hand, and the first pulls the gates wider so the carriage can pass. "Stall number five," the first brother says. "The praelat awaits. He wishes to interview the prisoner himself."

Allamonde and Marta guide the carriage slowly toward the stall. As if we have all the time in the world. But my heart races. I haven't seen Praelat Ortun in person since Darine. And I remember him from the hillside. He was there that morning. He witnessed the slaughter of fifty innocents, and he laughed.

Lighting is dim inside the fifth stall. Wisps of sunlight negotiate passage through cracks in the boards. Wall sconces are lit, and Praelat Ortun, his jowls hanging lower than ever, holds a gold-plated chamberstick. The stall smells of horses and straw and manure. It reminds me of Montauk and the day I met Stille.

"Please present the prisoner!" Ortun demands in his best chall voice. A voice that commands instant obedience.

I grab Stille, and Sylvia whispers from behind, "Be rough with him!" So I put my arm around his shoulder, and as we shake and tumble out of the carriage, I bite Stille's neck like a frisky colt might.

"That's not what I meant!" Sylvia scolds.

I shove Stille in front of Praelat Ortun. Out of the praelat's sight, I snatch a mallet leaning against the wall while everyone else gathers, their black robes and hoods firmly in place. Sylvia and Grist, to my left. Allamonde and Marta, to my right. Ortun raises his chins and peers down at us over the plaster cast that used to be his nose. Before I shattered it with a head butt at the chall in Montauk. I remove Stille's gag, and he coughs and dribbles spit.

"So this is Stille Vespers," Ortun says with distaste, his jowls swaying.

"My name," Stille says, eyeing Ortun angrily, "is Paul Guiscard."

"And my name," Allamonde says, pulling down his hood, "is Paul Guiscard."

"My name is Paul Guiscard," Marta says.

"My name is Paul Guiscard," Sylvia and Grist say over top of each other.

"What is the meaning of this?" Ortun protests.

"My name is not Paul Guiscard," I say, lowering my hood. "My name is Elan Montescue, and we've met before." With that, I leap forward and club Ortun in his left temple. He drops to the floor, face first, like a bag of potatoes.

"I think our dear praelat may have reinjured his face," Allamonde says with false concern.

"One can only hope," I mutter.

"Elan," Sylvia says. "We need to know the room in which the first brother is staying. Quickly."

Praelat Ortun has a trained mind, but not when he's unconscious. I remove the blackest fabric with the tightest weave that I can find. My right hand twirls my favorite crystal. I don't need Stille for this.

I am inside the praelat's head without obstacles. I scroll through his memories like lightning. Brother Mordecai is in the green room. Portraits of other men with dour visages and black robes – first brothers, I assume – line the walls.

But I am not finished. Praelat Ortun was not at

our villa that awful day – he was not among the nineteen red-clad hooded riders – but he arrived on horseback with two attendants one day later. I try to remember where I was that day. Oh yes, Gregor and I, still terrified from Father's and Willem's murders and constantly peeking over our shoulders for pursuers, hiked steep dense forested mountains toward the family Keep.

The two bodies are still in the courtyard. Father and Willem. No one has moved them, much less buried them. They continued bleeding long past their deaths, and the dirt under them is saturated.

Ortun walks into the farmhouse ruins. Steam rises pertly into the morning air, and periodic hissing leaks from the embers.

"What about the wife?" someone says.

"We're not here for her," he says snippily. "We're searching for the daughter. Six years old. Red hair."

He looks at his attendants. "A bouncy disposition," he exclaims lightly, and the attendants guffaw.

"Was she a witch?" one of them asks.

"No," he says, and then his foot strikes something. He leans over, and there are the charred remains of a small person.

"I may have found her," Ortun announces. He grabs the skull by its chin, then drops it. The bone is still hot to the touch. He fishes an iron-pronged comb from his pocket and stirs the smoking remains. Pearl buttons. Inlaid silver. The remains of a barrette in the shape of a butterfly. A partially burned hand-sewn shoe.

"I've found the girl," he announces.

"Are you certain it's her?"

"Yes," he says. "Who else would wear pearls and silver on a weekday morning? Or a hand-carved ivory barrette? No, it's her. The little girl. We can assure the first brother the mission was completed. Fully and successfully. The Montescue family is no more."

Ortun strolls back into the courtyard. He pauses at the two bodies, Father and Willem. "Are we certain they're dead?" he asks playfully.

The attendants are already horseback. "Praelat, there's only one way to be sure," one of them sings out, his horse rearing and wheeling. He tosses Ortun a rope, and Ortun cackles.

"Yes, of course, we must be certain!" Ortun yells like a child, then he ties the rope tightly against Father's left ankle. Ortun motions wildly with his hands.

The attendant spurs his horse hard, and Father's body leaps into the air as the horse gallops away. Around and around the courtyard they run, the attendants whooping and Praelat Ortun chortling. Father's body bounces and shimmies, his head skipping like a stone against the courtyard bricks.

At last they tire of the game, and Ortun instructs them to place Father and Willem's bodies next to Dezzie's charred corpse.

"They lived useless lives," he proclaims grandly, "but at least they will march into eternity together."

I emerge from the reading like a house afire. I stomp through stall number five, looking for rope, anything I can tie to Praelat Ortun's feet.

"What are you doing?" Sylvia asks.

"Leave me alone!" I scream. I find some rope and march back to Ortun's unconscious body. I rip off his left golden slipper and tie the rope around his fat ankle. I pull it as tight as I can. Then I stand and look for the nearest horse.

"Elan, stop!" Sylvia says.

I wave her away. I am not going to stop. Never, ever. I am going to find a horse, and I am going to ride it through the palace, dragging Praelat Ortun's useless body behind me. I will glance back in hopes of seeing his head bounce on the stones and bricks.

"Elan!"

It is Stille, and I stop. My breathing is fast. My heartbeat is faster. I am so angry I could explode. I could explode the entire world.

"You have to calm down," he says. "Whatever you saw in the praelat's memories, you have to stop. We have a mission, and this is not it."

I stare at him.

"Here, take my hand," he says, reaching for me.

I break down in tears. "You should have seen what he did to my father," I cry. My face is awash with tears.

He kneels beside me and takes me into his arms. "I can imagine. And I'm so sorry. But it's a memory. What you saw happened ten years ago."

"It feels like now to me," I say.

"It was ten years ago."

I sense Sylvia there. And the others. They are watching and waiting and holding their breaths. I lean into Stille's arms. They feel so strong and safe.

"The green room," I hear myself say. "Mordecai is in the green room."

33

Elan

I absorb Stille's voice. I know he's trying to soothe me. Say things to calm me. But I don't hear the words. Just the sound of his voice. I lean in and give myself over to it. My breathing slows. He and I are one.

After tying up and gagging Praelat Ortun, Sylvia led us through back corridors, the royal kitchens, the largest chicken coop I have ever seen, and then the moist steaming laundry to a single unmarked door, which let us into the royal wing of the palace. Sylvia told us she often went to the palace as a child with her mother, and she learned her way in and out of various places she wasn't supposed to be.

Sylvia orders a short break, and Stille and I sit heavily against the thick red fabric on the wall. Lighting comes from through ceiling windows.

Everything smells fresh. Like mountain water with a twist of lemon. So royalty really do breathe different air than the rest of us.

"How is she doing?" Sylvia asks.

"Much better," Stille says. He hugs me tightly, and I hear his heartbeat. Faster than mine.

"There is someone she needs to see," Sylvia says.

I sit up straighter. "Who?"

She smiles, and her eyes sparkle. Like they did before. "You'll see," she says. "Come with me. Stille, walk with us."

Sylvia leads us around the corner. The room is tiny but beautiful. Ancient tapestries line the walls and portray scenes of past heroics by dead heroes. Gregor could identify each one, I'm sure. There are four ceilings, each a masterpiece. An intense work of art. Staring in wonderment, I sit at a polished marble table.

And then I am alone in the room. Sylvia is gone. And Stille.

"Hello," a voice says. I stare at a silhouette against the candlelights. It is a man, old and short, and then I realize who it must be. I stand.

"Please sit," King Marcellus says, motioning adroitly with one hand. "Please."

I sit, and he eases into a seat across from me. He dresses simply, except for a doublet of exquisite blue satin. He is shorter than his portraits. But his face is gentler, and kind. His hair is gray, his skin old, his beard neatly trimmed. He offers a hand, and I take it.

"My name is Marcellus," he says. "My friends call me Marko."

"I don't think I can call you Marko," I say bashfully.

"You don't have to call me anything," he says. His demeanor is soothing.

"I'm here on a mission," I say.

"I know why you're here," he responds.

"You do?"

"I knew your father," he says. "Well, I met him once, anyways."

"When was that?" I ask.

"The summer he met your mother," he says.

"Oh, her," I say.

"Well, whoever Catherine was, *whatever* she was, she did us all a favor," he says.

"And that would be?"

"Why, she gave us you, of course."

I groan. "Be careful what you wish for, your majesty," I say.

"And why is that?"

"I'm not sure I'm anything to be grateful for."

"I would argue the contrary," he says. "Quite strongly, in fact. We are past the tenth Ebb, and the Riege needs sorcerers like you."

"What you need," I say, "is my father. And he's gone."

"Your father was a fine man," he says.

"The last great sorcerer of the era," I say proudly.

"Why do you say that?" he probes gently.

"Everyone said so," I say.

"Did they?"

"Yes," I say, surprised. "There wasn't anyone else."

"There may be another," he says. He has a way with his eyes. If he squints just so, it's like they're laughing. Not at you, but with you.

"Well, if not my father, then who?" I ask.

He takes my hand. The same way Stille does. "Rador-elan of House Montescue," he says as if bestowing a title, "*you* are the last great sorcerer of the tenth era."

I startle. My jaw drops to my chest. Stunned, I sit there – motionless and speechless – while the Riegian king strokes my hand.

"Your father was a talented sorcerer," the king says, "but his powers did not rise to your level. And you know what?"

"What?" I say after a pause.

"I think he knew it. Maybe not at first, but there at the end, I'm sure he knew it. And he was proud. Proud *as hell* that his daughter was poised to become the last great sorcerer of this woebegone era."

I let the king's words wash over me. He shifts in his chair, and I notice his boutonniere. A red corsage pinned to his doublet. My brain does a double flip.

"You can't be serious!" I say. I look at the corsage, then at him, then the corsage again.

"My name is Paul Guiscard," he says, chuckling. From inside his jacket, he withdraws a red crystal.

"How long, your majesty?"

"My whole life. My father, Albert, was a patron before me. I don't know exactly how far back it goes, but generations. The royal family has always believed the memory witches, Amelia in particular, were handled badly. If another one came along, we were ready to do things differently."

"I don't know about that," I say. "But you may want to steer clear of me. Amelia's mother wasn't a Karator spy."

"Where we come from and who we are," the king says, "are two completely different things. You are not your mother unless you wish to be. Our Master may have played a role in creating your powers, but that doesn't mean he owns you. You can be who you choose to be."

"Not if the Order takes over," I say.

He cocks his head sadly. "We are on the brink," he admits. "Brother Mordecai met with me last night. The discussion was not enjoyable. I have two options. War, which will bring misery to my people. Or abdication in favor of my son, Standish. I love my son, but he is not suited to rule. He will be a figurehead, and the Order will take charge. My daughter, Presella, is far better equipped."

"Then abdicate for her," I say. "At least try."

"I love how fearless the young are," Marcellus says. "But I'm a man of the world. It isn't that simple. The Riege has never been ruled by a woman. Troubled times like these may not be the right time to set a new precedent. Especially that one."

"I have a third option," I say. "I came here to

remove Brother Mordecai from the equation."

"If you and the patrons can pull that off," he says, "it changes everything. The Order is nothing without Mordecai. They will collapse like a cheap suit of clothing."

"So how can we get to the first brother?" I ask.

King Marcellus sighs. "We can't. He's holed up in a palace wing the Order has controlled for decades. It is fortified, and his best people protect him. You'll never get close enough to touch him with your suite of fabrics. And they're on high alert. That will make it even harder."

"You have soldiers," I say.

"Yes, and a few are even still loyal," he says with a rueful laugh. "Much of the palace, Elan, has turned against me. Some with pleasure, others with sorrow. But ever more, it seems, each day. They sense a changing wind. My commands have never carried less weight."

"I will obey you," a woman's voice intones from the hallway, "to the end."

I turn, and there is another silhouette. This one in battle armor and with long flowing hair.

"Presella," the king says, "I will not require that sacrifice of you. You have so many gifts. Throwing them away would serve no purpose."

Princess Presella strides into the room. Her armor, burnished and tied with Arcadian leather straps, rustles proudly with each movement. She is handsome, if not exactly pretty, and solidly built. Her long brown hair swings freely, and she carries a black-and-silver spiked helmet under her arm.

She wears a swordbelt over her hips, a dagger beneath her left armpit, and a row of glistening dirks around each thigh.

"Dying with honor has purpose," she says, standing tall in front of her father. "Better than expiring in a dungeon anyway. Which is where my loving brother will stow me as soon as he has the opportunity. I'm of more use as a symbol, a martyr, than a forgotten prisoner in a forgotten jail-cell."

"You are formidable, Pressy, but you are one person," the king says.

"My personal guard stands with me," she says. "Fourteen men, six women, all soldiers, all hand-picked."

"And four more," Sylvia's genteel voice chimes, Marta and Allamonde and Grist crowding behind. "Don't forget us." Suddenly the tiny room is filled. Stille leans against the wall off to the side, his look inscrutable.

"So twenty-five true and loyal subjects," Marcellus says. "Plus a memory witch and her brave *Anaiah*. I am honored beyond words and emotions. But the Order has hundreds. And the palace guard many hundreds beyond that. We will never get close enough to Brother Mordecai to kill him or for our young memory witch to use her tools."

My eyes adjust to the dim lighting, and the room takes on as many colors as the fabrics in my leathers. The four interlocking ceilings hide a multiplicity of gems, and they play tag with the inlaid threads of the tapestries. I bathe in a shower of colors.

I think back to my out-of-body experience on the Elden hillside. I did not touch a single person, living or dead, yet my powers, with the help of Stille's blood-stained shirt, summoned in full the memory of an unavenged atrocity. The boys' words ring eerily in my head. *You must get closer.*

I didn't have to touch anyone or anything. All I needed was to be close.

And I remember reading Agnes, and how my powers shaped and molded like clay her memory of the burned riders and horses. Yet another atrocity by the same man. I was not merely viewing her memory. I was a participant.

And in the flatlands, I overturned half a forest to save Stille and me with my upside-down spell. I didn't lay cloth on anyone or read memories. I was a mere sorceress with her human crystal reacting to dire circumstances. But the power was unmistakable.

In spare moments, I've pondered Anselm Grist's penetrating question – how do I plan to kill the man who murdered Father and Willem? I know who he is now. I know where he is. And he has a trained mind. Perhaps the most highly trained mind in the Riege.

I could try the upside-down spell, but would it work on a man like Brother Mordecai? And how many other people – innocent people! – would die if I brought down the palace?

You must get closer.

I realize I have no idea what the actual limits of my powers are. I have been told they exist, but I have not experienced them firsthand. Do I need cloth? Physical contact? Or are my powers so strong that, with Stille by my side, I need only get close to Brother Mordecai? And how close is close enough?

I need to trust my powers. Trust that they will rise to the occasion. I need to trust what Stille and I can do as a team.

I am the last great sorcerer of the tenth era. I will do – I can do -- what is necessary to fulfill my mission.

"Your majesty," I interrupt. "I'm not entirely certain, but I may not need to lay fabric on Brother Mordecai, or even touch him, to enter his mind. My powers are strong, and I have Stille with me. All I need is to get close. As close as we can. Stille and I will do the rest."

The king's head turns abruptly. "Elan, are you . . ."

"You have to trust me, your majesty. I can do this."

He turns decisively to his daughter. "Presella, where do we believe Brother Mordecai is staying in the Order's wing of the palace?"

"He's in the green room, your majesty," I say quickly, then realize I've just interrupted a king. "I'm sorry, I mean, I read Praelat Ortun when we snuck into the palace. Brother Mordecai is in the green room."

"And what obstacles stand between us and

him?" the king asks simply.

Apart from breathing, the room is silent. Even the floating colors seem to hold their breaths. No one wants to speak. Presella finally answers her father's question. So softly you have to lean forward to hear.

"That wing," she says, "has one entrance and a single main hallway with rooms branching off north and south. There are six rooms all told between the entrance and the green room. Each one, if garrisoned properly, would have at least twenty brothers, fully armed. Outside the entrance, the palace guard, which we must assume is now loyal to the Order, has fifty men, also fully armed and deployed in standard protective formation. Two hundred additional guards could be summoned to arrive within minutes."

The enormity of the task floats above the ancient marble table like a bad odor.

"So it won't be easy," Presella says, exhaling softly.

"And many on both sides would die," Marcellus says, his head slumped. "Perhaps everyone. Even Elan and Stille."

Presella sits down next to her father and lays her helmet on the table. She takes his hand, kisses it, and puts it against her right cheek. She leans into it, like a small girl nestling into a feather pillow.

Then Anselm Grist loudly clears his throat. "There may be another way," he says, scratching his beard, his unkempt white hair dangling down his back. "No one has to die, and Elan and Stille can get within an arm's length of the first brother."

Grist surveys the amazed faces of the people in the room. He pauses to enjoy the moment. Then he wheels to face Stille and me. "But you two are really not going to like what you have to do to get there."

34

Elan

Grist outlines his plan in a series of chopping hand motions. The detention wing of the palace, he says, has a row of jailcells they've closed off for years. The last jailcell is directly underneath the endroom in the Order's hallway. The devotions room. Only a stone floor separates the two.

"So," Sylvia says, "all we have to do is force Brother Mordecai into the devotions room, and dump Elan and Stille in the last cell in a closed segment of the detention area . . ."

"And Elan will be directly below the first brother," Grist announces triumphantly. "To do whatever it is she plans to do with the old bugger."

"Except there will be a floor in between," Presella says.

Grist shrugs. "Elan's a witch, isn't she? Surely nothing as immaterial as stone will interfere with what she has in mind for Brother Mordecai." His eyes sparkle, and his nose twitches.

"What say you, said witch?" Marta asks.

"I'm willing to try," I say. "I mean, what's a brick floor . . . "

"Stone," Grist corrects.

". . . when Stille and I combine our forces."

Everyone suppresses a grin.

"What I mean to say is, when Stille and I have joined together . . ."

"I think they get the idea, Elan," Stille says, blushing slightly.

"Why don't we just smash through the floor?" Presella asks.

"It would take too much time and make too much noise," Sylvia says.

"Even if we tried to be stealthy," the king says, "the detention staff are no longer reliable. The Order is expanding rapidly within the palace. Whatever we decide to do, it must be a quick strike. Before the brothers and their new palace friends can react."

The king turns to Grist. "And may I ask," he says, one eyebrow raised sternly, "how you came to learn so much information, and in such detail, about the detention area?"

Now it's Grist's turn to blush. "Well, your honor, I mean, your highness, you see, on one occasion, well, maybe two, I might have had a bit too much to drink, and then one thing led to another, and I may have become unruly, and there I was in the detention area. The jailers shoved me in that cell out of meanness and spite. And as I sat there sobering up, I could hear the brothers saying their devotions through the floor. Clear as day."

"And you remember all this from one time?" I ask.

"Well," he says sheepishly, "it may have been more than once. Possibly twice. Three times, tops."

Everyone frowns at him.

"Certainly not more than four."

"And another problem," Allamonde cuts in, "is how to persuade our dear first brother to relocate to the devotions room."

"That's the beauty of my plan," Grist says. "All we have to do is brandish swords, make a lot of noise, shout and yell and bang some drums, and maybe burn a few things. Smoke, lots of smoke. The brothers won't know how substantial the threat is."

"So as a precaution," Presella says, "they'll insist on moving Mordecai to the safest room on the corridor."

"The devotions room," Grist says. "The only room that can be locked from the inside. He is impregnable in that room. It's their safe room."

"It could just work," Sylvia says admiringly.

"Anselm, you still haven't told us why this jail cell is so awful," Stille says.

"Well, my good lad," Grist says, clapping him heartily on the shoulder. "I mean, how to put this, they closed it off because, well, the sewage pipes broke and flooded the area, which, I mean, as I suppose you could infer . . ."

"What you're saying is that it smells," Marta says.

"Badly," Grist confirms. "It's so bad they won't even keep prisoners there."

"Except you," Presella says.

"Apparently I was special," Grist says.

"I will defer to Allamonde," I say, trying not to laugh. "Will this experience be better or worse than hiding in a mortuary cart?"

"Well, my lady," Allamonde says, huffing then bowing twice, "we had limited options in Darine, we did what we had to do, and of course, in the end . . ."

"I'm teasing you, Allamonde," I say. "If this will get me within arm's length of Brother Mordecai, and if my powers can penetrate a stone floor, I'll find a way to endure the smell. Stille?"

"I'll do it," Stille says. "But everyone in this room will owe me a favor."

"Getting them into that cell unobtrusively will be more difficult than it seems," King Marcellus says. "If we are obvious, the brothers will learn of it promptly. There are eyes and ears everywhere in the jail."

"Then we shall be sneaky," Grist says. "Leave the young pups to me. Allamonde, I shall require assistance. The rest of you – focus on getting Mordecai into the devotions room! We'll drop these two in jail."

"Then let's move with all possible speed," the king says, standing. "Mordecai awaits my answer and I cannot stall him forever. Our forces weaken by the hour." We all rise, and before I can say good-bye, King Marcellus has departed.

Everyone else departs to plan and organize, including Grist and Allamonde, who require suitable disguises. Costumes, Grist calls them.

"And we'll need to figure out how to sneak your special coat into the jailcell," Grist says, one foot out the door.

"I won't need it," I say.

"But your fabrics . . .," Stille says.

"I won't need them," I say. "Not this time."

"My lady, I enjoy your confidence," Allamonde says, "but are you certain?"

"Yes, Allamonde. Quite."

The doorway empties, and Stille and I are alone in the king's room of magical colors.

"Well, Elan Montescue," Stille says, "we did what we said we would do."

"Yes."

"We said we would travel to Kimbar, and here we are."

"Yes." My eyes can't leave the colors circling in the room. They are soothing, almost mystical.

"So I have to ask," he says.

I meet his eyes. "Okay, ask!"

"Are you going to kill him?"

"By him, you mean . . ."

"Brother Mordecai."

Oddly, I do not know how to answer his question.

"I mean, I know your mission is to track down whoever killed your father and Willem," Stille says.

"And now we've found him. But we've never talked about, you know, exactly what you plan to do."

"Anselm Grist asked me the same question," I say.

"Yes, and what was your answer?"

"I didn't have one."

"Do you have one now?"

"Stille, are you getting cold feet?" I ask. I am more amused than concerned. I learn more about Stille every time I'm with him. I like that about him.

"I'm with you to the end, Elan. But I need to know what the plan is. Am I going to be a participant in another person's death? If so, I need to prepare for that."

"I'm not sure," I say.

"You're not sure?"

Suddenly I grab Stille by his wrists and shake them hard. I want to lean over and kiss him – his lips seem so delectable – but I fight the urge. This is not the perfect moment.

"There are things I need to make him see, Stille. Things he needs to feel. Words to be said. But I honestly haven't focused on the outcome. Will he live? Will I change him?"

"Will he die?" Stille asks.

"Yes," I say, "and I don't know. But this is how it has to be. The Fluence won't let me use my powers to harm someone. Not directly anyway. And I don't want to. But memories have power. I know I've hurt people over the years. Showing them memories they'd buried. Memories they thought they'd forgotten. Forcing people to relive the past, even tiny pieces of it, can have unexpected outcomes. Some good. Some bad. And some very bad."

The assorted colors in the delicate palace air wash over Stille's face. Like angels are scrubbing him clean. Preparing him for what lies ahead.

"What I know for certain," I say, "is I can't do what I need to do unless you are there with me."

Stille smiles. "I keep my promises. I'll always be there for you."

We hear footsteps in the corridor. I can tell by their sound it's Grist and Allamonde returning.

"I'm going to kiss you, Rador-elan of House Montescue," Stille whispers. "And you are going to sit there and let me."

I beam. It is now the perfect moment. "Okay."

Our lips touch at precisely the instant we mean them to. It's our first proper kiss. Not too hard. Not rushed. Not one-sided. Nothing hit-and-run about it. We pull our lips apart a second before Grist and Allamonde wheel into our room. Grist is cloaked in a brother's black robe, and Allamonde wears the uniform of a palace guard.

"Pray, did we interrupt?" Allamonde asks, glancing at Stille, then at me, then Stille again.

"No," I say, smiling.

"We had just finished . . .," Stille says.

". . . what we were doing," I say.

Grist throws greasy stained coveralls at Stille and me. "After you're done snuggling each other," he says, "you're to snuggle into these. Our story is simple. We've caught you stealing food from the Order, and now we're escorting you to jail. Don't say a word. Let Allamonde and me do the talking."

"You're not going to gag me, are you?" Stille says.

"We most certainly are," Grist says.

"Again?"

Grist shrugs. "And bind you as well."

"I'm already well trained at being a prisoner," Stille grumps.

"Practice makes perfect," Grist responds.

The detention area is underground. The only light comes from torches along the rough dirty walls. Water drips casually from the ceiling, and the floor alternates between soppy mud and hard-packed dirt. The damp air smells of spoiled raw food and human fluids. The guards, unlike those in the main palace, are unshaven.

"Section Five," Allamonde instructs the captain in charge.

"It's closed," he growls. "Fumes bad enough to kill a man."

"I am Brother Anselm," Grist intones. "These miscreants were caught stealing food from Brother Mordecai. From his actual plate. In his infinite mercy and wisdom, Brother Mordecai has determined to forgive these criminals and to take their future instruction, how shall I put this, into his own two hands."

Grist reaches over and harshly tousles my red hair. He smiles cruelly.

"But before they experience the joy of entering

into the first brother's personal service, he desires a suitable punishment. Something to get their attention. No more than a few hours."

The captain's mouth turns slowly into a grin, then he shrugs. "I guess he's the new master, or that's what I hear anyway."

"I hear the same, friend," Allamonde says from under his helmet.

"Follow me," the captain says, snatching a black grimy metal key from a peg on the wall. He grabs a long-handled torch and hands it to Allamonde. "I'll trust you to settle the two . . . criminals . . . in a cell. I'm not going back there."

"Yes, the fumes," Grist says. "We understand."

Once through the door, the odor is beyond anything I've experienced. Nausea rises in my stomach and into the back of my mouth, and my legs buckle. Grist catches me under my arms, then reaches into his robe for moistened towels. "Use these to cover your face," he whispers to me. Allamonde does the same for Stille, and then the two of them retrieve towels for themselves.

Once our gags and bindings are removed, Allamonde lights a dormant torch for Grist, and, the fumes acting as fuel, the flames leap nearly to the ceiling. This wing looks like someone used an upside-down spell on it. Fallen stones and debris are everywhere. Not to mention the cobwebs and dust and dirt. We are filthy after only a few steps. As we move swiftly to the last jailcell, rats and tar-lizards, their startled eyes like molten beads, scurry from the torchlight.

Gregor said I should be on the lookout for torches. Guess he was right.

The rusted iron-barred door to the last jailcell has fallen, taking a chunk of the wall with it. Inside is a single stone bench with a clogged drain in the middle.

"They kept you here?" I asked Grist, the towel still covering my face.

"A time or two," he mumbled.

I stare at him.

"But not recently, of course," he says with an injured voice.

Allamonde gestures with his sword back the way we came. "My lady, we must leave you, or the captain may come looking. We have done all we can. Now it is in your hands."

"And those of the Fluence," Grist adds. "Assuming she has any, of course."

Allamonde plants a torch in our jailcell's wall, and then the two are gone. I know I am fortunate to have such friends. People who two weeks before were living their lives as ordinary people. And then fate happened. Or rather, I happened. The first memory witch in a thousand years. They have rallied to my defense and support with no thought for themselves. And now they are risking their lives to create a diversion so I can enter the mind of Brother Mordecai.

Stille and I sit there for long moments. I listen for the ceiling, but I hear nothing. I focus on breathing into my towel. Stille is so frail. So fragile. He seems skinnier than when we met in Montauk.

His face is still bruised and swollen from the brothers. He says he's a fast healer, but even that has limits. I vow that when this is over – when our missions are completed – we'll take time for both of us to heal properly.

Stille and I should talk but we don't. Our time is upon us, and all we seek is quietude. I reach out my hand for his, find it, and squeeze. He squeezes back like he always does.

Now we wait.

Stille and I are a team. We will always be together.

35

Elan

"**D**id you hear that?" Stille whispers.

I come awake. We are still holding hands. I told myself I wouldn't fall asleep. The towel has slipped off my face, but the stench no longer gags me. How much time has passed? I don't know. Maybe fifteen minutes. Maybe more. The torch in our jailcell is burning low.

I listen intently.

"I don't hear anything," I whisper.

"There it is again," he says. "There's someone in the devotions room."

A chair scrapes on the floor above. Then it squeaks like someone sat down. I hear a voice. A man's voice. Deep and grating. "I think these precautions are silly," he admonishes. "Afterwards we shall discuss appropriate protection mechanisms and procedures."

I hear murmurs. Other brothers are placating him. I cannot make out the words.

"Very well," Brother Mordecai says, his voice dripping with affront. "I understand. I shall be here in prayer and ready to emerge at the first available opportunity."

The hinges shriek as the door closes in the devotions room. The first brother leans back in his chair, and the chair protests. I stare at the ceiling. Brother Mordecai is directly over me.

My eyes meet Stille's. We are now both very much awake. It's time for the greatest sorcerer of the tenth Ebb to see what she can do against Brother Mordecai, the best-trained mind in the Riege.

I lean over and delicately kiss the burn mark on my right wrist. *If you're out there somewhere, Dezzie,* I think, *I've never needed your help more than now.*

I close my eyes and visualize black cloth with a tight finesse weave. I see it floating in the air. Rolling slowly over. Undulating in shimmering light. Each fiber is like a perfect strand of hair.

And then I focus my will on the man above me. I visualize placing the fabric on him. I sense his presence, and then I am past his presence. I am almost in.

And then he swats away my intrusion. My mind stings, as if he hit me physically.

Well, well, a witch, he thinks. *Trying to force her way into my mind. I wonder who it could be? We should have killed you with your father! I'm only sorry I sent that fool Ortun to confirm your death. I should have done that myself.*

I visualize a range of fabrics, including some I know and love so well. Every color from pure white to darkest blue. Mordecai bats each away like they are flies buzzing around his head in the summer. With each imagined cloth I almost penetrate his mind, but the first brother repels each attempt in the nick of time.

I have an insight. This time I visualize Mordecai's own black robe, which already rests against his skin. His mind pauses for an instant since the robe is familiar – it is part of him! – but the slight delay is enough for me to push through. His defenses dissolve like a mirror shattering.

And then he does something I don't expect. He laughs! I hear him inside his mind, and also through the ceiling.

Well, if you insist on being my guest, then welcome! But be careful what you wish for. You may not enjoy the ride.

I grip Stille's hand even harder, and he returns the pressure, as I force my will into sorting the first brother's memories. He responds by flipping hundreds of them at me, maybe even thousands, like playing cards. One after the other, faster and faster. I feel the impact. Not pain exactly. But it slows me down.

You don't get to choose, the first brother thinks. *Let's see what memory I can find that might interest you. Ah yes, dear old daddy, the failed husband and father. The last great sorcerer of his era. Who couldn't even devise rudimentary security protections for his family!*

Mordecai pulls me inside his memory from that awful day. The one I witnessed hundreds of times through Gregor. We are riding. I can almost feel the horse as he thumps along. Attacking the farmhouse. The grappling hooks swinging menacingly onto the roof, ripping holes and felling beams. Barking orders and setting the villa on fire. The servants racing for their lives out the back. Mordecai's momentary pause before he decides to let them live.

Then seeing Father rush into the barn. A glimpse of Willem on the second floor. Hiding in the hay. Everything burning. Willem's face stretched and cracking. He is a nine-year-old boy about to be murdered. Mordecai directing his men into the barn. The fight is short, and father is wounded. Willem is beaten savagely. They are both dragged before Mordecai, and all the horsemen gather to watch.

Mordecai talks to Father. I tune out the words. Disgusting filth. The Order's hatred of the born-and-bred runs deep in Mordecai. Father says something. Then Mordecai beseeches the skies, noting the penance they have paid, before calmly piercing Father through the heart with a rapier. The terrible agony on Daddy's face. A man in his prime dying too early. I want to take him in my arms and tell him it's all right. And Willem's haunting throes, compounded by a young boy's visceral fear of dying. I think of Willem as my older brother, but on this day he is a little boy, nine years old.

If I were in your shoes, Mordecai thinks. *I would be angry. Very angry indeed. I would be enraged. You should want to kill me. Destroy me. Well, here I am. Come out, come out, wherever you are!*

My blood boils. My head is so tight I want to destroy something.

"Stay in control, Elan," Stille says, and I realize I'm gripping his hand so tightly I've probably cut off his circulation. "He wants you to be angry. Don't give in to it."

I realize Mordecai has not shown me anything I haven't seen before in other memories. Hateful haunting awful things. My training kicks in, and I tune it out. Now is not the time for outrage, and I am not a vigilante. I am not Amelia. I have a mission. To avenge my father and Willem. When I was younger, I wanted to kill their murderers. Now all I want is to make Mordecai see what he did. Truly see it.

And I remember that snippet of Mordecai's memory. Father said something to him moments before the rapier pierced his heart. Something Mordecai didn't focus on. Father's mouth moved, but the first brother didn't watch or listen.

I clench my jaw, and I force the memory backwards. Mordecai grunts in pain, and Stille squeezes harder. He's feeling all this as much as I am. I slow down the memory as my father speaks. Now I realize why Mordecai heard no words. There weren't any. Father mouthed them. I reverse the memory again and slow it down further, gritting my teeth as Mordecai summons his will against me, and there it is. Clear as day. Father's last words, mouthed in the face of the man who murdered him: "Elan, be strong. I love you."

My heart dances! Father knew that someday I would be inside this monster's mind and that I would be witnessing his murder as a memory witch. He knew! He knew! He knew what I would become!

The first brother tries to turn the tables. He plays roulette with his memories, each one seemingly worse than the one before. Inflicting torment and pain on others is the one constant of his life. Joining the Order at sixteen enabled him to indulge his cravings, especially as he rose through the ranks. By the time he became first brother, he had richly earned the title of first torturer. The lives he has twisted or ruined are almost beyond counting.

My greatest hits! Mordecai thinks. *Enjoy!*

Then Mordecai scrolls back to his earliest memories. And I see Gregor as a child. Younger and smaller than his vicious sibling. I squirm as Mordecai metes out all manner of punishments. In one nasty segment, he squeezes Gregor's head like a melon, then pushes it towards the hearthfire. I can see the furious red embers. Hear Gregor's squeals and protests. I know Mordecai must stop short because, in my lifetime, Gregor is not disfigured. His head is not burned. But in this memory, my heart races as Mordecai pushes Gregor closer and closer into the flames.

It's their father that interrupts the crime. "Morty, Morty," he calls from outside the room. Then there are footsteps, and Mordecai pulls Gregor back from the flames. "Is everything all right?" his father asks from the doorstop. "Yes, Father," Mordecai lies. "We were just roughhousing." Gregor lies on the floor gasping and whimpering. "Well, enough for tonight," their father says, lowering his eyes at Mordecai. "To bed with both of you."

So you have a nickname, I say into Mordecai's mind, the first words I have spoken to him. *Morty! Hi, Morty!*

Father was an idiot, he snarls. *Mother, too. Neither understood me. Neither understood the world.*

Whatever you say, Morty!

I engage in a brutal tug-of-war with Mordecai over which memories to view. I choose one, then he repels it for one of his own choosing, which I wrest from him and fling to the side. I am sore. And tiring. I want him to make him see the damage he has caused.

You don't understand me either, he says triumphantly. *You haven't shown me a single memory I didn't enjoy. You have to be strong to lead. You must relish that which you inflict. You can't be a leader if you feel other people's pain.*

You can't be human either, I respond. I hear his laughter, both in my mind and through the ceiling.

Mordecai is winning. I am losing strength and willpower. It is time to play my trump card. I squeeze Stille's hand. There is a pause, then he squeezes back. We are still a team. We are still in the fight.

It takes every ounce of energy I have left, but taking a deep breath, I muster my strength to locate and pull to the surface the one memory we've both avoided. The slaughter of the innocents. The fifty boys in nightshirts on the dewy hillside one chilly spring dawn in Elden.

I wondered when you would get around to that one, he says.

Well, here it is, Morty, I say.

What you can't seem to get through your thick but pretty skull, he says amiably, *is that I'll enjoy seeing it again.*

You're not going to see it, I say.

Oh no?

This one you're going to feel. As if you were there. As if you were each boy feeling the blade of your sword on his neck.

There is silence above me.

I visited the boys from the hillside. I relived their torment. They offered their pain as a gift to me. I am now regifting it to you.

Mordecai fights back with all his strength, but I force him, my heart pounding with exertion, to become each boy, standing there in a clean white nightshirt, shivering, stamping his feet, and then experiencing the sword strike. One boy after another boy after another. Mordecai bucks and heaves and groans. I feel him weaken. By the time the fiftieth boy falls onto the wet grass, there is silence above me. Mordecai and I are there together in his mind, and then it is merely me. Alone in a dry echoless chamber.

And then my spirit flies back into my own body, and I know Mordecai is no more. As I leave his mind, I catch a glimpse of him in the devotions room. Bloodstains from both ears, and down his nose. His mouth agape. His eyes open but unseeing. His hands ripping into the arm fabric of his chair.

I settle back into my own body with an enormous sigh. Relief washes over me.

"Stille! We did it!"

His hand is limp in mine.

"Stille?"

The torch has burned out in our jailcell. I say a quick spell, and it flashes to life. I see Stille, frail and white and motionless. His head lolls against the wall. His eyes are closed.

"Stille!" I yell.

I feel for a pulse, but there is none. I put my hand to his mouth, but I feel no breathing. I place my ear against his chest. Nothing.

I shriek for Grist and Allamonde. I shriek and I shriek. Finally, Grist comes running, one hand over his nose, a torch in the other.

"Stille needs a doctor!" I scream. "Fetch one as fast as you can."

Grist kneels before Stille, staring urgently into

his eyes, then throws a despairing glance my way. "Yes, my lady," he says, then races out. It is the only time Grist has ever called me "my lady."

I breathe into Stille's mouth and pump his chest. Nothing works, and I know Grist won't get back in time. The truth descends like an anvil on my heart.

Stille Vespers is dead.

Epilogue

Elan

I tell myself I should smile. Everyone expects it. And for a few seconds at a time, I can oblige. But more than that is a bridge too far.

I avoid stopping at the ruins of our villa. I don't know what I would say to Father or Willem. Their spirits are long gone anyway. It is late afternoon when we reach the treeline. The flatlands are behind us. The steep forested Northern Reaches stretch fearsomely in front. Home, I think.

We are done for the day, so the five kingsguards, our escort, dismount and picket their horses. Three men and two women, they are beautiful in their blue-and-gold uniforms, shiny black boots, and exquisite epaulets. Princess Presella, now Queen designate, chose them personally.

Marta stays mounted. She has studied me the entire trip. She knows something is wrong. She is magnificent in her long glossy raven hair and tight black leather riding suit, her dagger with the silver hilt displayed prominently. Along with her red corsage.

Sylvia wanted to join us, or so she said, making excuses. She believes herself too old, Marta told me, to face Gregor. I told Marta that Gregor would be delighted to see his sister. He probably forgave her years ago. Probably doesn't even think there is anything to forgive. Sylvia was a girl who did what was necessary to survive a monster. Marta shrugs. There is nothing to be done, she says, about Grandmother.

My heart pounds as the last rider canters to the group.

"How are you feeling?" I ask.

"Fine," Stille says, but I know it's a lie. "Getting stronger every day. Like I've always said . . ."

"Yes, I know, you're a fast healer," I say, forcing a smile.

"The healer said it will take time, Elan," he says. "I came close to dying there in the jail cell. Anselm took me aside. Said he was sure I was already gone. Guess I'm tougher than that."

"Yes, Stille, you are," I say, fighting back tears. "I've never met anyone tougher."

He leads his horse to the others, and I feel the rubystone pulsing contentedly in my pocket. Stille died because of me, so I did what I had to do. If there is a price to be paid, I should be the one to pay it. Not Stille. He deserves to live, and if I had to use the rubystone to bring him back, then it's on my head. My conscience. Our Master uses people, like Kortok, then discards them ruthlessly when he's through. As if a person could be disposable. I need to be – I *am* – different than Our Master.

I watch Stille dismount and picket his horse, and I realize I would give my life for him. As he gave his life for me.

Stille never once cried out. Never once asked me to stop as the escalating fight with Mordecai drained me of all my strength. And him of his.

I tell the kingsguards they should wait here for us to return from the Keep. They protest weakly, but I stop it with my hand out.

"I need to do this by myself," I say. "With Stille."

"And me," Marta chimes.

"You should stay as well," I say.

"No way," she says. "I've longed for years to meet my famous Uncle Gregor. The greatest tutor of the tenth era. Surely you wouldn't deprive me. He's family."

Marta smiles. She is so gorgeous when she smiles. Her explanation is as phony as the carnation on her riding suit. And she knows I know it. Sylvia instructed her to stick with me all the way, and that's what she's going to do. I purse my lips and nod. She'd follow, at a distance of course, even if I told her not to.

Word of what happened has spread quickly throughout the Riege. And the Order has disintegrated. In some towns, challs have been burned. In others, they have been occupied and the brothers thrown out. King Marcellus was right. Without Mordecai, the Order has splintered into a million pieces, no two the same. Who knows what will rise in its place. There is a vacuum. Something will fill it. Whether it is good or bad, or worse, no one knows.

At the last village we rode through, people lined the streets. I don't know how they knew when we were coming, but they did. They stared at me and also at Stille. They didn't cheer. They didn't throw catcalls. They just looked. Wondering, I suppose, what all this means for their lives. I'm glad they didn't yell questions, because right now I have no answers.

The next morning, Stille and I, with Marta in the rear, head into the mountains to the Keep. I take it slowly for Stille's sake. His recovery has been difficult. One day he's improved, but the next he flags. I can't tell anyone what happened. Not even Stille, and that eats at me. I've kept secrets from him before, and it didn't go well. But how do I tell him this secret? That he died, and I used the rubystone to bring him back. It is the mother of all secrets. I don't know how, so I don't tell him. Someday I'll have to. But that day is not today.

The excitement builds in my heart and soul the closer we get. We pass the crossroads and continue uphill. The smell, the air, the forest – I even begin recognizing individual trees. The sunlight shines differently on my skin this far into the mountains. I have been gone only a few weeks, but it feels like years. I am so much older than I was. Gregor said I needed experience, and I got far more than I bargained for.

Another two days of familiar landscape to the Keep. I know the way. In all kinds of weather. In all seasons. I am not just *going* somewhere. For the first time in my life, I am *returning* somewhere. I am coming home.

As we make the final turn, I see the Keep in all its ancient majesty. The massive gray walls with perfect footholds for my narrow feet. The narrow slits where archers would loose arrows at attackers. The window to my room, now dark and tight. The Keep looks the same yet different. Like any home, I suppose, when you've been away. Then it hits me – I should not be seeing the Keep if Gregor has warded it properly. But I *am* seeing the Keep. Which means it isn't warded. Which means . . .

I drop off my horse and race across the rocks and prickly underbrush to the Keep. This can't be happening. First Stille, but now Gregor? Have I lost everyone I care for? The iron-framed front door is locked, and I panic. I try to calm my nerves, but it doesn't work. I'll probably find Gregor cold in his bed, I think. Or maybe at the bottom of the main stairway. Like the time he fell when we argued and he broke his leg. This time he probably broke his neck. Desperately, I run around to the back by the kitchen. By the patio and jimberry trees.

And there he is! Sipping tea and reading bloody Eusebius. His eyes light when he sees me, and he gamely pushes himself up from his chair. But I don't let him finish. I skip over to his chair, push him back into it, and plop onto his lap. I kiss his old wizened barely-haired head time after time. I have never been so happy to see another person in my life.

He laughs and clucks exactly like I knew he would. He hugs me like that time I ran away to the crossroads and he found me by the ravine. Like he's never going to let go of me. "Oh, my child!" he says over and over.

I grab both his shoulders but shake them gently. "You scared me!" I accuse him. "The Keep isn't warded."

Gregor immediately becomes my tutor again, and he raises a finger. "Well, dear child, I wanted to make sure you could find your way home. One never knows, of course, and you have wandered off course on more than one occasion. And . . ."

"I forgive you!" I say. "But don't do it again. My heart couldn't take it!" And we begin hugging and rocking again.

"You're crying," Stille says softly. He's snuck up and stands there, grinning. Even Marta, usually the sourpuss, can't entirely stop herself from joining him.

"We're *both* crying," Gregor exclaims.

I quickly stand up and help Gregor to his feet. He's aged in the weeks since I've left. Even with his cane, he can barely stand. He has lost weight, and his skin is jaundiced.

"Gregor, there's someone I need you to meet." I say. "His name is Stille Vespers."

"A pleasure to meet you, sir," Stille says, stepping forward with an outstretched hand.

Gregor turns to me. "Is this Stanislaus?"

I nod my head.

"Stanislaus?" Stille asks.

"I'll tell you later," I say.

And then Gregor and Stille shake hands, and I feel like two large pieces of destiny's jigsaw puzzle have fallen into place. I nearly prevented this moment from happening, and then I gave everything to make sure it could.

As Gregor meets Marta, his grandniece, for the first time, I grab Stille by the neck. "How are you feeling?" I ask.

"You need to stop asking me that," he scolds.

"Some days you're better," I say, "but then some days you're not."

He shrugs. "Life isn't linear," he says. "That's what Uncle Martin used to say."

"Well, I want it to be," I say. "I want every day to be better than the day before."

"It is when you're with me," he says, and I pretend to scowl while tagging him lightly in his shoulder. He tries but fails to hide his grimace.

That night, after a light dinner, Marta settles into her room, and Gregor, at my request, offers Stille the room next to mine. I've made up my mind. I know what I'm going to do. There is a barrier between Stille and me. Maybe it's only in my head, but it's there, and I created it. I need to do something to feel close to Stille again. To regain what we fought so hard to become together. Stille once saw me exposed, but he can't remember it. There is only one way to be as close as two people can be. Skin to skin. Maybe the time is ripe to show him something he won't forget.

As I head to the stairs, Gregor waits for me at the bottom, leaning heavily on his cane. It's late, and he should be in his room. Instead, he is agitated and holds a paper in his hand. He waves it.

"This came a few days ago," he says, his voice shaky. "Someone brought it from the crossroads. It concerns you. I didn't know when was best to tell you."

"What is it?" I ask.

"News."

"What news."

He tilts his head. "Oh, my child!"

"Gregor, what is it?"

"Catherine has returned," he says, shaking.

"My mother?"

"Yes."

"What does she want?"

"You," Gregor says. "She wants you."

THE END

Acknowledgements

The author wishes to acknowledge with gratitude the assistance of those who read drafts of this story, including his wife, Julie, as well as Erica Gravely, Donna Royston, and Martin Wilsey. Special thanks to Luca Oleastri and Paola Giari for the cover art and to Victor Rook for his assistance in preparing the story for publication.